'Left me positively breathless'
ANGELA MARSONS

'A chillingly authenic, bang-on-trend thriller'
LISA HALL

'A murder mystery story with a modern twist. Enjoyable read'
THE TIMES+

'Blisteringly fabulous dark crime'
NORTHERN CRIME REVIEW BOOK BLOG

'Intensely creepy . . . truly addictive'
LIZLOVESBOOKS.COM

'Outstanding . . . Perfect for readers who like their police
procedurals fast paced, twisty-turny, and served with
a side order of grit. I loved it'
CRIME THRILLER GIRL

'A great read'
SWIRL AND THREAD

'A contemporary thriller that keeps you on your toes'
RACHEL'S RANDOM READS

'Fast-paced and exhilarating plot . . . I can't
recommend it enough'
BECCA'S BOOKS

Alex Caan has spent over a decade working in information systems security for a number of government organisations, and is currently specialising in terrorism studies. A lifetime passion for writing was sparked by the encouraging words of an English teacher in school, and eventually led to Alex successfully completing an MA in Creative Writing and writing his debut novel *Cut to the Bone*.

www.alexcaanauthor.com

FIRST
TO
DIE

ALEX CAAN

ZAFFRE

First published in Great Britain in 2018 by

ZAFFRE PUBLISHING
80–81 Wimpole St, London W1G 9RE
www.zaffrebooks.co.uk

A CIP catalogue record for this book is
available from the British Library.

ISBN: 978-1-78576-188-1

Also available as an ebook

1 3 5 7 9 10 8 6 4 2

Typeset by IDSUK (Data Connection) Ltd
Printed and bound by Clays Ltd, St Ives Plc

Zaffre Publishing is an imprint of Bonnier Zaffre,
a Bonnier Publishing company
www.bonnierzaffre.co.uk
www.bonnierpublishing.co.uk

Omeed and Zahida, for Mum
MKAZORHZZI, always follow your dreams

Prologue

She couldn't watch him die. Not actually see the life escape from his eyes. She thought she would be immune to it by now. What was left to make her care? Not much. Not the blood, the screams, the pleading. Yet she couldn't look into his eyes and watch them mist over with the fog of death.

He was so unaware of what was going to happen. She stood at the foot of the bed, his chest rising and falling, his face creased in some nightmare. Not the one she had embroiled him in. Something else, something more personal. She felt a twinge of envy then, that she couldn't be part of that intimacy. The thoughts inside him, shut off from her. She wondered if his brain was pricking at his subconscious, trying to rouse him. Danger is staring at you. Wake up.

He didn't. He just carried on sleeping. She edged closer to the bed, barefoot, silent. Her fingers reached out, lightly felt his skin. Warm. A memory of someone else. A missed heartbeat. She became reckless then. She decided to give him a chance. A chance she never had.

She sat down, and the bed moved with her. She shook him gently. If he woke up, she would let him live. But he didn't, his breathing became shallow, and then deep again. It was a sign. It was meant to happen. This was all part of the plan.

She tilted his head back slightly, and ran her finger over his throat. It felt so solid, like cord, or steel. Would she have the strength? She closed her eyes. And remembered. She remembered the beginning. She remembered a time when she wasn't like this. And she remembered the moment she had changed. When they had changed her.

And that filled her with anger, an energy that coursed through her every cell, a hatred that needed to be sated. She took the hand saw from inside her jacket. Reckless again. She was leaving so many clues, but she no longer cared. She looked at the serrated edge, and she looked at the hardness of his throat.

Then the memories came again. And they brought with them the strength. She placed the cool metal against his soft skin, and began to move it. Side to side, each stroke filled with more vigour, as her purpose grew and she knew that what she was doing was the right thing. The blood first poured, then spurted, as she cut, struggling against the gristle, the veins. A mess of flesh and red liquid, her fingers drenched, her face splattered, the white bed sheets covered.

As she hacked away, she didn't stop, and she didn't look into his eyes.

When she was satisfied that he was gone, she looked up.

His eyes were open.

He had woken up, he had felt the pain! That wasn't meant to happen. The empty glass caught her eye. There should have been enough in there to keep him asleep, to keep him from feeling what she was doing. It hadn't been enough.

She started to sob.

She had killed him. Horribly and with no mercy. And he had felt it. She had become one of them. A monster.

Chapter One

The group all wore masks, the mouths turned up with threatening grins, the skin pure white. Their bodies cloaked in black, only the trainers and boots differentiating them. Detective Sergeant Zain Harris couldn't even tell their gender, let alone race or age. Their menace was broken as they walked past him, and asked him for some weed.

'Go fuck yourselves,' he told them.

'Chill bro,' one of them said, the mask unmoving.

'I'm not your bro.'

The group burst into hysterics at a comment Zain didn't hear, and they wandered off. He felt like chasing them and smacking them into next week. Instead he tried some grounding shit he had learnt during his mandatory 'if you want your job back' therapy nonsense. Engage all five senses and you'll be anchored.

Great. So what could he see? The group were disappearing into the night, joining the thousands of others dressed in similar gear. He could make out the silhouettes of the hordes against the street lamps, against the police strobe lights on every car they could get into St James's Park. Fireworks were being let off randomly, like flares or warning shots into the purplish night sky. He heard clashing voices, as protestors screamed at police, who remained silent, letting the sirens do their talking.

Around the protestors were lines of his colleagues, dressed in uniform, unlike him. Solid yellow blocks of high-vis jackets, broken by armoured vehicles, cars and horses.

The acrid stench of horse shit, smoke and gunpowder from the fireworks filled his nose, lining the back of his throat. His stomach, devoid of food and water, retched against the staleness.

Zain bit back the thought that he didn't know exactly which side he was on. Anonymous or the State. He didn't like to dwell; the answer was too complicated, even more than it had been before. Zain could be loyal, he could be devoted and believe in something. The State technically employed him. Anonymous though, they crossed the lines and asked the questions he wasn't allowed to sometimes. He felt an affinity with them, with their bravery and their disregard for rules when they caught the scum that the law failed to convict.

Except, who made the decision about who was scum in the first place? There had to be some mechanism to discern that, right?

'Yo, bro,' said another voice.

Zain got ready for another *giveussomeweed* or *gofuckyourselves* exchange. The masked figure stopped in front of him.

'What?' said Zain, baring his teeth.

'Zain, man? Didn't realise you were coming these ends. Been long time bro. How you been?'

The mask was pulled off. It was a cousin, Rakim or Kasim, he couldn't remember. From his mother's half of the family. She was the daughter of a Turkish diplomat and an Indian journalist. Rakim or Kasim had the olive-skinned, dark-haired look that could belong to either side. Zain had the same complexion, but with his Turkish grandfather's bright blue eyes, and his English military father's features.

'Yeah, well . . .'

'I mean, I knew you were always a bit off-centre like, but you a proper hacker?'

'I do my bit,' Zain said, looking away. He had done more than that when he was younger. He had even been part of the Anonymous movement for a few months, before being recruited by extremists. Zain didn't look like anyone else in his family and had grown up feeling a sense of alienation every time he faced the mirror. And that's what had started his demise, his willingness to try and belong to something, anything, that could give him a clear identity. Bastardised forms of religion and anarchists were his favourites. But his hacking skills just weren't up to the level of Anonymous, so he had never got very far.

Zain had never truly fit in growing up. His parents were the definition of *opposites attract* – from very different backgrounds, they had met in a war zone, fallen passionately for each other, and then spent the rest of their lives pushing against each other. Loneliness was a frequent part of Zain's life, and despite excelling at academia, he found himself vulnerable to voices that could speak to his emptiness. One of the generation first to be radicalised online, Zain had fallen easily into the hands of predators who wanted to use him to carry out their warped agenda. Brainwashed, but not brain dead – as he became further embroiled in a terrorist cell, making physical contact with his online groomers, Zain's moral compass kicked in. He was trapped and he wanted a way out. And that's when counter-terrorism and MI5 offered him a lifeline. Detective Chief Inspector Raymond Cross from SO15 had come to his rescue. Zain turned double agent for him, and from then on the teenage Zain was marked, the secret services taking an interest in him and what he could do for them. Through university, Cross had been a mentor to Zain, and afterwards Zain had done stints with GCHQ before turning to SO15 and covert operations. Until that had gone horribly wrong, leaving him almost dead.

'Nice one, bro. It's why I'm here, need one of these guys to help me run some business shit.' Rakim or Kasim's voice cut into his thoughts.

'I don't think that's what they do. They're not guns for hire.'

'There must be some, innit, willing to turn to the dark side. You sure you won't bro? Do a favour for me innit? Family rates?'

Rakim or Kasim grinned at him. Zain shook his head, said he'd be in touch, maybe.

'Nice one, bro.'

Zain put his hands tightly into his jacket pockets, pulled his hood up, and headed away from the park. He wasn't feeling this; he didn't know why Unit 3 had been dragged in. They were special ops, under the command of the Westminster Police Crime Commissioner Justin Hope. They weren't here to patrol a riot, that wasn't their remit. Detective Chief Inspector Kate Riley, his boss, had asked them to blend in. To try to stay one step ahead of the crowds, by infiltrating and manipulating them if need be. They weren't the only ones. SO19, the armed response unit, were on standby in ARU vans. MI5, the security services, and SO15, the counter-terrorism command unit who worked with them, were also dotted around and running their own covert surveillance.

He had been part of that set-up once, knew how that joint-operation stuff worked, and how when things went bad, they went bad really quickly.

Zain could think of better ways of spending Bonfire Night. He was missing a Krav Maga class for this bullshit. And he wasn't even sure this was proper anti-capitalist Anonymous protesting. So far most people he had seen without their masks were just kids.

Actually, *enough*, he thought, he was going. He needed to get home, and get some food inside him. He started heading towards where his car was parked, only to get a frantic message come through to his earpiece.

'Zain, I need you. Something's going down.'

Chapter Two

Zain was standing in a side street by the Albert Arms pub next to Detective Sergeant Stevie Brennan. She was wearing jeans, and a padded bomber jacket like his. Although he wondered if *bomber* was an appropriate term to use now.

Part of Unit 3, like him, Stevie had given up her previous Met-liaison role within the team, but she was still responsible for any officers that were loaned to them, or any PCC officers that were part of an investigation. She also coordinated interviews, searches, took witness statements and was training to be part of SO19, regularly attending firing ranges for practice.

A good person to have your back, Zain had always thought.

In front of them a group of protestors were baiting a small line of Met officers.

'Like a fucking emaciated blue line,' said Stevie. 'Where the hell is their back up?'

'Probably us.'

'Fuck.'

'Yeah. What are we doing here anyway? Waste of time.'

'The edict was for all resources on the ground.'

'Edict?'

'Riley's words. More like Hope's probably.'

'Still. It's freezing, and it's not like anything's going to happen. There's more cops in St James's Park than I care to even think about.'

'Maybe,' said Stevie. 'Only . . . You know what I thought when I turned up? All these people, look at them. Thousands of them are hidden behind their masks and cloaks. I couldn't tell one from another.'

'Clues in the name, Stevie. Anonymous?'

'Facetious fuck. You know what I mean. And I thought, shit, imagine if something did happen here. Imagine if the worst happened, where would you even start to look? Every suspect looks pretty much the same.'

She shivered, and her hand went to her shoulder. Zain didn't ask about it. He had more than enough injuries lurking like phantoms in his own body to want to call attention to any that Stevie had.

'So let's hope no one turns up dead then,' he said. 'Where's Rob anyway?'

Detective Sergeant Robin 'Rob' Pelt, also in Unit 3 , was supposed to be infiltrating the riot with them.

'No idea, and honestly don't want to know. Since he started seeing that anti-fox hunting woman he's become a zealot. Does my head in. Glad she dumped him.'

'That's a bit unfair. I think she woke up some moral fibre in him.'

Rob had dated Monica for four months. The relationship had ended, but the animal-loving vegan had left Rob with a new outlook on life. He was as bad as an ex-smoker these days, determined to convert everyone else to his viewpoint.

'Woken up some sort of crap, that's for sure, nothing moral about him. And shame his animal-welfare love doesn't extend to the female of the species. He's still a womanising arsehole.'

'Well he's missing all the fun.'

The protestors were jeering, making no sense, nothing coherent to Zain anyway. Just noise circling into the air, hurting his ears. It all felt pointless, until one of them lit a rag stuffed into a glass bottle.

'Oh shit,' said Stevie.

'What is this, the nineties?'

Zain and Stevie started moving quickly towards the figure holding the lit bottle, its black cloak billowing in the breeze.

'Hope he catches fire,' said Zain.

'That can be arranged.'

They were a couple of feet behind the protestor with the flaming weapon, ready to disarm as soon as they got close enough. The Met officers in turn were closing in from the front, trapping the little group. Zain worried about the Molotov cocktail being hurled into the pub at the side, which could cause serious damage and potential casualties.

He began manoeuvring himself to stand in the path of the armed protestor, acting as a stop gap, hopefully. He should be seen, dressed in his casual attire, and hopefully make whoever was lurking under the Guido Fawkes mask think twice. Think about the people inside the building.

Stevie stayed where she was, in case the group decided to retreat, so she would at least be able to follow if not thwart their attempts. But they didn't seem to care; instead they were inching their way towards the officers that were creeping towards them.

The figure holding the Molotov cocktail turned suddenly, looking at Zain. He felt the same uneasiness he had been feeling all night when staring into the solid white masks with their drawn-on features, their uniform disguise. It was all too familiar: dehumanised opponents. He swallowed hard, staring into the eyeholes, the only discernible features.

There was a thickness in Zain's mind, as he recalled his incarceration. During a botched surveillance with SO15, Zain had been kidnapped and tortured for days. Held in a Portakabin in Portsmouth, about to be beheaded. Every day men with their faces hidden would come and beat him, and one in particular would come only to pull his toenails off, one by one.

Zain felt sick as the masked figure came closer. He thought about letting his cover go, telling the figure to drop the Molotov cocktail, stand down. Instead he stayed fixed, unmoving, caught in what felt like a battle of wills. His nostrils filled with a chemical, not petrol, something else. He didn't get a chance to think much beyond that, as he watched the bottle arc through the air. He tried to work out where it would fall, try to limit its damage if he could. Too late, he saw where it was heading, and ran with every breath he could muster, but he couldn't reach it in time. The Molotov cocktail smashed the windscreen of a parked Honda, and Zain could only watch as the flames spread and in seconds turned it into a fireball, followed by an explosion, renting the night into a hundred pieces of burning rain.

Zain fell to the ground, choking, as screams and chaos surrounded him.

But his brain registered something. A last thought. A last vision. Something was wrong. Very wrong. And it wouldn't be until much later that it made sense to him.

Chapter Three

The body was lying face down, the dark hair exposed behind a Guy Fawkes mask that was still secured to the body's face with an elastic band. DCI Kate Riley watched her breath fog in front of her as she walked towards the lone police officer standing guard. It had been a long, busy night, culminating in a blast which had put her officers' lives at risk. Five hours later the rising sun had transformed the world around her. Kate had sent the rest of her team home as the protestors had begun to disperse. It was as though exposure to morning sunlight would bring them into the glare of discovery, their power of anonymity slipping as the sun slicked up into the sky.

When the masked body had been found it was nearing eight, with St James's Park returning to its status as a shortcut for the civil servants and office workers who used it to get from the Tube to Victoria Street and its surrounding areas. Kate's own team were situated in a building close by, many of her colleagues taking the same route. The body was in a secluded spot, hidden among some thick bushes that kept their foliage in winter. It was close to the lake, and closer to the Buckingham Palace end of the park, away from the protestors.

Kate introduced herself to PC James Alliack. He had been given the night off, one of the few Met officers afforded the privilege. They needed someone awake in the morning to give the impression of business as usual.

'New baby. Works a treat to get out of most things,' he said, smiling.

Ironically, he was probably getting more action than most of his colleagues had the night before. They had mostly ended up babysitting the crowd. Barring a couple of incidents, it had been relatively peaceful. It would have to be Zain at the centre of the biggest action. Coincidence, that was all it was. Though Justin Hope was convinced Zain attracted trouble; in fact he insinuated that Zain stirred it.

PC Alliack was in his early twenties. Kate could see the unmistakable marks of youth on his face, despite the dark circles and lack of sleep smudged under his eyes. A nervousness marked by the way he couldn't hold her gaze for too long. She wouldn't want to be that green and inexperienced again. She couldn't bear to live through those years and uncover that darkness once more.

Born in New England, Kate had been forced by events to give up her identity and relocate, entering witness protection with her mother Jane. Only the boredom of that existence didn't sit well with her, so she had asked for a transfer to another country instead. And here the ex-United States Capitol Police detective, who had also done stints with the Department of Homeland Security, had reinvented herself. The new name, the change from blonde to brunette, had all been relatively straightforward. Impressed by her PhD in Criminal Justice from Brown University, the Met had snapped her up, with some faked references the US government had been obliged to give her.

The only thing that often threatened to give her away, was the American accent she couldn't quite tame. Even though she tried, it slipped through, especially this early. Alliack looked at her curiously as she spoke. 'I'm guessing there won't be many people coming to the party today then? Have you requested support?'

'Yes, ma'am,' he said. 'I've been told to let SOCO do their part first.'

The Scenes of Crime Officers, the forensics experts. They would be fresh after a full night's sleep, and were the most useful presence in these situations. They would gather the evidence that people like Kate would need later. She felt her own tiredness in every cell, and fought it back. Her heart was beating faster than usual, fuelled by the many cups of coffee she had drunk. She probably shouldn't be leading on this, but there were few senior officers around. Plus it was a body, post-riot, in St James's Park. That didn't go under anyone's radar and demanded the PCC's attention and involvement.

'What's their ETA?'

'Should be here any minute.'

'How was the body discovered?'

'Jogger.'

'What would we do without joggers and dog walkers?'

Alliack laughed, unsure if he should in these circumstances. His rawness was endearing in a way, but worrying if he had to have any sort of involvement in the case.

'What happened?' she asked.

'He was jogging through the park, got a cramp, stopped to massage it. Saw something, came to investigate, and saw the blood. Ma'am.'

Kate looked at the sprawled figure. While cloaked, the exposed neck seemed to be quite thick, the shoulders broad. She estimated the height to be over six foot. It would suggest a male, but she didn't want to assume just yet. Not until the pathologists did their job. Kate stared again at the body, the pooled red around it, mixed with mud.

'Did the jogger touch the body at all? Before he called us?'

Alliack shook his head, but tell-tale redness crept into the corners of his face and he averted his eyes.

'Has anyone else been in contact with the body?' she asked, slowly and deliberately, her voice in a lower register than she normally used. It was something she had learned during her Reid technique training, standard for all US law-enforcement officers. Men responded to lower voices more than higher female ones. It shouldn't have to be done, but often in work she used it to make herself heard. She needed the truth, no matter how worried Alliack was about saying whatever it was he was so obviously holding back from her.

She heard him swallow, his Adam's apple almost bursting through the skin on his throat.

'I did,' he said finally. His shoulders hunched forward perceptibly. 'I checked for a pulse, just in case. I know from external examination they look pretty badly done in, but I just wanted to be sure. Was I wrong?'

'No, you did the right thing. We can eliminate ourselves easily, as long as you didn't move the body out of situ, and God help us if they had been alive and we didn't do anything. I'm assuming you didn't feel a pulse?' Kate arched an eyebrow, hoping it would help to reduce the tension.

'No, ma'am, or I would have called an ambulance.'

Kate didn't respond, instead taking in the surrounding area, trying to piece together how the body might have got to where it was. Nothing to suggest what had happened could be seen by her naked eye, but they were set away from where the main action had taken place, so possibly forensics would find something. She looked for tracks indicating that the body had been dragged to its final point, but again there was nothing she could see.

She was itching to turn the body over, take the mask off. She tried to judge from height and weight if she could tell the sex, but apart from the exposed bits of neck indicating a Caucasian victim, she didn't want to assume. The short hair was matted with dried blood and dirt. She tried to see if there was a style to it, something gender specific. She thought then of Stevie; from the back her short hair could have been a man or a woman's.

'Now what, ma'am?'

Kate looked through him, feeling a sense of dread she couldn't explain. She rubbed her arms to get some warmth into them.

'We wait.'

He took a step back, involuntarily, as though she might have seen him. That wasn't possible, he was so far away, watching her through his manipulated sunglasses. From the outside they looked like shades, but they were telescopic lenses, the latest in subtle espionage equipment.

He touched the arms, to adjust his view, focusing on Kate Riley clearly. So this is what she had become, this was the new her. He had wanted to see her in action, see what he was up against.

She didn't look like much. Five ten, brown hair to her shoulders, a jacket concealing the shape of her body. There was no resemblance to who she had been, to the bitch that had ruined his life. He felt an anger bubble in his throat. Her stance was the same though. Erect, sure of herself. Always walking as though she was being propped up by the rod of justice. Fuck her and her righteousness.

He breathed and moved further back into his hiding place. He had to control his anger, the urge to tear her apart. That would came later. Kate Riley would meet her end, in him. For now he had only one task. To keep watching her.

Chapter Four

The cold air was brushing Kate's ears, and she could see frost on the ground. It looked almost beautiful in the bright sun. All she could hear were the birds. It felt picturesque, until she looked at the trauma lying in front of her. PC Alliack seemed to be looking everywhere except at the victim, or at her.

'Your first dead body, I take it?'

'That obvious, ma'am?'

The same masking laughter he had done before. She thought back to the first time she had seen a corpse. She had been to enough family funerals prior to starting her career, but coming to a crime scene, and realising you were too late, that no one was being saved, was different.

She had been part of law enforcement across Washington, the very power heartland of the nation. The place where politicians and the influential all mixed against a heady cocktail of ambition and corruption. It was probably why the idea of London had been so attractive to her, and she hadn't been disappointed by its reality.

'Mine was fairly tame,' she said, breaking the awkward silence that had fallen between them. 'Homeless man, beaten to death for a bottle of beer and his coat.'

'Nice. I mean, not nice, I meant . . .'

'I know. I thought it was ironic, here was someone who by the standards of our materialistic world had nothing, yet somebody thought the bits he did have were worth killing him for. I remem ber I felt utter sadness. And a sense of powerlessness. There was nothing I could do for him. He was dead, and his final minutes were probably horrendous. It seemed so innocuous, but it threw me. I became really depressed after it.'

She stopped to check she wasn't revealing too much or making PC Alliack feel worse. He was staring at her, intensely, hooked on her words.

'What happened?' he said, in a whisper.

'It took a long time to get over it. I saw other murder victims after that, but that man, he never left me. It was the smell, it lingered. Sounds crazy I know, but it was there at random times, like a sensory memory that triggered at inappropriate times. And that hopelessness kept coming back. What was I? Just there to clean up after the fact, not do anything useful?'

She had changed so much, she had moved her world quite literally, and been in some tough battles over the years. Yet that first time was still fresh, she could recall it in an instant. She saw herself back then, educated to the eyeballs, but on the street she was so raw.

'Isn't that part of our job though, ma'am?'

'Yes. And that was what got me through it. I realised I wasn't just there to mop up. I was the last chance for the dead. When their final breath had left them, I was there to be their voice and to make sure they were still heard. Make sure the evil that had fallen on them wouldn't go unchallenged.'

'You found who did it?'

'Yes. Another homeless man. On the streets because the mental health system had failed him, because society had failed him. He should have been in a hospital getting help, instead . . .'

'Sad.'

Kate thought pointless was a more appropriate word.

'Well look on the positive, PC Alliack. We're in the open air so at least you won't have the smell of death to contend with. Until the autopsy of course.'

As if on cue, she saw the forensic pathologist assigned to the PCC making her way through the park.

Dr Rani Kapoor was in her early thirties, with a singsong voice, as though she had stepped out of an animation movie rather than a morgue. Kate didn't like to think it was forced: the pathologist trying to fight the stereotype of the job by always being so cheerful. It irritated her, but she let it go.

'Sorry, sorry, my team are all stuck. Flat tyre so the Batmobile is currently being rescued by the AA. Imagine the look on the face of their mechanic when he rocks up and there's a van full of my lot with their face masks on.'

Even her laughter trilled. Kate felt her insides tightening. She was tired, needed sleep, more coffee, but more importantly some answers.

'Dr Kapoor, this is PC James Alliack, he found the body.'

'Lucky you,' said Dr Kapoor, putting down the metallic case she was carrying. 'Did you touch or move it in any way?'

PC Alliack gave the same details he had already given to Kate about how the body was found, and what he then did. He seemed a lot more relaxed talking to her than he had to Kate earlier. Maybe it was the authority chain – Kate was his superior – or maybe it was just her personality? Really, she must be tired, she thought. Second guessing if people liked her. She had given up that garbage years ago; she was here to do a job. Who she pissed off, or what people might or might not think about her, was of no consequence.

From her case Dr Kapoor pulled out disposable overalls for herself and Kate. They both suited up in the white plastic, Kate immediately glad of the warmth, if not the sharp smell. Dr Kapoor pressed above her right collarbone and began dictating the scene. No more need for manual audio recorders; they were now built in to the forensic suits. Like airplane black boxes, the recordings were removed as the overalls were destroyed. They stepped close to the victim, and the smell of PVC was replaced by the distinct smell of human decay.

'That's odd,' said Dr Kapoor. 'Given the temperature and the fact we are outside, there shouldn't be such an overpowering aroma.'

'It might have been here a lot longer than we thought?' said Kate doubtfully. The protest was the night before and the figure was clearly adhering to the dress code.

Dr Kapoor didn't reply, her face serious, as she studied the body, dictating her observations into the air. She went back to her case, and took out a small digital camera. She started to take shots of the scene and body, then filmed it carefully, taking small steps as she covered the ground painstakingly. This was the Dr Kapoor that Kate preferred, the professional one she could engage with.

Dr Kapoor handed Kate the camera, asked her to do another video scan of the area and body. Meanwhile the pathologist inserted a digital thermometer into the right ear of the victim, and watched her machine beep until she had a reading.

'Ok so this is a KX67, new thing we're helping to trial,' said Dr Kapoor.

'Trial for a thermometer? Aren't they a few centuries late?'

'It comes highly recommended. Records the temperature of the body, the air or room temperature, and takes into account readings for humidity and other pertinent environmental factors, runs an algorithm, before finally churning out a probable time of death.'

'Does it work?'

'I'll take manual readings during the post-mortem, use the liver and rectum temperature to compare the results it gives me, but I've used it in a couple of cases now and the results seem valid.'

The KX67 beeped three times. Dr Kapoor went to pull it out, but it was stuck. She tugged at it harder, and then gasped. The victim's ear had come off with the machine.

Chapter Five

Kate looked at the fleshy stump at the end of the thermometer. Blood and internal veins that had attached it to the head were hanging off the ear, making it look like a fake prop for Halloween. A holiday the British still didn't have the hang of, she thought, as images flooded her mind. New England Fall evenings, the trees riotous colours of red, orange, gold. The noise, the excitement, the atmosphere on the night of 31 October. Her brothers tormenting her, Kate standing up for herself even back then. Her parents looking on, so normal. But when a layer of normality was peeled away there was a darkness that eclipsed most horrors she could attribute to that night. She closed that door before it even opened; it was not the time or the place to be thinking of her past. She was doing too much of that lately.

'Well this is a first for me,' said Dr Kapoor, laughing, as she bagged the torn body part and the KX67, and described for her notes what had happened.

'Ears don't usually un-attach themselves from heads unless they have been cut,' Kate said coldly.

Dr Kapoor moved in closer, using her fingers to trace the bloody hole where the ear had been. The remaining flesh was deep brown, but it was hard to tell if there was any other damage.

'I don't think it was removed with a blade. There's no visible sign of any adhesive or connecting matter, without which the ear wouldn't have remained in place. No, I think I simply pulled it off. Question is how, what's happened inside to make it so loose?'

Dr Kapoor checked the hands next. They were covered in black gloves, bits of leaves and mud. She then traced her fingers around the body, following its shape gently.

'Just checking in case there's anything directly under the body that might get moved when I turn it over,' she explained. 'Curious. See here, there's splash marks on the trouser legs and boots, but the back of the cloak is clean. I think we can rule out the body being dragged to its current location.'

'The splash marks would suggest the victim was alive at some point in St James's? Did you check the reading on the KX67? Did it give a reading?'

'Yes, but it suggested a body temperature of 40.2 degrees. That would be impossible even under normal circumstances. I think it's met its match in testing. A dislocated ear. I'll report back to the manufacturer.'

Dr Kapoor took a phone from a pocket of her suit, dialled her team.

'Look, just show some initiative, and get here somehow. Get taxis and claim them back through expenses. I need this place examined asap. Something isn't right.'

She tutted when she ended the call.

'Honestly, they have a combined IQ of thousands, and can give you an academic paper worthy of a doctorate on some of the most complex science around, but when it comes to common sense, I do despair, DCI Riley.'

'You said something didn't feel right?'

'Are you OK to assist me moving the body?'

'Yes, of course.'

Dr Kapoor covered the gloved hands of the victim in plastic bags. They were positioned as though the victim was asleep, the right hand at ninety degrees and close to the shoulder, the left hand arched at a higher angle over the head. Dr Kapoor put covers over the boots next.

'The cloak doesn't seem to have any folds in it, from the back anyway. None of the clothing does. It's very odd: even if the body had been carried here rather than dragged, there should be something.'

'You think it was positioned after the act?' asked Kate.

'Possibly.'

She motioned Kate over, and asked her to grab the body at shin level. Dr Kapoor took hold of the body at shoulder level, and counted them in. On three they moved the body over onto its back. Kate felt a moment of horror as the masked face stared up at her. Dried blood congealed at the sides where it touched the face, and more blood had spattered down the torso. The ground that had been hidden under the victim was pocked with puddles of more red and brown, where blood had leaked and congealed with the soft earth.

For a moment Kate pictured her mother Jane. And then her father. His orders had led to an assault in which Jane had been physically broken. When Kate had found her after the attack, her mother's face was a bloody, damaged mess, with pools of red on the wooden floor of their family home. Kate blinked the image away, guilt always palpable that it was her actions that had caused the attack on her mother. Always ready to pinch deep inside.

The front of the body was covered in mud, but Kate couldn't tell if that meant it had been in contact with the ground by being pulled across it, or if it was just from where it had been lying. Dr Kapoor looked more intently, shook her head. She took out her digicam again and began taking photographs while describing what they could see.

Satisfied she had taken a note of everything, and that her external examination was done, Dr Kapoor put her hands on the mask.

'Ready to see who we have under here, DCI Riley?'

Kate nodded, as the pathologist began to pull the smiling white plastic off.

Chapter Six

The mask was attached to the head using an elasticated band. Dr Kapoor felt around the back of the skull, and brought the elastic over to the front. The mask made a sucking noise as she gently eased it off, holding it above the face for a few seconds, before moving it aside.

There was absolute silence as the two women stared at the mutilation in front of them. The pathologist's hands started shaking slightly. She checked the back of the mask, covered in blood, and put it in an evidence bag, hands still not steady. She then began to dictate for the recording. Kate felt her insides move up to her mouth.

'The victim appears to be male, age difficult to determine in current state. The face is . . .' Dr Kapoor stopped. Kate didn't quite know how to describe it either. 'The face seems to have sunk into itself. The nose is flat, the cheeks have turned into the skull. The eyelids are closed, but further into the sockets than they should be. Blood has leaked from the eyes, the nose and the mouth. There are no obvious signs of actual trauma, no cuts or bruises I can see. There may be more detail during the post-mortem, once the surface plasma has been removed. For now, it appears as though the face has simply collapsed in on itself.'

Dr Kapoor started to feel the body, pressing gently into the torso.

'What do you think?' said Kate. 'What can do that? External trauma?'

'I'm not sure. If the victim's face had been battered there would be a lot more bruising, lacerations and it would be much messier. Apart from the blood coming from the eyes, nose and mouth, there doesn't appear to be that level of physical damage.'

'Unless it was done with a lot of control?' Kate had studied the psychopaths of the world as part of her doctorate, she knew all about rituals and obsessions. She had then seen at first-hand how someone could slowly deconstruct another human, taking their time and making sure each contact was one that fulfilled some disgusting need. Whether the perpetrator was a damaged individual or a terrorist. Or a father.

'Possibly,' said Dr Kapoor. 'I just . . . I honestly haven't come across anything like this before outside a lecture or seminar. I need to get the body back to University College Hospital and do a thorough examination there. I need X-rays, and tox reports and something more . . .'

She stopped mid flow, then started dictating into her suit again.

'Visual of a raised lump, a blister possibly, to the *lobulus auriculae*, on the left side.' She ran her finger over where the left earlobe joined the face, and Kate saw what she was referring to. It looked like a lump, or a giant zit, that had burst. 'Approximately three centimetres in diameter.'

Kate held her breath, unsure of what, if anything, it meant.

'I'm breaking with protocol to begin an examination of the body *in situ*,' said Dr Kapoor.

The cloak was stitched shut, it was one you pulled over the head, so Dr Kapoor took out small scissors and started to cut the material from the throat down. Kate saw the bits of stubble growing into the skin; definitely male then. The neck was relatively clean, the material must have protected it to some extent.

Dr Kapoor pulled the cloak back, revealing a striped white shirt, which was covered in the unmistakable patterns of blood and viscera. It was tucked in neatly at the waist, which struck Kate as being odd. Dr Kapoor took pictures, before starting to unbutton the shirt. She did it carefully one button at a time, and asked Kate to film as she did, so they had a record of each alteration made to the way they found the body originally. Kate held the camera at an angle, but her eyes were fixed to Dr Kapoor's hands as they worked. When all the buttons were open, she pulled the shirt back gently.

'My God!' breathed Dr Kapoor.

Kate dropped to her knees, and stared. The body was covered in lesions, boils and craters. Some of them had erupted, accounting for the blood that soaked the victim's shirt. She looked on, sickened by what she was seeing, yet resolved to keep focused. She moved in closer. As she did, one of the boils on the body burst. She felt warm fluid spatter her cheek. Dr Kapoor looked at her intently, a worried expression crossing her face.

Neither of them moved. This wasn't a stabbing, or anything involving a physical weapon. Kate's mind reeled at what it might be, second guessing and coming up with theories she didn't like the feel of.

'You need to call the Royal Free,' Dr Kapoor told her. 'Put them on alert.'

'The Royal Free? The hospital?'

Kate couldn't stop the thought entering her head. It was where the Ebola patients had been treated.

Chapter Seven

Zain watched the ambulances line up, four of them, on Birdcage Walk. The location reminded him of a different time, meeting Kate Riley, a conversation on a knife edge. He had landed on the blunt side, but still felt cut. He had nearly been killed in a previous case, and knew his recovery was not full enough for him to be back on active duty. Once again rules had been bent for him. Desperation had made him grateful back then. Now, he wasn't so sure. Not about the role, Unit 3 and most of all not about Kate Riley. She had saved his life, she had given him back his career. He owed her. Still, there was that scene in his head, a night in Winchester when they might have crossed a line, if he wasn't so messed up. Become more than just colleagues. You couldn't switch that off. And against all of that, he resented her. He felt as though he owed her a debt, and he would never be able to pay it back. Loyalty and resentment. Zain's brain just didn't do normal anymore, and he had given up trying to work it out.

When Kate called him earlier that morning, Zain was at the Accident and Emergency unit at University College Hospital, being checked out for smoke inhalation and minor skin damage caused by flying burning debris. Stevie was being checked out in another cubicle and seemed to be OK. He wasn't so sure about himself. The heat, the impact of the explosion, losing consciousness for a few minutes.

Kate had been sketchy on details during the call, saying only that a body had been found, and it was being taken to the Royal Free for the autopsy. She asked him to take charge of the investigation once she was there. It was only when he got to the scene that Michelle called him. Michelle Cable was the IT and systems analyst for Unit 3. She had secured Kate a communication channel and it was through this that Zain had been given more details. About suspicious pustules being found on the male victim and as a precaution Dr Kapoor had asked for containment. Nobody was allowed near the scene, only the hazmat team when they got there. And no word of this through any open channels, or normal mobile conversation.

Zain felt insulted, he did understand what covert meant. He had worked for SO15 and GCHQ, he wasn't some rookie. He had remained on the perimeter of where the victim had been found until the ambulances had turned up.

Inside each ambulance was a Multi-Disciplinary Team of two, wearing deep blue hazmat uniforms. Both members of the MDT had their faces covered with clear plastic helmets. It creeped him out, felt like an overreaction. They didn't know what they were dealing with. Suspicious pustules on a dead body? Fuck that shit.

The doors of the vehicles began to open one by one, the MDTs assembling in groups, discussing tactics. Zain was told to keep his distance, stay on the perimeter of the park. He couldn't even see Kate from here. A sliver of worry ran through him for her. He tried to ignore it. Failed. Berated himself for caring so much. She was his boss, nothing more. He didn't believe that even as he thought it.

'DS Harris?'

Zain turned to look into a plastic encased face, a man with brown eyes and a wide nose. Every inch of him was covered with something. They must have comms equipment built in, thought Zain, or how else could they be heard or hear him?

'What's the plan?'

'We are going to take our vehicles in. We have a route mapped out, based on the suggested location of DCI Riley and the victim. We are expecting to find three live subjects that need containing, and one deceased subject. Is that your understanding?'

'Yes, that's what she said.'

'Anyone else found in the area will also be contained, let me make that clear.'

'Fine by me.'

'My teams will load up the subjects into the vehicles, after which we will proceed to the Royal Free. We will need patrol bikes to clear the traffic before us. Can that be arranged?'

'Yes, sure, no problem. See what I can do, Doctor . . .?'

'Apologies, Professor Nick Gerard.'

Top level surgeon, Zain thought. He knew they called themselves professor when they were consultants. A leftover from the days surgery used to be performed by the local butcher.

'Once we have them back at the Royal Free, we will hold them in isolation units, where the MDTs will treat them. We will run tests, look for any symptoms that might manifest, keep them under observation, give them some psych support. Anything we can to find out exactly what we are dealing with.'

'Sounds intense. I feel like we should be doing something more? Putting out a national alert, a warning? Telling anyone who was here to check themselves?'

'Check themselves for what, DS Harris? We have no idea what we're dealing with yet. Panicking the general populace is not a strategy, it's the path of creating more problems.'

'I know that, I'm not an idiot.'

'I didn't suggest you were. Public Health England have planned for scenarios like this. We are now going to execute those rigid strategies without emotional interference. So are we OK? Can you get us the security we require?'

'Yes, no problem.'

'Good, in that case, we will commence with the extraction.'

Knob, thought Zain. Extract the stick from up your ass first.

'I'll just wait here I guess, and follow you to Hampstead.'

Zain felt patronised, but surgeons were built like that he knew. He had enough experience of them, putting him back together over the years. The physical Zain was at least stitched back to some level of functioning normality. But even the best surgeons couldn't glue back his fractured brain properly.

Professor Gerard walked briskly, updating his blue MDT army, who filed back into their ambulances. The doors closed, and the vehicles started their slow crawl into St James's Park. Heading to Kate, and the dead body.

Chapter Eight

Kate watched as James Alliack made a call to his wife. His face was pale, and he hadn't stopped shivering since she had explained to him what was going on.

'It's going to take a while, as I was the first officer to respond; I'll have to go and watch the autopsy and process the case. I might not be back until late. Very late. I'm not sure. I'll call you and let you know, yeah?'

His eyes looked into Kate's, but she had no answers for him. She instead watched Dr Kapoor take swabs of the erupted boils and craters, and take the temperature again, this time in the other ear.

'Listen, give Amy a big kiss from me, OK? Tell her Daddy loves her, and will be home soon,' said Alliack. 'And, you . . .'

Kate shot him a warning look, and shook her head.

'I love you, see you later?' he said, and ended the call. 'I will see her later, won't I?'

'Of course. It's just a precaution that's all. We can't take any risks, and since all three of us have come into contact with the deceased, it just makes sense.'

She wasn't convinced it did. There had been thousands of people in the park the night before, and who knew what route the victim had taken to get there. What if the virus was airborne? Imagine the number of people on a London Underground train, or on a bus. She shut those thoughts down quickly; she was being irrational. Dr Kapoor was just being cautious that's all; it was the professional thing to do. There was no need to jump to conclusions that might cloud her judgement. She would not be the one to fall to pieces today, especially if it turned out to be something else, something innocuous.

She thought of her mother then. How would she cope without Kate there to look after her? That was an emotional punch she didn't need. In her former life, Kate had turned witness for the FBI against her own father, but he had extracted his revenge when he got the chance. And it was on Jane mainly, because the thugs he had hired had messed up their timing and Kate wasn't home. The injuries they inflicted on Jane, caused by using a baseball bat repeatedly to her head, had left her with prosopagnosia, the inability to recognise faces. Kate and her mother had been forced into witness protection, but there would be no independence for Jane for the rest of her life, and it was Kate's duty to care for her. And if there was no Kate, who would? She stifled the guttural emotive response inside her, and focused instead on the lesions on the deceased's body.

'Do they look familiar at all? Have you come across them clinically, or through your academic work?' Kate asked Dr Kapoor.

'They look like something medieval, pictures I've seen at conferences. I haven't come across anything like this clinically. And until we know what it is, I think it's dangerous to give it a name.'

'Yes of course.'

At least the cheerfulness had gone, and it was professional Dr Kapoor she was working with.

Kate knew the names already. Smallpox, Ebola, plague. Any number of poisons, like Ricin. They could be looking at anything.

This could be a biological act of war, or it could be nothing, an unfortunate skin condition that the victim had. Kate wished she thought this latter theory was likely.

'The body has finally cooled to thirty-seven degrees,' said Dr Kapoor. 'That's what a living person may have.'

'So it spiked? What might cause that?'

'I have no idea. Fever of some sort, but I wouldn't expect it to last once the victim was no longer alive.'

'And we're sure he's not?'

'Yes.'

Kate saw PC Alliack had sat down, his back to a tree, as he stared out across the park. She didn't like the phone in his hand, the possibility he might text someone. She walked over to him.

'Can I take that please?' she said, holding out her hand. He grasped it close to his chest, and looked at her as though she was about to mug him.

'For what?'

'It's just standard procedure in these circumstances. I've asked Dr Kapoor to do the same,' she lied. 'Please, Constable.'

Kate had to grab the phone from him as soon as he made the effort to hand it to her. She felt for him. He had been given the supposed easy shift, allowed to stay home when they thought things might get ugly. Instead, he had been plunged into something he couldn't imagine. She just hoped for all their sakes it was nothing.

'DCI Riley,' said Dr Kapoor. Her voice was higher pitched, excited almost. 'I think I have a name for you.'

Chapter Nine

Dr Kapoor had kept herself busy as they waited for the hazmat team to arrive.

'I will not be letting my team anywhere near the body until I know what we are dealing with. I'll do the autopsy and any other forensic work that needs to be done once we're at the hospital.'

'They will still need to process the crime scene,' Kate had said. 'There must be a hell of a lot of evidence that needs to be collected and sifted through.'

'That's fine, and they will, but only under heavy supervision from PHE and DCD. They have a response team there, they need to be alerted.'

Kate didn't like the sound of that. Public Health England or the Department for Communicable Diseases being informed would widen the pool of people that could potentially leak information. Yet she knew it had to happen, if it hadn't already.

'I'll leave it with PCC Hope to orchestrate,' she said. Her stock answer for anything difficult she needed time to deal with. He had some uses.

Kate had joined the PCC's Unit 3 with great ambition, taking a role she finally thought might bring her back into the guts of a capital city. She hoped for the big cases, the complicated ones that would test her, that required her. Over the months, sitting in witness protection, Kate had felt the mould start to set in. Unit 3 was meant to be her greatest achievement, a fuck you to the men that had destroyed her and her mother. The men she had in turn also helped to destroy.

Only what she found working for Justin Hope was another man who was using his position to his advantage. Helping those he felt he needed, or who would be of benefit to him, practicing law enforcement at the highest political levels, just this side of corruption. Just like her father. Only her father had well and truly crossed that line.

For now though, Kate was stuck with PCC Hope, and she was learning to live with him as her direct supervisor. Her previous manager had gone off work due to illness after clashing with PCC Hope and had never come back.

Kate wasn't sure where her loyalty lay, but she couldn't leave her team to PCC Hope's political machinations. The teams under him had expanded considerably, more of the Met's budget had been allocated to him, so he was distracted these days. It meant that she had some freedom at least. But a potential murder with a biological weapon, in his and The Queen's backyard, would surely have him suffocating her once again.

She walked over to the pathologist, who was crouched low near the body. Kate felt as though she had given up the pretence that they would be safe. The blood spatter had caught them both, so they had been exposed to whatever it contained. Dr Kapoor had explained that it wasn't some creature harbouring inside the victim that had caused the pustule to explode, but a build-up of gasses. It was normal during the decay process, and might explain the abnormal temperature readings. It felt like being trapped in an episode of *The X-Files*, too surreal. So she would do what she did best, which was cling to the logic involved in procedure.

'What is it?' Kate said, bracing herself. Dr Kapoor looked confused at her words. 'You have a name?'

'I don't mean for the pathogen or whatever we're dealing with. I mean for the victim.'

Kate felt excitement bristle through her, her senses alert, despite the stress of the situation.

'How did you manage that?'

'The good old-fashioned way. Searched his pockets.'

Dr Kapoor handed Kate a wallet. It was empty except for an ID. Issued as standard by the government to all its employees, the lion and unicorn prominent in one corner. She had read it represented England, the lion, and Scotland, the unicorn. If Scotland ever became independent what would happen to the mythical creature?

The man's face was clear in a passport-sized photo; he had been attractive, in what was probably his late forties if the picture was recent. He had a preppy-style cut to his hair and his face was angular, his eyes brown.

Her heart skipped when she read the name, and the job title.

'You've got a live one,' said Dr Kapoor.

I've got an absolute nightmare, Kate was thinking. PCC Hope would definitely be all over this one, as would half of Whitehall and the secret services, given the apparent nature of the death. GOVERNMENT OFFICIAL DIES THROUGH SUSPECTED BIOLOGICAL WARFARE ATTACK. If it was him of course; the face had sunk so badly it was hard to tell. And it was odd that the wallet was empty except for the ID. As though it was there on purpose.

'There's no department name,' Kate said. 'He could work for any of the branches of the Civil Service.'

'Yes, but whichever one it is, he's pretty much heading it up. And I think a Google search would easily tell us.'

Kate took the hint, and searched the name on her phone, but didn't get time to explore further as she heard the ambulances containing the hazmat teams pull up.

Chapter Ten

Kate bit back her anxiety as the ambulances emptied. She was faced with ten individuals, moving in groups, heading towards her. James Alliack swore, his breathing now laboured, as panic took hold of him completely.

A man with brown eyes and heavy brows came close to Kate. There was a team of two around him, a man and a woman, dressed in the same blue suits and clear face helmets.

'Professor Nick Gerard,' he told her. 'I'm leading the MDTs, coordinating your safe passage to the Royal Free. You're DCI Kate Riley I take it?'

Kate nodded.

'So the procedure will be as follows. One team will contain and transport the deceased. The others will be responsible for yourself and your colleagues. We are going to decontaminate you and dress you in biohazard suits, and then place you all into the back of our ambulances. Does that make sense?'

None of this made any sense to Kate, but she nodded silently again, showing her understanding.

'We have a containment unit ready, that will allow us to work on the body without coming into contact with it. We've also set up an autopsy suite in a mobile isolation unit back at the Royal Free, to minimise risk to others. We need to conduct an autopsy at speed, get the remains tested, try and identify what pathogens might have caused this. Hopefully conclude that there were none, and that the marks on the body are a result of something else entirely.'

'I like your optimism.'

'Essential when faced with a crisis such as this. I was responsible for treating the Ebola victims. I had to compartmentalise back then, and I will do so again now. Let's not panic, until we have to.'

'And will we have to? If you find that this is worth worrying about?'

His eyes grew darker, and stared intensely into her own.

'We have procedures in place, DCI Riley. For every eventuality. Even this.'

Kate called Hope to update him. She didn't tell him about the ID, only that Dr Kapoor suspected a Category A virus. Category A's, she went on to drive home the point, included diseases like Ebola, plague (bubonic, septicemic, pneumonic) and smallpox. Hope had let her speak without interruption for once, actually listening to what she said.

'I am going to be in isolation at the Royal Free. I will be asking Zain Harris to take the lead on this for now.'

'You think your team are still best placed to carry out this investigation? I think we should hand it over to PHE or DCD. It's beyond our remit to deal with something like this.'

'I know, but until we're sure, we can't create mass hysteria. People think Cat A's are airborne, or you can get them from close proximity.'

'If the victim was leaking blood in the way you have suggested, anything is possible.'

'Of course, sir. I just think if you let us carry out this initial part of the investigation, we can probably get some answers that would be delayed if too many people are involved.'

'I hear you,' he said. Then silence as he pondered his next move. She always imagined him like Cardinal Richelieu from *The Three Musketeers*, always plotting. 'I am going to be speaking to my counterparts across the services later today, they will be made aware and put on high alert. I will ask them to let us lead on this, and I will ensure a media blackout. I know how they think and what they can offer us. You have four hours to carry out your investigation.'

Kate would take it. It meant four hours in which there wasn't a mass panic and a breakdown in everything that was normal. It would have to be enough, she just hoped they could get some answers quickly.

She ended the call as the MDT began to spray her with infection control liquid. It smelt like bleach, and stung her eyes and nose.

'I hope that's not corrosive,' she said.

No one spoke, as they began dressing her in a biohazard suit. It felt odd, the heavy plastic being put over her forensic coverings. She felt uncomfortable and started to sweat, despite the frozen air around her.

The last thing to go on was her helmet. It felt leaden, the breathing apparatus attached to the back causing the whole thing to feel weighed down. It was switched on, her breath now being filtered before it was released, and any air coming in also cleansed.

Dressed in the hazmat suit, breathing as though in a sci-fi movie, she was then sprayed again. This time she couldn't smell the bleach, the suit she wore impenetrable even by molecules stuck to the air.

Professor Gerard walked close to her.

'Follow me to the ambulance assigned to you.'

Kate did as he requested. She spotted the MDT responsible for moving the body into a plastic bag. For a moment she imagined herself in a similar position, her own lifeless body being carried by strangers to be disposed of. She shuddered, despite the clawing heat of the layers of protective clothing she wore.

The MDT walked her to a line of ambulances. What looked like a giant protective cot for premature babies was waiting by one. It was zipped open and the body was placed inside. There were plastic holes cut around it, which were plastic arm covers, with gloves attached at the ends. She remembered seeing the same when the Ebola patients were treated; they allowed doctors to touch the patients without there being any actual contact.

The body was placed inside the ambulance, and Kate saw Dr Kapoor get into another one. Again she looked quite calm. James Alliack was being carried into a third ambulance, supported on either side by members of his MDT. Kate suspected he had been given a sedative to calm him down. Satisfied that everyone was safe, Kate climbed into her ambulance.

Inside was a plastic sheet. She was asked to step behind it, before it was sealed, like a zip lock freezer bag. She was now contained in half the ambulance, as the rest of the MDT got in. The doors shut behind them, and the vehicle started to make its way to the Royal Free.

Chapter Eleven

Zain got into his Audi A6, his official assigned ride from the Commissioner. He thought he might have got an upgrade on his return, although Stevie had pointed out quite quickly that he was lucky they didn't demote him and give him a banged-up second-hand vehicle.

DS Stevie Brennan had thawed a lot since Zain's return. She'd hated him to begin with and tried to antagonise and block him at every opportunity. Pissed off that he got a promotion over her, to act as DCI Kate Riley's second in command, she had made her annoyance clear. Things happen though, and people change. Stevie had been through some major shit of her own, and it had brought them closer. They weren't exactly best mates, but there was something there.

Zain started the car up, ready to follow the ambulances. The Royal Free was the only centre in London geared up to deal with potentially lethal outbreaks. He dreaded to think what would happen if this was such an outbreak. How would they cope with the demand?

He had arranged for there to be police escorts on motorbikes with the ambulance, and also an unmarked car in case back up was needed. The PCC hadn't started out with many staff, so previously any serious investigation always meant winding up the Met by stealing their staff and resources to help out. A new recruitment drive however had brought in a host of new officers, mainly ex-Met ironically, with money taken from the Met itself. It now meant that there were enough bodies on the ground at the PCC headquarters to allow some tasks to be done in-house.

He switched his stereo on. Sufi music his grandfather had sent him. Arabic religious chants against the duff drum, recorded in Konya where the dervishes ruled the spiritual waves. It was great music to think to. He used it to practise his Krav Maga routines sometimes. An Israeli martial art to Arabic incantations. A kind of peace in the Middle East.

Zain was all about the peace these days. He was so fucked up by the drama of his life that he needed any calm he could find. His own past, the bad choices he'd made, and the addictions he used to keep his nightmares curtailed. Every day felt like breathing in sludge, taking in a lung full, and choking. He slammed his steering wheel to the beats of the music, and pulled out into the traffic. His phone rang as he set his satnav to the hospital. He pressed inside his steering wheel; it was DCI Kate Riley.

'How are you even calling?' he asked, trying to quiet the voice inside him that said how great it felt to hear from her, know she sounded OK.

'They have comms built into these suits, so I can use my phone. And yes, I'm using the secure app you and Michelle sent over,' she explained, although sounding slightly pissed off that she had to. 'Harris, I have a name for you. Potentially. Dr Kapoor found ID on the victim, are you OK to follow up? And you need to treat this with the utmost care. Only when you are sure we have the right person, and that this isn't some plant, do I want you to take it to Hope.'

It was still there wasn't it, he thought. The trust issue. He didn't blame her, but still, it hurt. Zain had been conflicted after his initial recruitment to Unit 3. It followed on from his kidnap and torture ordeal, his medical reports declaring him unfit, but Hope ignoring them on the say of Zain's ex-boss and mentor from SO15, DCI Raymond Cross. PCC Hope had then asked Zain to carry out surveillance on DCI Kate Riley and her team for him, something he was ashamed he had done. That was his past though, one of the many fucked-up things he had done. He just wished Kate could get beyond it. It only added to his confusion when dealing with her. If she didn't trust him, why had she bothered to save him so many times? Why did she build that bridge, one where Zain had become dependent on her kindness. Loving and hating her at the same time.

'Yeah sure,' he said. Casual, cool, unaffected. He listened as she told him the name on the ID. He whistled. 'What the actual fuck? How is that possible? That's going to put some real crap on us, we're going to have all sorts sniffing around. My old bosses for one.'

'I am aware of that. At present only myself and Dr Kapoor know the details, and I would like it to stay that way.'

'You know that just means this might be something way beyond what we thought? Government arsehole gets whacked by some weird biological shit? This is going to be nuclear when it gets out.'

'Which it isn't, not until we're sure anyway.'

'Yes, boss.'

'PCC Hope's given us four hours to carry out our investigation. After that, we lose control of it.'

Zain changed direction and drove in silence, before parking by the PCC head office. They were now just off Whitehall, the building entered through an archway that was hidden unless you knew it was there. The outside was the brown yellow stone familiar to all the buildings around there, stolid and historical in its look. But the inside had been revamped with the latest technology.

Zain took his laptop from under his car seat, and connected to a secure wireless network accessed via the PCC building. He checked his uniquely generated passcode, which changed every thirty minutes, on his phone. It was an app he and Michelle had developed, to stop them having to carry, and possibly lose, physical fobs. Once inside, he had access to the PCC search engines and databases. He typed in the details Kate had given him.

In less than a minute he had the information he needed on screen, and a home address. He set his coordinates for St George's Wharf, opposite the MI6 building. Odd place for someone like this to live. Not just because it had a price tag that would blow most people's minds.

'So, Julian Leakey,' said Zain. 'Let's see if this is you we've found. And, if so then why the hell is the Permanent Under Secretary for International Development lying dead in St James's Park covered in plague like pustules?'

Chapter Twelve

The ambulances parked in the basement of the Royal Free. Kate could hear voices as the MDTs began to alight, and staff from inside rushed out with more equipment. She understood how containment worked, and the need to be very careful. But if this was the manpower it took to handle just four cases, she felt despair at the city having to cope with thousands and potentially hundreds of thousands if this was an attack or an outbreak.

The doors to her own ambulance opened and Professor Gerard got in, making the other occupants leave. It was just the two of them, partitioned by a plastic sheet.

He couldn't meet her eyes.

'Problem?' she asked.

He didn't move, or react to her words. She saw the intercom sign then. Whatever the plastic wall between them was, it was flimsy enough to appear to be a curtain, but strong enough to act as a sound barrier. She pressed the intercom, and repeated her question. Professor Gerard looked up at her.

'Potentially. Your colleague, Dr Kapoor, is causing quite a stir. She would like to personally proceed with a physical autopsy of the deceased.'

Dr Kapoor was rising in her estimation. It was the sensible thing to do. She and Kate had potentially been exposed to what-ever it was the victim had died from; keeping others away from the sort of contact a post mortem would involve seemed like a rational choice.

'I would rather treat you both in an isolation unit, run some tests, see what we might be dealing with. Before anything else.'

'Can't we do both? Run your tests in the mobile isolation unit you set up for the autopsy, while we carry it out?'

Kate had just given her weight to Dr Kapoor's request. It was now the force of law enforcement and the PCC versus hospital administration.

'It's not about the logistics. What is more pertinent to this case is that we won't be carrying out a physical autopsy.'

'What do you mean?'

'We are forbidden to do so in cases where a Category A virus is suspected.'

'I don't understand. You said you wanted to do a PM when you collected us?'

'Yes. It will be done using the iGene table. It's a digital autopsy. We will scan the body. We will also collect samples using the isolation bubble you saw us put the body in.'

'I see. And Dr Kapoor wants to carry out a physical one?'

'Yes. She seems to think because you may be infected, it won't pose a danger to yourselves. I cannot risk the bodily fluids of a Cat A victim running freely like that.'

'Dr Kapoor can do the autopsy, but she will do a digital one. You have your isolation unit set-up, test us both there at the same time.'

'We aren't prepared to test live patients in the mobile autopsy suite . . .'

'How long would it take to get the containment unit ready? With what we need?'

'I don't think that's a reasonable request at this late stage . . .'

'How long?'

'An hour at least . . .'

'You have twenty minutes to turn it into a mobile testing unit as well as an autopsy suite. Dr Kapoor may also be trying to minimise risk. You are aware of Locard's principle?'

'Of course. The forensic principle that every contact leaves a trace.'

'Imagine the fallout if we take whatever we are carrying anywhere into a packed hospital, and the risk we are exposing people to.'

'We are able to isolate you both, it's what we've done in the past. There are no concerns for us.'

'With all due respect Professor, you knew then what you were dealing with. It was Ebola. It had a name, a modus operandi, or whatever you guys call the way a virus works. This is an unknown at the moment. You put together the mobile unit, and we have a tight chain of contact, and it's minimal. From the backs of these ambulances straight into a secure box.'

Professor Gerard studied her carefully. Kate clenched her stomach muscles, and stared back. She would never lose at this game. She had practiced too many times on her stubborn mother, not to mention the sort of people she had had to deal with both in her work and personal life. Jane's illness was causing memory loss, and her inability to recognise faces she saw everyday was always a reason for her to act out. And the men from Kate's past? Well, Professor Gerard was nothing in comparison to people like her father.

Professor Gerard looked away, blinked first. Kate didn't expect anything less. She would not be cowed, not after everything she had been through.

'Twenty minutes. Get the team in to take my samples, I'm ready for them.'

Ready to find out what it was she might be carrying. And if it was fatal, just how long she might have to live. She thought of her mother. And then she thought of Eric. They had barely begun, and it was already potentially at an end.

Dr Eric Sandler had come into her life after his involvement in a recent case she had taken the lead on, his expertise as a forensic cyber psychologist helping her understand a whole new way of being in the virtual universe around her. She had always struggled with relationships; she blamed her father for that, the way he drip drip bullied her mother over the years, even before she knew the extent of his corruption. He had been a member of City Hall, her brothers in law enforcement like her. They were the face of respectability, well connected and trusted. Only, her father had come from nothing and was determined to make something of himself, even if it meant flouting the very rules he was meant to be upholding.

Using his position he had created a veritable empire of corruption. Backhand deals, threats, gangland support, covering up the worst crimes, which he was almost certainly involved in too. Drugs, prostitution, murder. He had expected Kate to follow suit, follow him into the family business. Only she wasn't Kate Riley back then, she was Winter Morgan. And she had refused. She had gone along with him at face value, but in reality had gathered evidence for the FBI. And when her father was brought to court, it was her testimony and evidence that had landed him in prison.

Except her father was no fool; he had covered up most of his past. So the sentence was small, and Kate/Winter and her mother were whisked off into witness protection. But before they could go, her father had exacted his revenge, leaving her mother for dead.

Only Jane had stood up after that. She had opened up about her past, talked about the violence she had suffered at her husband's hands. And it was her testimony, coupled with medical records and statements given in confidence, that had given Kate's father a longer sentence. But with her mother so dependent on Kate, there was no realistic way Kate could indulge in a relationship that would pose a danger to her ability to care for Jane. So she had made desperate and damaging choices, sleeping with men who were unavailable when she needed to feel some human contact.

The last of these had been Ryan, the small-town American who had relocated to London, and who had become her mother's primary carer for most of the day while Kate was at work. Ryan was very much married to Chloe. Kate had crossed too many lines with that relationship, and had had to let him go when she and her mother changed location from North London to Pimlico.

She missed Ryan. She had trusted him to look after her mother, but her new set-up meant she had fewer concerns about her mother's safety. Jane and Kate now lived in an open-gate prison, in effect.

So she had allowed herself to start dating Eric when he'd asked her out, and his commitments to his role at Cambridge University meant they rarely saw each other.

Things had seemed to fall into place. But now, once again, Kate was being pulled away from normality, to the place of greatest risk.

But the victim might hold the answers they desperately needed. Kate wondered how Zain was getting on confirming his identity and potentially his last movements. A DNA match would be best, and they'd need that quickly.

Chapter Thirteen

Zain was livid. He was just about to arrive at the Leakey residence, when he got a call from Deborah Scarr, requesting his presence back at the Police Crime Commissioner's HQ. Deborah was the Executive Assistant to the PCC for Westminster. Her orders were Hope's, although she was a lot more pleasant to deal with.

Zain parked his Audi in the underground car park, accessed via a tiny side alley opposite Westminster Abbey. It was blocked off at one end, with a wooden door to the side, which rose up like a shutter to let vehicles in and out. No room for a U-turn; you either got in first time or you got stuck. Zain was used to it now, easily snaking his way through.

Sitting in the dimness, surrounded by empty vehicles, with water streaming down a wall where the ancient guttering had given way, Zain felt anxiety rub him. Kate had trusted him with this, and he didn't know if he could hold his own with Hope. There was a time he didn't have these slivers of doubt, but that was before. Before he was brought low by men who wanted to inflict as much pain on him as they could, for a cause he had once naively supported. Sometimes he felt as though it was retribution.

That life seemed so distant now. Zain had instead become the hope of the security services how someone with his background should really be used. And in the end he had felt used, and abandoned. He'd found out later that those same security services were going to let him die in the Portakabin his kidnappers were holding him in. The terrorists who had taken him were going to be allowed to behead him on camera, and broadcast it worldwide. Until a last-minute rescue attempt had been put together. The reasons for which he was never fully told.

So now, he didn't trust himself, or anyone else. Well, maybe Kate Riley. That was about it. He had seen her honour and integrity. When the world was full of so much underhand bullshit, she stood out as something so much better. And what was he doing? Was he in any fit state to be taking this on? He'd been sitting in A & E only a few hours before, half choked. He still had cuts that were stinging when he touched them, and he reeked of smoke.

He opened his glove compartment, feeling around for the only other thing he trusted. The plastic packet was familiar now. He no longer needed to examine it every time; the Chinese writing barely registered. He should scan the image and see if an online search could translate it for him. But he didn't really want to know. He was convinced it was snake venom or alligator balls he was consuming.

Plastic foil in hand, Zain popped a green tablet through and swallowed it with reflexive precision. He then took a second. One was never enough these days. Not since his last case. And his second brush with death.

He closed his eyes and breathed in the leather of the seats, the aroma from the pine needles his sisters had sown into parcels that clung to his dashboard. The tablets couldn't be working yet but his heart was already crashing against his ribcage in anticipation of their effect. Zain got out and headed to the secure lift, up to see the PCC, to see what the knob wanted.

Chapter Fourteen

Unlike the temporary office on Victoria Street, where PCC Hope commanded a top-floor view across London, mainly into Buckingham Palace's backyard, the new offices in St James's were more subdued. They were on the second floor, with views across Horseguard's Parade. The office was more traditionally decorated, in muted wood and leather, the odd Persian rug placed around the room. It reminded Zain of a gentleman's club he had been to, the sort where membership was exclusive and only available to those with money, Masonic connections, or some sort of posh breeding. Zain was usually mistaken for the waiter on the odd occasion he had met his father or grandfather at these places.

There were two guards outside the door leading to the PCC's office, both armed with Heckler and Koch MP5SFA3 semi-automatic carbines. The women ignored him as he winked at them, and bowed theatrically. He then showed them his ID, which they instructed him to run through a scanner on the door. It bleeped green, they checked the ID manually, and then pressed a button to let him in.

They must be bored shitless, he thought.

Inside the anteroom was the formidable Deborah Scarr. She had grey hair, tied tightly into a bun, and was wearing a maroon suit. Zain held out his ID for her to check, which she did by running it through a machine on her desk. She then took his thumbprint. It all seemed so tedious. She knew who he was, but rules were rules, he supposed. Although armed men trying to get in would simply shoot the guards and Deborah, sod the ID crap.

'Surprises me every time it clears you,' she said, amusement across her patrician features. 'But who am I to query state of the art technology?'

'Deborah, looking glamorous as ever.'

Zain kissed her on the cheek, holding himself a moment longer to take in the Chanel No. 5 she wore. It reminded him of someone from his past. Before the torture, and the pills and the nightmares. When he could actually get it up. Impotence on top of everything else just seemed like an unnecessary kick, and in some ways the harshest.

'So what have you done now?' she said. 'He was rather desperate to see you.'

'Usual stuff. DCI Riley has done a disappearing act and left me to clear up her mess. You know how it is.'

'Yes, I really do. I hope she's going to be OK.'

'What have you heard?'

'Kate's being taken to an isolation unit at the Royal Free. Unknown pathogen potentially killed a man in St James's Park. Maybe a virus, possibly contagious, she and two others at least have had direct exposure to blood and body fluids from the victim. Anonymous protest night before, horrific possibility there could be dozens of carriers that had contact with the deceased. Is that enough for now?'

Zain smiled at her. She always had his back, and had just given him a lowdown on what exactly the PCC knew. So no potential name, which meant no leak. This was good. A leak would mean that someone knew about the ID found on the body, and they would have had to have cracked the PCC internal secure communications network to find this out.

Zain walked towards the double doors that led into PCC Hope's office. He was about to knock, when Deborah stopped him.

'One last thing,' she said. 'Julian Leakey. Permanent Under Secretary for International Development.'

Zain felt his heart nearly burst, as panic and anger overtook him.

Chapter Fifteen

Professor Gerard had concluded there wasn't enough time to set up testing facilities in the autopsy unit, so he had ordered both Kate and Dr Kapoor to have their samples taken while they were still in their respective ambulances. Kate's arms were aching, where they had failed to take blood properly. She had warned them she always had a problem giving samples; her veins were just too difficult to detect. There was a space in the plastic wall guarding her where they had attached a robotic arm, carrying a needle and syringe. Another space in the wall was filled with a plastic arm, with a purple glove on the end. Professor Gerard watched as one of the nurses, dressed in a hazmat suit, put his arm into the tube and glove. He then began roughly looking for veins on Kate's arms. Satisfied he had one, he began directing the robotic arm with the needle towards the place using his voice. The robot plunged the needle in, but the vein had run away, so all that happened was Kate winced and then was left with a bruise.

The second and third attempts were no better, but the fourth managed to fill a vial. She then had her throat and eyes swabbed. Less traumatic, but still unpleasant.

'There we go, all done,' the nurse had said.

Kate would have hit him if there wasn't so much protection between them. It felt like the most paranoid game of safe sex she had ever been involved in. This made her laugh unintentionally. Professor Gerard had shot her a look.

A few minutes later, Kate was told the autopsy unit was ready, and was led from the back of the ambulance to where they had put the mobile unit.

Kate was walked through a plastic tunnel, a covered pathway for her and she assumed for Dr Kapoor. She was still in the hazmat suit, so the sealed tunnel seemed like overkill. Once through the tunnel, she was at the door of what looked like a trailer park cabin. Her mother would turn her nose up for sure.

The door to the mobile unit was locked by a secure code, which Professor Gerard typed in, before motioning for Kate to go in. She walked in and the door shut behind her, an electronic beep telling her it was locked from the outside. She was essentially trapped inside the metallic box with Dr Kapoor. And a dead body riddled with an unknown lethal substance.

Dr Kapoor was busy with the autopsy already when she arrived. Kate hadn't come across a digital autopsy table before. She knew they existed, and had been intrigued by them.

'They were developed in Malaysia,' said Dr Kapoor. 'Religious reasons to try and avoid an autopsy.'

'Do they work?'

'The evidence so far is that they do. There have been cases where the iGene found things that were missed by a physical autopsy done on the same victim.'

'How?'

'Think about it, DCI Riley. Physical autopsies can only go so deep, and are subject to a lot of human error and observation.'

'You back them up with CT scans though?'

'Yes, we do. However, we rely on the physical autopsy itself mainly. And this way, anyone can carry out the autopsy, long after the original one.'

'Have you got shares in iGene, Dr Kapoor?'

The pathologist laughed, flicked a switch on the table, causing it to hum to life, like a desktop computer slowed down by a full memory.

'You can take that off, by the way,' said Dr Kapoor. 'We are essentially inside a giant hazmat suit. And please, call me Rani not Dr Kapoor. I think we've been through enough now to qualify as intimates. And we are currently the first line of defence against whatever we are dealing with.'

Kate was glad to be out of the suit, although she'd needed some assistance from Dr Kapoor to get it off. Dr Kapoor was in her white forensic outfit, although it looked fresh. She indicated for Kate to put on a fresh one too, pointing to where it was hanging. Kate pulled a curtain to, and changed.

'How does it work?' Kate asked, coming back to the table. 'I don't know the details, but would like to.'

'Of course. So a normal scanner is used for the body itself. They put the body in a special leak proof bag, which doesn't block these X-rays. It is used to check for internal damage. Magnetic resonant imaging, MRI, is then used for the soft tissue. It takes three and a half thousand slices of the body using computer tomography, CT scanning, 0.5 millimetres each. The process we normally X-ray the body with.'

Kate imagined the body being placed in the cylindrical scanner, as it made noises around him, like a powerful vacuum cleaner.

'Then they use 3D imaging. It amazes me, to be honest. It has taken images so far into the body, where I would probably need an electric saw and medieval instruments of torture to get to myself.'

The digital autopsy table was slightly smaller than a snooker table, with a touchscreen on the top, and wires running off it. There were three USB keys, all with memory sticks in them. The two women stood on opposite sides to each other, allowing the pathologist to run her hands across the width uninterrupted.

Dr Kapoor touched a corner of the table, making the table screen light up, with the same quality as a giant iPad.

Another touch, and the victim's body leapt out at them from the table. Dr Kapoor used her fingers to manoeuvre the 3D image, which looked as though it was hovering in mid-air.

'He looks like someone's made him into a character in a computer game,' said Kate.

'Are you there, Professor?' Dr Kapoor called out.

There was a cough, and Professor Gerard confirmed his presence. He and the rest of his team were watching the digital autopsy live back at the main hospital. Seeing and hearing everything that Kate and Dr Kapoor were.

The 3D body was grotesque naked. Kate looked at the ruptured pustules on his torso, and the full bobbled ones, like pockets of limestone had seeped under his skin. His body hair was matted with blood and pus, and she could see his stomach was concaved. She guessed it had probably sunk, like his face. Yet his legs and exposed genitals were unscathed. No boils or spots, and hardly any blood.

Dr Kapoor picked an image of a scalpel, used her fingers as though using a smartphone, tapping the chest, expanding and contracting. The image changed from flesh, to muscle, to nerves, to bone. Underneath that lay his organs, before she brought it back to the top image where he was human again.

'They haven't changed the method for a post-mortem for a hundred years,' said Dr Kapoor. 'When you think how many advances there have been, this critical function has not moved on. I can say, hand on heart, the scalpel-led autopsy is no longer the gold standard.'

Dr Kapoor touched the body, and it seemed to lift off the table, as she rotated it, zooming in to particular points.

'Just checking the equipment,' she said. 'You ready to go in?'

Kate nodded.

Dr Kapoor clicked on the scalpel again, touched the body with it. The skin disappeared, revealing the muscle and blood vessels below.

Chapter Sixteen

Justin Hope surveyed him. That was the only way to describe it. His eyes travelled up in an instant from Zain's muddied boots to his faded jeans, his tight T-shirt under his jacket and unzipped hooded top sticking out the back. The smudges of charred soot on his cheeks, the tiredness hanging like mountaineers under his eyes. Zain felt light headed, from lack of sleep mixed with whatever the green pills were starting to do to him. Yet he also felt strangely awake. He wouldn't trust himself to make any important decisions, and fuck he needed some rest, but he was alert, pumped. Maybe his body was releasing adrenaline and pushing him to limits he didn't have.

Yeah, as if there were any limits left his body hadn't already traversed. Zain had been to the brink of everything he could tolerate already. To a place where there was nothing left to give. He swallowed, his throat tightening under PCC Hope's intense stare. The man could wither you without saying a word, but Zain was no fresh recruit. And he had stuff on Hope, stuff that meant he didn't have to be scared or care what he thought of him.

Zain had kept records and evidence of his role as PCC Hope's spy, the things he had been asked to do. He was keeping them for a day when he needed to pull in favours. That day would be a momentous one, but he wasn't going to play that card for PCC Hope's usual self-aggrandised bullshit.

Still, respect was due. Justin Hope was the only black face at his level in the country. The second most powerful police officer in London after the Met's Commissioner, the indomitable Sonya Varley. Hell, between them, Hope and Varley were probably the most powerful cops in the country. Even the Prime Minister seemed to defer to them. That was real power, real success. It wasn't in the material wealth you accumulated, or the titles others gave you. It was when you did the impossible.

PCC Hope often described himself as the impossible man. Born and brought up on a council estate, by Afro-Caribbean parents, he had clawed his way to the very top. Zain thought about scum rising to the surface, but still, PCC Hope must have kicked like a maniac to break through. Then again, so had Varley. It said something when a woman and a black man were London's gatekeepers of justice, controlling access to the most important offices in the land. They had sledgehammered the glass ceiling.

Zain would give PCC Hope respect for that. Even if he was a slimy, untrustworthy dick. Zain felt the hypocrisy burn inside him. He was in no position to judge. Not with his own track record.

Unlike the rough and ready 'blend in with the crowd' look Zain was sporting, Hope was immaculate in a suit, definitely designer, and manicure, with nothing out of place. Polished. Poised. Poisonous.

Zain swallowed hard again. Fuck his stupid throat that kept constricting under the scrutiny. He was not some limp-dicked nobody, he was DS Zain Harris. He had credentials, he had paid his dues. He stared back, his eyes locking with Hope's.

PCC Hope smiled, revealing the fake even teeth to go with his faux-everything else. The anger was crawling through Zain, and he didn't know why. He thought he had made peace with this man, had accepted him for what he was. The clichéd necessary evil, a man forced to be to survive. Zain could get that, surely? PCC Hope had to capitulate to the rich and powerful, because he needed their favours regularly. The PCC, Unit 3, Zain's car, the team's resources. They were the result of the murkiness under which PCC Hope operated; they benefited from his questionable behaviour.

Zain looked away. Wondered how Kate was. Hope was reading his mind, or so it felt.

'Any news from the Royal Free?'

'No,' said Zain. 'Sir.' Respect where it was due. Disrespect coursing through his mind.

'I do hope she survives.' There was malice in every syllable.

'No reason to think she won't, sir.'

'Yes, quite.'

Zain wondered if the unsaid word PCC Hope wanted to say was 'shame'. 'Last communication I received from her was that tests are being done. On her, Dr Kapoor, and on the victim. We still don't have an ID.'

'Don't we?'

Fuck you and whichever lackey you've got spying for you. 'Not officially, sir. We haven't got a face.'

'How do you know this?'

'DCI Riley has a secure phone. We're communicating using an app Michelle Cable sent her. It means no one can intercept or hack into our conversations.'

'Not even Anonymous?'

Zain stayed quiet.

'I see. And is it legal whatever your connections have given you?'

'It works, and it's keeping this from going public. I say does it matter?'

'You work for the PCC, DS Harris. Yes it matters.'

'And what would you rather happen? That this leaks? That a panic starts? You want to see London break down? The protests last night would be child's play compared to ten million people thinking they might be infected with some . . . whatever it is . . .'

'I am aware of the dangers of mass hysteria. In thirty minutes I'll be at an emergency meeting of COBRA.'

Zain was incredulous. COBRA was the national committee that involved the Prime Minister, representatives from the intelligence agencies, the armed forces, most top government departments. They met to combat national crises, when the proverbial was about to hit the fan. They were being too hasty, he thought. The autopsy was still going on, the tox report wasn't even processed. They didn't know what they were dealing with, and if they thought they could keep a COBRA meeting secret? It would blow the whole thing open, and any type of investigation they could even begin to attempt would be fucked even before they started.

'I have already briefed the comms department, they are issuing a code thirteen emergency blackout on all news and media. No one is legally allowed to report this for the next few hours, and anyone doing so will face public prosecution.'

'Good luck blocking social media.'

'There are ways, as you know. We will contain this, in all respects.'

PCC Hope smiled at Zain. It felt worse than being bollocked.

'I think you're familiar with one of the participants at the COBRA meeting. DCI Raymond Cross?'

There it was. The blow, the punch to his balance. The past in one name. Zain felt his pulse race at thoughts of the darkness that had been.

He looked out of the window, trying to steady himself. The dusty emptiness behind St James's Palace, where military parades were held on memorial days. The red expanse which led to the green of St James's Park.

'It's a mistake, the COBRA meeting. You are going to send up red flags . No one will let it go unnoticed.'

'The heads of MI5, MI6 and Counter Terrorism will be in attendance. I think we can hold a secret between us, don't you?'

'And what about the security, the catering, the receptionists, the drivers? All the invisible people you lot probably don't even notice anymore. Can you trust them not to let even the slightest thing slip? Even the rumour that a meeting took place will send people into overdrive.'

'We can cover ourselves.' Zain heard the irritation in Hope's voice. What was unsaid. *Zain Harris you are also invisible to us and a nobody. You don't get a say.*

'COBRA is going ahead. I want to update them on whatever it is we know.'

'You know everything I do, sir.'

Hope steepled his fingers in front of his face. It was a signature move. Was he praying or sharpening his fingertips? Either way, it was a warning that he was thinking deeply, and he was thinking about how to come out on top. How to crush his opponent.

'A name, DS Harris.'

Deborah had already told Zain that PCC Hope knew the name. She had given him that warning at least.

Zain weighed up the options in his head. Kate had said to keep quiet. Still, Hope already knew, so revealing it wouldn't cost anything, not really. And instead, it might be some sort of alliance with him.

Zain repeated Julian Leakey's name. A beat. PCC Hope raised his eyebrows, as though hearing it for the first time. Then relaxed his fingers.

'I can't reinforce how sensitive this is, DS Harris. Leakey was one of the top civil servants in the country. He had access to everyone. And everything.'

'We don't know it's him for sure. There was only an ID found on the body. Doesn't mean it's him. We are looking for him. It's what I was doing before you called me here. Sir.'

'Why would someone else have Leakey's identification?'

'The possibilities are there.'

'Have you tried contacting him?'

'Yes.'

'Try harder.'

Zain kept his mouth closed. Start counting, stay grounded, let your senses do the anchoring. He heard the advice in Kate's voice. Always in her voice, no matter which therapist he got. Kate had taken on the role of his conscience. Or rather his conscience had taken on her voice. A meaner, more twisted voice whispered to him then. *You are obsessed with her.* Zain shut it down, clamping his jaw tight as he did.

Obsessed. Was it too strong a word, or was it simply the truth? She had rescued him. He loved her for it. And hated her for it.

'I was on my way to his residence, sir.'

'So you said. By yourself? What are you going to do there?'

'His wife is home, alone. She hasn't seen her husband since yesterday morning.'

'Doesn't that give you your answer?'

'Not necessarily. He keeps rooms at a gentleman's club somewhere in Mayfair. Often uses them. Someone is checking he wasn't there, but they are a bit cagey about revealing members' details.'

PCC Hope raised an eyebrow, but nothing more. Genuinely new information or another fake response? Zain couldn't tell. PCC Hope would be a killer poker player.

'So you are heading to Julian Leakey's home address. A site where he was potentially infected with an unknown substance that may have caused him to die horrifically, and you are going in alone, unprotected?'

'I spoke to his wife briefly. She isn't feeling unwell, sir.'

'And we know how whatever this is works, do we? She isn't going to have a delayed reaction of some sort?'

Fuck. He was right.

'I suggest, DS Harris, you find yourself a protective suit and some experts at this sort of thing. Quite honestly I will not risk the lawsuit if I send you in to a hazardous situation without protection. I've put in a call to the DCD, they are sending a team to meet you there.'

Zain felt the air rush from him. Department for Communicable Diseases? It properly hit him then. Leakey had died horribly by all accounts. And Zain was about to retrace his life, his last known steps.

And somewhere along the way, at some juncture he didn't even know yet, he would hit ground zero. The source of infection. And if he wasn't prepared, he would die just as savagely as Leakey had.

Zain rarely cared for his life. Except in those moments when he felt it under imminent threat. And that's exactly what he was feeling as he left PCC Hope's office.

Chapter Seventeen

Kate felt her breath catch in her throat, and genuine fear run through her. How had this happened? She looked again into the open corpse of what they had to assume was Julian Leakey. No pliers were needed, as with delicate touches Dr Kapoor simply removed the ribcage. The organs were weighed by the scanner, based on density and size. It seemed odd, there was no damage to any of them. Dr Kapoor was expecting some level of trauma at least, yet there was very little. Blood vessels that could burst under stress, some internal bruising, possible patches of haemorrhaging. Nothing that could explain the level of blood loss, and ultimately death.

'Cardiac arrest is visible, but that would always be the end for most people, no matter what injury was sustained,' explained Dr Kapoor. 'Actual cause, it's not there.'

Dr Kapoor checked the laptop that they had been given as part of the makeshift autopsy suite.

'I thought it might be an error,' she said, pointing to the screen. Kate followed her gloved finger, saw where it was indicating, and felt her stomach tighten, a shiver run up her spine.

'Only one way to be sure,' said Kate.

Dr Kapoor touched the head. Normally, she would need a scalpel to serrate the skin. Now with just one touch, she began to peel it back, taking the thick dark hair with it, as though the victim had been sporting a wig. Underneath, his skull was covered in the detritus of the skin that had been cleared away. This is where she would have been forced to use an electric saw, under normal circumstances. Now she simply touched the skull, and it disappeared. Revealing the horror underneath.

The skull came off, and Kate stared at what the iGene table was reflecting back to her.

'I don't understand, where is the brain?' she asked.

'Are you seeing this, Professor?' Dr Kapoor said. There was a tapping sound before Professor Nick Gerard's deep voice came over speakers hidden in the corners of the Portakabin.

'Yes,' was all he said.

Dr Kapoor looked up at cameras hanging from the ceiling like birds frozen in mid flight, hoping to prod a more detailed reaction from the professor possibly.

'Is this what I think it is?' said Kate. She felt her skin crawl, and an ache start in her head. She watched as Dr Kapoor tapped, and the contents of the victim's mouth were on display. More deep copper colouring. Dr Kapoor did the same to check the ear canals, and then again where the nasal cavity was. All of it covered in the same gooey, copper red detritus.

Kate looked in disbelief, as Dr Kapoor walked slowly around the table, her movements laboured as though the suit and the day had taken their toll, tired her out. This can't be true, Kate thought. How did something like this happen? It was the stuff of science fiction, of nightmares. Only it was now here, in this room, a reality.

'Dr Kapoor . . . Rani . . . I need to be sure. What I'm seeing here . . .' Kate stopped. How did you even frame the question? 'It looks as though the victim's brain has simply dissolved and poured out of every orifice it could?'

Dr Kapoor stared at her hard, then simply nodded.

'Yes, DCI Riley, that's exactly what seems to have happened.'

The pooled blood and the puddles of lumpy flesh they had seen in the park. Kate could finally make sense of it, of what had killed their victim. Or at least what it had done to him, the very final assault on his body. The pain he must have endured, as he literally burned up from the inside out. How could a man enduring that much go ignored? Someone must have seen him, or heard him? And how had he managed to find his way into the very heart of a public park?

Kate needed to sit down. And then her mind went there, the place she tried to keep it from going. If she had been infected, this was her fate too. She looked at the ravaged body, and imagined herself in his place. Then thought about the nightmare if whatever had done this was out there somewhere, waiting to take hold and cut down thousands of unsuspecting people.

The watcher had been following Kate's movements since the morning. He had tracked her as the day had burst alive, following her to St James's Park and from his vantage point seen the chaos that had ensued. The precautions being taken as Kate had been suited up and sprayed down. He felt something inside him hope that she was infected with whatever they were trying to contain.

The watcher was no fool. He knew which protocols were being observed, what was being played out in front of him. And then he felt cheated. No, it would be too easy a death for Kate Riley, dying like this. She had to suffer. And not suffer the pains of a disease, but suffer in every way possible.

Kate Riley had dismantled his life. And the lives of those he was working for. Trapped in a metal box, contained on the premises of the Royal Free hospital in one of the most expensive neighbourhoods in London, that was not how she would be allowed to die.

The watcher dialled a number.

'So she's very much alive, for now,' he said.

'Keep her that way,' said the voice on the other end. 'There are plans in place for her. Meanwhile, while she is locked away . . .'

'Yes, I was thinking the same.'

It didn't need to be said. With Kate Riley unavailable, her mother Jane was alone and vulnerable. And it was Jane Morgan who would be targeted next by the watcher. With a long overdue message from her beloved husband.

Chapter Eighteen

Vauxhall was typical for London. Gay fetish clubs jostled alongside Nandos and the MI6 building, penthouse apartments looked out over council estates, and traffic ran through it and over the bridge on a constant loop.

Zain pulled into the underground car park of St George's Wharf, having explained to the security who he was. He didn't tell them who he was visiting. They saw his badge, and rang in his number to the central Met switchboard that verified all police officers were where they were supposed to be. The two security men had hardened faces and eyes that suggested they had been around a bit. They might prove useful later, Zain thought, if he needed some more perceptive information on the Leakey set-up.

Zain waited for the hazmat team to arrive. How he would explain them away or sneak them in unseen was beyond him. He would play it by ear when they turned up. He walked out of the car park, headed to where the wharf was.

The flats were jutting glass, cutting into the London skyline and carrying price tags over seven figures. With the River Thames to one side, there were restaurants, bars and even a hairdresser on the complex. It reminded him of Kate Riley's home, the enclosed fortress she had shut herself up in. St George's was too open and accessible for her, no doubt.

She must be reading his thoughts. His phone rang, the caller ID telling him it was her. Zain checked she was connected to his secure app.

'Boss, I'm at the Leakey apartment building. About to go and see his wife, just waiting for pest control.'

'Pest control?'

'PCC Hope got DCD involved, they're sending me a team.'

'More people know then. Information is supposed to be sacred, especially in an investigation like ours.'

'You can trust me. After the last time . . . I'm embarrassed how I behaved.'

'I wasn't accusing you, Zain.'

'Still. I think I just need you to be sure, and hear it from me.'

'What's their ETA?'

'Any moment now. You're right though. Trying to conduct a subtle investigation into this is going to be pretty tough.'

There were two beats of silence on the other end. Zain saw a clipper bouncing on the waves of the Thames. The wind picked up around him, as rain spat at his face. He closed his eyes against it, welcoming its coolness and the feeling of being cleansed.

'I think that is the sensible approach, given the circumstances,' said Kate.

'What do you mean?'

'We've just finished up with the post-mortem.'

'Before you carry on, I think we should control the details we share across the app.'

'I thought Michelle secured it?'

'She did. I think it might have been breached though. PCC Hope knows everything we do. I've asked her to ghost it and create a replica with different encryption, use something that is even more secure.'

'Ok. When Michelle clears it, I'll send you what we found during the post-mortem. All you need to know is that the hazmat team, well, just follow their advice, OK?'

Zain was sure nothing they had shared was a secret from PCC Hope. The fact Zain knew about the hack into their app should make him sit up though, realise that Zain was no idiot, and that his time of spying on his own team was pretty much coming to an end.

Unless the new app got breached as easily. Or was he just being paranoid? Maybe it wasn't the comms but something more old-fashioned: human intel that PCC Hope was squeezing? They were a much bigger team now, with dozens of bodies working for the PCC, and random officers would be assigned to Unit 3 while they dealt with this investigation. Any of them could have let the name slip.

'I'm not wearing a suit,' he said.

'I have a duty of care towards you, Zain. I would recommend you take every precaution you can.'

Duty of care. Zain couldn't help feel something inside soften at the thought of Kate feeling protective. He bit it back, wanted to ask her what exactly they were dealing with, but until Michelle sent them the new app he wouldn't put that sort of information out into the open.

Kate signed off, and Zain got a text through from the hazmat team. At the security gate the two guards were bewildered, staring at the team dressed in their white plastic outfits with plastic helmets. Zain decided to go with the description he had already used.

'Pest control,' he said lightly.

The security guards exchanged looks, then waved them through.

Chapter Nineteen

The Leakey's lived on the twelfth floor. The security guards had let them use the lift reserved for goods and contractors doing work, allowing Zain and the two hazmat members to go up discreetly.

'I'm Jake Sands, this is Emilia Crake,' said one of the team when they were alone in the lift. Zain refused their offer to suit up, despite Kate's pep talk. Somewhere deep inside, the damaged part of him was hoping he would get infected just so he could sue Hope. Irrational whispers, his constant companions, he tried to drown out.

'The wife is going to be distraught anyway, if I turn up dressed like you frea— Dressed like you, it will make it impossible to get any sense out of her. You search the apartment; I'll say you're forensics. I'll deal with her. If she opens the door and she's got plague all over her face, don't worry – I'll run faster than you straight out of here. Deal?'

They weren't impressed. He needed to stop being facetious, but he couldn't help himself. Tiredness had pretty much switched off any civil neurons in his brain. Not that they did that good a job at transmitting most of the time anyway.

Outside apartment 1201, Zain stopped. He felt a flicker of anxiousness, but then put it away. No Category A deadly diseases were airborne; you needed some sort of contact with bodily fluids to catch them, or something needed to come into contact with your bloodstream. He had to hold on to that certainty for now at least. With Kate tied up in hospital, too much was sitting on his shoulders for him to let his usual doubts get in the way.

He breathed in, and knocked.

DS Rob Pelt was watching through eyes that were blurring because he had seen so much footage. And he was only watching footage that was suspect.

'It's like a constant stream: people in masks, cloaks, disembarking from tubes and buses and just messing around. I don't get it.' He heard his Mancunian accent coming through stronger than normal. Unlike the rest of the team, he'd managed some sleep, so was alert at least. He had sent DS Stevie Brennan home after the hospital to get some rest, but didn't like to think how tired DCI Kate Riley and DS Zain Harris would be.

His role in Unit 3 was primarily to organise the SOCOs, check CCTV and, most importantly, to liaise with other agencies, especially Met stations, to source personnel and resources. Those bodies on the ground would be vital if this case turned out to be as complex as they thought.

Michelle Cable was in the zone, engrossed in some computing stuff he wouldn't even begin to understand. And actually he didn't really care to. He took whatever Zain and Michelle told him as fact; they knew what they were talking about. Or at least they sounded like it.

'What you working on?' he asked.

'Security. Zain thinks our comms app has been hacked.'

'How does he know?'

'It's an instinct, he's not ours.'

'Ah yes, that well known scientific principle of instinct. Brother to the other well-known scientific fact, gut instinct. Too right.'

Michelle ignored him, furiously tapping away on her keyboard instead. Rob went back to his laptop. He'd asked Michelle to project his laptop screen onto a bigger computer monitor, so he had a clearer view while he still kept the convenience of driving through the laptop keyboard and touch mouse he was used to.

He stretched his legs under the desk, and stretched his shoulders and back. A massage from a date a couple of nights before had left him extremely sore. He thought she'd dislocated his spine at one point. It had seemed kinky when she suggested it, but in practice it was one of the most agonising experiences he had ever had.

He thought again about Monica. She was always on his mind. Four months, his longest relationship by far. And she had changed him. Given him a religion in some respects. He realised the rest of the team were getting bored of his vegan preaching and his campaigns for animal protection, but he didn't care. They were probably pissed their vacuous little himbo had developed something solid to cling to.

The screen filled with more masked figures, all of them indistinguishable from each other. This was going to be impossible. He didn't even know what they were looking for, and searching these images made him aware just how much they didn't know and how much they needed random luck to make headway in this.

'OK I think it's done,' said Michelle. 'I have a new comms app, and this time, nobody is cracking it.'

She pressed a few keys, and Rob felt his phone buzz. Message from Michelle.

'Should I open attachments from suspicious contacts?' he asked. She gave him the sort of look she probably reserved for her children. Rob heard voices heading their way, and looked up to see Justin Hope with a man he didn't recognise. The man had grey hair and was dressed in a smart dark suit, a raincoat over one arm and a panama style hat held between thick fingers.

The two men headed towards the lifts, PCC Hope leading. The other man seemed to be searching for something, or someone, momentarily locking eyes with Rob, but more interested in checking the empty desks around him. Rob went back to watching his videos, but couldn't shake off the idea that the man was looking for Kate or Zain. And whatever exactly it was that he wanted with them, Rob wasn't sure either of them would be happy about it.

Chapter Twenty

Anya Fox-Leakey sat poised, regal almost. At any rate, unmoved. She was sitting in a cream armchair, by an unlit fire. Zain was sitting across from her in its matching pair. He imagined Anya and Julian having warming Scotch on cold evenings, as flames cracked logs. She was barefoot, her soles resting on a cushion. He stared at the toenails, they were unpainted, but clean and cut neatly. She caught his lingering gaze, looked curious.

'Can I get you a drink? Or one for your colleagues?'

Jake and Emilia had been a bit of a shock to Anya; she wanted to know what they wanted. Zain said it was standard if someone was missing; they would be doing a cursory examination. She asked him if he had a warrant. Zain told her that they weren't searching the flat; no one was under investigation for any crime; repeated that it was just a cursory examination. And yes, he did have a warrant for that. Hope had rushed him one through; they weren't taking any chances with this. Time was already way ahead of them, and they needed to catch up fast, or risk something apocalyptic.

'No, we're fine. Thank you.'

'Have you found Julian?' she asked. Zain didn't reply at first, then he showed her pictures of the shoes and the jacket that Julian had been dressed in. Anya stared at the images, with deliberate concentration. 'They match items he has in his wardrobe. Are they his? I couldn't say, although I do generally buy most of his clothes.'

Anya was blonde with clear blue eyes, and sharp cheekbones. There were lines around her eyes and mouth, soft markers of her age, which was possibly somewhere in the early forties. Julian was forty-seven according to the official HR file they had managed to access from DFID.

'Where did you find these?' she said, handing Zain back his tablet computer.

'I'm sorry, Mrs Leakey . . .'

'Please, either call me Anya or Mrs Fox-Leakey. I kept my maiden name after I married.'

'Of course, Mrs Fox-Leakey. Well, I'm sorry to have to tell you that it's not the best news. We found a body in St James's Park this morning. Those items of clothing are what the deceased was wearing, and we found ID that belonged to your husband.'

Zain hated breaking death to families. It was the worst news you could give to someone, especially when it was unexpected. This was different, though. She seemed so unaffected he almost relished telling her, trying to push her for a reaction of some sort. She seemed to be taking it calmly. Her face remained impassive, her eyes deep in thought. Only a slight frown crossed her forehead.

'I don't understand, DS Harris, shouldn't we be sure it's him? Have me identify the body?'

That was her first thought? No trauma at possibly being made a widow, or asking what happened to her husband? Her first thought was about police procedure?

'We thought we could spare you the pain.' It was true to a point. Zain didn't add that the face was unrecognisable, that in essence there was nothing viable to identify. Kate and Dr Kapoor were working on a 3D reconstruction, trying to get it as life-like as possible so they could email it to Zain for Anya Fox-Leakey to confirm. In the meantime, Jake and Emilia would be looking for something they could do a DNA match on.

'I think the pain is more acute sitting here not knowing?'

'I apologise, Mrs Fox-Leakey. An ID is not possible at the moment.'

Anya stayed silent, staring into the unlit logs, as though mesmerised by a fire that wasn't there.

'How bad is it?' she whispered. 'I'm not a fool. The fact you won't let me see him, there must be a reason? What's happened to my husband, DS Harris? And what exactly are that forensic team doing in my apartment?'

There was a note of hysteria creeping into her voice, which Zain tried to calm. He needed her to stay focused, and not have some sort of delayed breakdown to hearing about her husband. Although her original lack of emotional response was already giving him that feeling again. The one he was warned about taking too seriously. The one he had developed back in GCHQ and SO15, where paranoia and suspicion and second guessing were used to fill in any gaps of information.

Her husband was potentially dead, and it didn't take a genius to work out that the lack of ID meant it wasn't pleasant and the body was probably in a disturbing state. Sure, hysteria was in her voice now, but Zain would have expected some type of upset previously. Unless she hated him. Although the rich might process things differently to normal people, he thought. Was that it? She sounded like she had breeding. Her children were away at boarding school; they had their permanent home in a Dorset village somewhere. Zain had painted a picture of the Leakeys already, and he couldn't help the judgements that were forming in his mind.

Who had the money? Was it his or hers? His salary was not enough to pay for a riverside crib like this, and she said she was a home maker. What the hell did that mean, anyway? Was she a housewife, or did she build houses? The sodding rich, he thought.

Zain bit back his venom. He heard Kate's voice in his head chiding him. She had that polished accent, her New England roots always coming through. It was accentuated when she spoke to her mother. Her American accent came out then without any form of adjustment. Zain didn't know why she felt the need to disguise it so much in her work life.

He wondered what she was doing. There hadn't been any updates since he'd spoken to her earlier. Zain had no idea how long the blood tests would take, when would they know what had infected Julian Leakey, and whether or not Kate and Dr Kapoor were carrying it.

He looked hard at Anya Fox-Leakey. He didn't like her coldness, and he was determined to find out exactly what her secrets were. They could impact on too many people if she kept them to herself.

Chapter Twenty-One

Kate was wondering how PC James Alliack was doing. He had been a mess back in the park and she didn't like to think what state he was in now. She dialled Professor Gerard using a laptop.

'Not great,' he said, his image slow on the Skype chat. 'He tried to escape the isolation unit he's in. He keeps demanding to speak to his wife, and becoming hysterical. We've had to sedate him, I'm afraid.'

Kate felt for him. A new baby, a life he was only really just beginning. No wonder he was in pieces, thinking how it was all going to come to an end. Sedation was probably best for him. The not knowing would drive anyone mad.

The throbbing in her head was growing worse. She asked for some paracetamol, which was supplied via a first-aid box already in the cabin. They had bottled water and snacks to keep them going. The air was being recycled, pumped into the room cold, and she was feeling the chill now, dressed in only her plastic suit. Kate removed her latex gloves to take the tablets.

'Can I take your temperature?' asked Dr Kapoor.

Kate stopped mid swallow, then gulped down the paracetamol. Nothing like a medical professional to give a loud echo to your panic and worry. She knew how things worked, knew the containment and quarantine was a total overreaction. You didn't get Category A infectious diseases or pathogen-driven viruses by sitting next to someone or touching them. She remembered a lecture where she was told that unless an Ebola patient vomited directly into your mouth, or bled into an open wound, you were unlikely to get it just from being in close proximity. The nurses who got infected did so because they were cleaning up the diarrhoea, stomach contents, plasma and blood of those that had severe symptoms and a protracted stage of the disease.

Fighting through her logic though was the scene she kept recalling. The burst pustule, the blood hitting her face, hitting Dr Kapoor's face. Particles of it might have entered her mouth. She remembered a metallic taste, the iron stronger in memory recall than it probably was in reality. It was how the brain worked, its mechanism for defence amplified dangers and negative experiences to prevent you from being in harm's way. And she hoped that's all it was.

Except the headache was still severe.

Dr Kapoor took out a digi-thermometer.

'Woah,' said Kate. 'That's not the same one as you used on the body?'

'We do learn about the transfer of diseases in medical school,' said Dr Kapoor, and she inserted it into Kate's ear.

'I hope my ear doesn't suffer the same fate as Julian Leakey's,' said Kate.

Dr Kapoor left it in for a few seconds, until it beeped. She removed it and showed Kate the reading. So, she definitely had a fever to go with the headache. It was nothing though. Probably tiredness, coupled with being out in the freezing cold all morning, and the stress of the whole situation.

Kate watched Dr Kapoor take her own reading. She showed it to Kate. It was the same.

'I've been trying to talk away my headache. I hate taking tablets for minor complaints. There is a technique, if you chase the head pain you can alleviate it. Close your eyes, focus in on where the pain is, and then ask yourself again, where is the pain and follow it to that point again. You soon pick up the pain is in different places, and that way it diminishes and dissipates.'

'As a doctor, I thought prescribing medicine would trump what sounds to me like nonsense . . .'

'Quite the opposite, I see what dependence on drugs can do to people.'

'And has it worked, Rani? Running around your brain, trying to pin down the pain? Has it disappeared?'

Dr Kapoor looked at the thermometer in her hand, her eyes glazing slightly as she wandered into her own subconscious. She walked over to the laptop, and dialled Professor Gerard.

'Professor Gerard, I need to report abnormal body temperature and some base symptoms we are both having.'

Kate watched as Dr Kapoor's mouth moved. She couldn't take it in. Is this what was happening? Was she infected with something? She looked at the clock. They had about two hours left. Justin Hope's voice was clear in her mind; she had a four hour window in total to make headway. After that, it was out of his hands. There would have to be a press briefing and Public Health England would start mobilising.

Kate couldn't let that happen. She knew what people were like. Rioting, looting, the breakdown of morality. It would be survival of the fiercest, the cruellest, the most selfish. Cynicism worthy of Zain Harris, she thought.

'Professor Gerard, any idea when the tox results are going to come back?'

'We are testing them in-house, we have the labs and protective equipment set-up, so I am expecting an imminent result. Although, you are aware we are only testing for known pathogens? From what we can observe, the deceased isn't displaying the signs which would directly link him to one type of pathogen or infection.'

'You think it's a mutation?' said Dr Kapoor.

'We can't rule that possibility out. The skin lesions are very much what we would expect in an outbreak of a plague-like virus, and the internal haemorrhaging is consistent with Ebola symptoms. But the brain, what happened there, it's very unusual.'

'Professor, something has just occurred to me,' said Dr Kapoor. 'The mechanism for delivery of whatever it was. Since the organs were relatively untouched, I'm thinking the brain may have been the primary source of infection?'

There was quiet as the Professor mulled over Dr Kapoor's words.

'Let me broaden our search criteria, and start looking for other signs. It might be how this was delivered to the deceased, and might help to work up its life cycle.'

Professor Gerard dropped the call, and Dr Kapoor sat down on one of the chairs they had been provided with. Plastic hospital chairs that could easily be wiped down, and were an anathema to comfortable seating.

'What exactly are we dealing with Rani?' asked Kate.

'I'm not sure. Potentially someone has managed to genetically modify known pathogens to create something new.'

'How?'

'These viruses all have genetic make-up. They can be manipulated to behave in certain ways if the right knowledge is applied to them.'

'You mean someone can potentially make a synthetic version of these diseases if the right knowledge is applied to them. Ebola is an example of a retrovirus, made from ribonucleic acid, or RNA. It means they mutate very quickly. Smallpox has a DNA structure that can be altered.'

'It's not quite as simple as that, Kate. But yes, in a way. Someone with the right level of knowledge could potentially create a synthetic version of these diseases and, more than that, could potentially mutate the code to create something else.'

'So someone has deliberately tampered with the genetic make-up of these Cat A viruses, and infected a top civil servant? That sounds like bioterrorism to me, doctor. Why would they infect *him* though?'

Dr Kapoor was stroking her hands, self-comforting, bringing herself to the point where she could say what she had to say next.

'It seems too fantastical to be a coincidence. If what I am saying is true, this isn't something you could manufacture in your bedroom or even most laboratories around the world. This would have to involve the best minds, plenty of resources and . . .'

Dr Kapoor bit her lip, a sign she was chastising herself before she voiced an opinion she knew she shouldn't. Kate rubbed at her eyes. She had studied human behaviour, was au fait with the Reid technique, the FBI's interrogation manual. It was difficult to just switch off and have a normal conversation sometimes, without looking for the silent behavioural clues people gave off.

'You see, our deceased over there, he can't be patient zero. He can't possibly be the test case.'

'They've tried this out on someone else?'

'How else could they know what its effects might be?'

'Yes, of course. And the planning, to wait until the night of the protest, to pick the Guido Fawkes mask and the cloak, the perfect disguise. Opportunity to both kill and dispose of the body right under the eyes of the law.'

'Only, the Cat A viruses we are dealing with, the ones we know about, they don't work instantaneously. Ebola takes two or three days to show up in terms of symptoms, and thereby in bloods.'

Kate processed this. They wouldn't know for days if that's what they had been infected with? Kate would just have to wait to see if she was infected?

'Same for diseases like smallpox and plague. They incubate inside a host, and slowly they manifest and wreak havoc on the body. The savagery inside this victim was consistent with something that happened quickly. I couldn't see any haemorrhages that had healed, no past bleeds. They were all happening fairly close together. Whatever took hold of him, it did so within hours and possibly even minutes. The skin, his immune response system, must have gone into a frenetic over drive, forcing antibodies to send warning signs to his brain and body.'

'If the aim was to kill Julian Leakey, and at the moment I am working on the hypothesis that he was the sole intended victim, because not to is something I can't yet grasp or comprehend, whoever was responsible would know that this would work. Julian would die within a specified time. So yes, I see, someone else must have been used as a guinea pig, as a test case. How could you mutate viruses like these that take days to work, and make them behave like this?'

Dr Kapoor ran her fingers over her head, and arched her elbows behind it. It was the pose people adopted when subconsciously they were sending the message that they were superior to their audience. In Dr Kapoor's case it was probably because of the knowledge she had that Kate didn't; nothing more malicious, Kate hoped.

'You see, that's my discussion with Professor Gerard. Viruses, particularly haemorrhaging viruses, take time to work. However, substances known as neurotoxins can have an effect in minutes at the right doses.'

'What are neurotoxins?'

'Neurotoxins are complicated.'

Kate looked at the clock, looked at Dr Kapoor.

'I don't have time for complicated, Rani. Please, give me enough details for it to make sense, but not so many that we lose precious time.'

'Neurotoxins are complicated because we need them to function, so some are OK. We also use some to isolate and treat pain in the human body. For example cytotoxins are used regularly in hospitals to treat acute pain such as arthritis. They shut off certain parts of the brain, to prevent it from sending signals to other parts of the body. When you injure yourself, for example, let's say your foot is cut off. Your foot doesn't know how to react, except to bleed. It's the nerves in your body that have the pain signal transmitted to them.'

She looked at Kate to make sure she was following.

'I understand this, but I'm guessing you're about to tell me the other side. When neurotoxins are doing anything but help the human body?' Kate was hoping to speed up Dr Kapoor's explanation and alleviate the tension she was feeling.

'Precisely. Botulinum is the most dangerous neurotoxin. It's available as Botox of course, for beauty treatments. But botulinum is a horrendous poison. Tetraodontidae, we know them as puffer fish, their liver is home to another neurotoxin. In the right doses neurotoxins can have catastrophic effects. And that's the essence. Give a neurotoxin in the right dose, and the effects can be immediate.'

'What do they do? Could they ravage a body like our victim?'

'Generally no. Ok, sorry, I know you want fast but I have to give you some detail. There's what we call the blood brain barrier in all of us. The brain needs blood to function, but it also carries compounds in it that aren't necessarily good for us. So there is a separation of brain and actual blood vessels. And that's me telling you in layman's terms here. What neurotoxins do is breach that barrier, and they get into the brain and the nerves and tissue inside it, and they break it down. They cause paralyses, organ failure and quite a painful death as your body closes down.'

'Haemorrhaging?'

'Not in the amounts we saw.'

Kate considered what she was hearing, and came to the conclusion before Dr Kapoor started to explain it to her.

'I think someone has not only mutated these Cat A viruses, but they have worked out how to use a neurotoxin to both deliver and speed up their effects,' said Dr Kapoor. 'If this is the way I'm describing it, I think we might be looking at one of the most sophisticated and dangerous bioweapons in existence.'

'And who would have access to such a thing?' said Kate, thinking out loud.

'Exactly.'

Kate sat down on one of the plastic chairs. So what had happened here? Had a foreign government just carried out an assassination on British soil? Or even worse, had our own government done the same? Why would they? What exactly did Julian Leakey know that made him so dangerous that he had to be eliminated like this?

She knew she shouldn't, but she had made the assumption it was him. She needed Zain to get a confirmation quickly, so they could focus on finding out why he was targeted, before someone else ended up dead.

Chapter Twenty-Two

Zain watched as Anya Fox-Leakey drank her hot tea. She had insisted on black tea with lots of sugar. Zain had followed her into the kitchen-lounge, with its stunning views across the River Thames. Everything was white and silver chrome, neat and sanitised. More than that though, there was the feeling of space. It was probably the floor to ceiling windows that did that.

Zain had asked for coffee. He needed sleep and green pills, but a strong black coffee would do for now. His cup was resting on a side table, while Anya folded her legs underneath her and drank slowly.

'What exactly did your husband do, Mrs Fox-Leakey?'

'He was a civil servant.'

Zain bit the inside of his mouth. That much they knew.

'On a day to day basis? What was he involved in? Did he ever discuss his work with you?'

'Not really. He was responsible for administering the foreign-aid budgets that we agree to.'

'We?'

'We, as in the nation. Whoever the government of the day thinks is a worthy cause, or who may bring us some political kudos if we help out. You know, the lurid headlines that fill the tabloids, the undeserving foreigners who are stealing all our taxpayer's money in aid. That's what Julian did, he wrote those cheques.'

'Had anyone threatened him because of his work?'

'He's not the face of DFID. There is a cabinet minister for that, for the hate mail and the threats. The civil servants get on with doing the real work.'

'I thought you didn't know much about his job?'

'I know about the Civil Service though. My father is employed by the Foreign and Commonwealth Office.'

Zain wondered if it was the actual FCO or a cover for a role in MI6. He was always suspicious because of his own stint with GCHQ when he met members of the FCO who were spies.

'Has your husband been concerned about anything of late in terms of his work? Any particular patterns of behaviour you notice might have changed? For example was he spending more time at his club than usual?'

'No, not that I can think of.'

'Forgive me, Mrs Fox-Leakey, but you seem to be taking the possible murder of your husband with a lot of calm. How was your marriage?'

Anya sipped her tea, and her eyes narrowed as she stared at Zain.

'Hope, DS Harris.'

At first Zain thought she meant Justin Hope. Was she one of his pals? *What the hell?*

'I'm not going to believe it's Julian, not until I see the body myself. So there is hope that this is some sort of nightmare, mistaken identity, whatever you wish to call it. It is not my husband. And for the record, because I know this is going to be put on a record somewhere, we are very happily married. I've known Julian for over twenty-five years, since we met at Cambridge. And we've been married for coming up to fifteen years now. I love my husband and to think . . .'

Anya stopped, as the teacup in her hand started to clatter against the saucer it was in. Zain got up, and took it from her. Her hands were still shaking as she wrapped them around herself. He wondered if it was just a show for his benefit, or if it was all sinking in and she was finally realising the enormity of the situation.

Zain checked his phone, to give Anya time to compose herself. Still nothing from Kate. He was waiting for the 3D scan of the face that might belong to Julian Leakey. There was a message from Michelle; she had attached a new comms app that would hopefully be more secure. Zain downloaded it onto his phone.

'Sorry, I just need to call my colleague,' he said, stepping out of the lounge, onto a balcony that faced towards Westminster. He could see the Houses of Parliament and Big Ben, the wind whipping his face and probably distorting his voice as he checked in with Michelle. He could make calls using the app, but until she gave him a unique user ID and password, he wouldn't be able to send messages.

'How are things?' she asked.

'Not good. The wife barely reacted. And she hasn't told me anything I didn't know already. Apparently they're all happy clappy and no issues. Sort of people that make me sick.'

'Don't be jealous, or bitter.'

'I'm clearly both, and I don't give a shit to be honest. Anyway, I have no idea why anyone would want to kill her husband.'

'You sure it's him?'

'Unless things are more twisted than we thought.'

'Did you tell her how he died?'

'No. PCC Hope wants details like that on lockdown, until the moratorium, or whatever bullshit he calls it, is over.'

'We've got about two hours left before we lose our hold on this.'

'And I think I'm done with Anya Fox-Leakey. I need to speak to his work colleagues. There has to be some dirt on him, otherwise why would anyone do this?'

Zain saw that a message had come through from Kate. It was the 3D remodelling of what they thought the face of the dead man would look like. Zain walked back into the lounge, where Anya was still seated, scrunched up tissues in her hands.

Zain showed her the picture he had just been sent.

'Mrs Fox-Leakey, is that your husband?'

She looked at the picture, and then looked at Zain.

Chapter Twenty-Three

Zain raced through the streets of London, his blue lights flashing. He hated using them, but he had no choice now. Time was not on their side, and unless he got some answers quickly they would be forced to give up the investigation. He had no doubt MI5 and SO15 were itching to get their hands on this. Kate had called him as he was leaving the Leakey residence, letting him know her concerns about it being a possible bioweapon attack.

'Fuck, OK, well that means MI5 are probably all over it already. Why are we being allowed to lead on this?'

'PCC Hope asked.'

'Simple as that? But that's mental! I still don't get how that man commands so much power.'

'We don't have long. I think they will keep us as the face of this investigation, no matter what. MI5 are hardly going to start broadcasting their involvement or doing press conferences with their agents. Anyway, I thought with your history you might relish the thought of working alongside your former colleagues?'

'I'm not being someone's bitch again, pardon my phraseology, boss. We lead on this, that's all there is to it. And since when did you seek permission from anyone, boss?'

The DFID offices were in Whitehall, part of the beating heart of the nation's governance. The PCC headquarters weren't too far from them, and, despite itching for a change of clothes and a shower, Zain didn't have the time to stop and check in. He drove straight there, parking in Whitehall, displaying his PCC permit in the window in case anyone tried to tow him or fine him.

The DFID offices were built in the same limestone as the other Whitehall buildings, grey yellow, with windows covered by thick net curtains. Zain had to wait at the entrance while security dialled Julian Leakey's office. It took a good ten minutes before anyone came down to see him, another ten minutes from the window PCC Hope had given them. Zain was pacing, checking his phone, with security looking at him surreptitiously. He'd be clocking himself as well if he were one of them.

The man that came to find him was Simon Wells, who introduced himself as Julian Leakey's executive assistant. He was in his mid twenties probably, blond with light facial hair. He was dressed in trousers and a jumper. All a bit casual for the Civil Service, thought Zain.

'Apologies for keeping you. Mr Leakey isn't here yet, but I'm sure he would be happy to assist with any police business, Detective. If you follow me you can wait for him upstairs?'

Zain got the sense that Simon was trying to protect Julian Leakey, assuming that police business would be office gossip and possibly not something he would want shared. That sort of loyalty was touching, but Simon's irritating positivity was not.

Leakey's office was at the top of the building, floor six, with views over Horseguard's Parade, the same view as PCC Hope's office had, though from the opposite direction. Behind thick doors were four desks, two were occupied by women about the same age as Simon and two were empty. A door led from the room into, he assumed, Julian's office.

'Mr Wells, would it be OK to have a quick word with yourself in Mr Leakey's office please?'

Zain felt the two women staring at him.

Simon obviously wasn't sure what to do; it wasn't protocol to let anyone into the office, but then Zain was a cop. The tussle in his head came to a halt, and he agreed, taking Zain through the closed door.

Chapter Twenty-Four

The closed doors had suggested a much bigger room beyond them, but the actual office barely had room for a desk and chair, and a couple of chairs for visitors. Simon offered one of these to Zain, and took one himself.

'I'll get Clara to get us some coffee?' he said.

'That won't be necessary. I've had a lot already this morning. Thank you, though.'

Simon smiled, but his nerves were echoing off him, his left foot tapping under his chair. Zain scanned Julian's desk, which was covered in files, memos and a desktop computer. A phone was on the floor to the side.

'I try to keep it organised, but it's organised chaos according to Julian,' said Wells. There was a familiarity in the way he said Leakey's name, a fondness even. Or was he posturing for Zain, trying to show that he was on a first-name basis with the man who effectively ran DFID? Zain didn't care, instead he took out his phone and showed Simon the 3D fit.

Simon's face was a study in emotions. His smile was replaced by curiosity in his knitted eyebrows, before his eyes opened slightly wider in recognition and finally shock as he realised what being shown a 3D fit of a face with the eyes closed meant.

'I'm sorry to break it to you, but we found Mr Leakey's body this morning.'

Simon was staring from the phone to Zain and back, his hand over his mouth. He started to hyperventilate, and suddenly loud sobbing erupted from him. Zain was taken aback. It was the sort of reaction he had expected from the wife, not the PA. Even when she had confirmed Julian's identity, Anya Fox-Leakey barely did more than shed a solitary tear. Her whole 'she was living on hope' argument felt about as genuine as her crying.

Still, she didn't exactly fit the mould of a bioterrorist. And he didn't think she could access that sort of weapon, let alone hate her husband enough to carry out killing him. Then again, what did he really know about them? He was hoping Simon or some of the other staff might be able to help. But Simon was blubbing away. Zain tried to be sympathetic, but he didn't have the time. Or the patience.

'Must be a shock,' he said. Simon's answer was to cry louder. 'Let me get you that drink? Clara you said?'

Zain popped his head out of the door, where Simon's cries had clearly been heard. The two women were standing up, half-way across the office.

'Sorry, which one of you is Clara?'

A woman with straight dark hair and a hair band stepped forward.

'Do you mind just getting him something please, anything that can help with shock?'

Clara nodded and hurried out of the door. Zain smiled at the woman who was left.

'You alright? What's it like working here then?' He tried to speak over Simon's sobbing, but instead closed the door on him. 'Sorry I didn't catch your name?' said Zain, holding out his hand.

'Emma,' said the woman, taking his hand in hers. She had shoulder length auburn hair, and glasses. 'Is he OK?'

'Yes, I'm sure he will be fine. I'll need to speak to you and Clara as well when I'm done.'

Emma nodded.

'How is Julian as a boss?'

Emma shrugged her shoulders, but didn't say anything as Clara came in with a mug of coffee. It was hardly going to numb shock, but then the Civil Service probably didn't have a supply of alcoholic shock absorbers. Hot chocolate or tea with copious amounts of sugar would probably have worked better, he was thinking.

Zain was curious though. He expected Simon to give him a haloed version of Julian Leakey. But with Emma's nonchalant shrug, he knew she would be the one to give him a dose of reality. And tell him who the real Julian Leakey was.

Chapter Twenty-Five

Kate's headache was worse, and inside the forensic suit she was feeling feverish.

Dr Kapoor took Kate's temperature again. 'No change really.'

Kate wasn't surprised. She could feel her body start to ache in the joints.

'I wonder how PC James Alliack is getting on?' she said.

'I can ask Professor Gerard when we next speak to him.'

As if on cue he called the laptop. Dr Kapoor answered.

'So test results are back,' he said.

There was a pause. Kate wanted to shake the man.

'Negative.'

'What exactly does that mean?' said Kate.

'We tested Julian Leakey for every one of the Category A viruses, but he has none. There was no presence of smallpox, Ebola, plague. Nothing at all to link to any of those.'

'I thought it took days to be sure?'

'Normally yes, but during the Ebola outbreak we developed a more sophisticated test locally. It hasn't been trialled enough to be released to others yet, and I do have to caveat it strongly, but we believe it is so sensitive it can detect the presence of Cat A's in their early stages after infection. A product similar to say an early-pregnancy-test kit.'

Kate bit back the reprimand that he was using the pregnancy analogy because they were both women.

'What if they are mutated? Dr Kapoor said someone could manipulate the genetic code?' she said instead.

'They could change its behaviour potentially, but not eliminate the core of those diseases. We would still be able to partially match their DNA even if there had been substantial changes to how they work.'

'So what is this? Something new we haven't seen before? I saw his body, Professor, I saw what this did to his insides in the autopsy. Normal viruses and diseases don't simply melt a person's brain.'

Even on the grainy Skype images, Kate could see Professor Gerard was taken aback by her abruptness, but she didn't have time to placate grown-ups; she needed some answers quickly. Her mind was already reeling from all the scientific jargon she had heard.

'We checked for antibodies in his blood, to see if his body was fighting any form of unknown virus and we tested for antigens to see if anything had invaded his system. There was nothing there.'

Kate wanted to believe this, but if it wasn't a virus then what the hell had happened to Julian Leakey? She knew she should be relieved, but instead she was worrying about exactly what had gone on.

'What are we looking for, then?'

'We're exploring Dr Kapoor's theory about neurotoxins.'

'Have you found any evidence yet?'

'Nothing so far. I've accelerated tests on the brain-tissue samples we took, but they can take slightly longer. We only have tests for specific neurotoxins we have identified, and there are hundreds out there we have no tests for. Neurotoxins tend to be diagnosed when symptoms of poison manifest in live subjects.'

'So what does this mean for us?' said Kate.

'We tested your blood samples for any type of pathogen, and again there is nothing to suggest your immune systems are creating antibodies to fight an infection, especially from a Cat A. We also tested for antigens to detect any invading virus.'

Kate felt some relief, but the aches were getting worse and she was feeling nauseated.

'What about the neurotoxins? Could we be infected with those?'

'It's unlikely. You aren't displaying any symptoms, and I don't think you ingested enough blood for there to be any risk. I can't be completely sure, but if you are in agreement, Doctor, I would like to remove you both from quarantine?'

Dr Kapoor checked with Kate. What could she say? It didn't make sense. Julian Leakey had died of something, and she had been exposed to his blood. Did she go home and wait for her own body to start manifesting symptoms? Would she be putting her mother at risk? Her team? Eric?

'Oh, DCI Riley, there is something interesting that came up in our testing of the samples Dr Kapoor took. The results were quite startling.'

'How so?' said Kate.

'Well, Julian Leakey's shirt? The one he was wearing underneath his black cloak? It was drenched in blood. We assumed it was his. Only, when we tested the sample, that isn't the case.'

She held her breath.

'He seems to have been covered in someone's else's blood along with his own.'

Kate felt her pulse pick up and her heart start hammering. Then she felt the acidic burn of bile at the back of her throat. She rushed to the steel sink and emptied her guts into it. A few seconds later she heard Dr Kapoor do the same behind her.

If they weren't infected with anything then why the hell were they both so ill? And why was Julian Leakey drenched in another person's blood, and who did it belong to?

Chapter Twenty-Six

Simon's view of Julian Leakey, well the view he could give through protracted sobs, was the one Zain was expecting. Julian was an attentive boss, attuned to his staff's needs, with great rapport and interpersonal skills, loved by anyone who came his way.

'You make him sound like a saint.' This was met by more histrionics from Simon. Zain was exasperated, and led him out of the office, asking instead to see Clara and Emma. Clara didn't add anything much to what Simon had said. Her praise was less sycophantic but still gave the impression Julian Leakey was the sort of person who didn't have enemies, who treated everyone with respect. When Clara left the office she went straight to Simon, consoling him, and the two began to talk in furtive whispers.

When Zain asked to speak to Emma, they stopped whispering. They watched Emma walk across the office towards Zain, and then they began to whisper again. Zain closed the door on them, harder than he should have, but they were irritating the hell out of him.

Emma was nonchalant about Julian's death when Zain broke it to her. She didn't seem particularly intrigued either when he said it needed to be kept quiet for now. They were all signed up to the Official Secrets Act and knew the results of reneging on what he was asking them.

'I get the feeling you're not exactly a Leakey cheerleader, unlike your colleagues?'

Emma took her glasses off, and started to clean them unconsciously using the end of her shirt. She checked the image of Zain through them, then carefully placed them back on her face. She looked right through Zain, then over his shoulder.

Zain waited. Inside he was screaming at her to get on with it.

'It's a bit disrespectful to speak ill of the dead,' she said. Zain's heart sank. Great, so she wasn't going to bury Leakey under meritorious diarrhoea like her other two colleagues, but was instead going to say nothing. 'Some people though,' she went on, 'don't deserve that sort of respect.'

Zain heard applause inside his head.

'That's quite a strong opinion?' he said, trying to keep his voice calm.

'It's an honest opinion. The man is an obnoxious bully. Was. Pardon my French, detective, but he was a complete and utter wanker.'

Zain was impressed. Most people buckled under the nerves of speaking to cops, talking far too much drivel, clamming up or just making up things they thought the police want to hear. Rarely did you encounter someone apathetic enough to communicate clearly.

'I mean, don't get me wrong. He had changed of late; was a lot better. After Natalie left, you know? After she did what she did. I'm sure Simon must have mentioned it to you?'

Zain shook his head.

'I can't say I'm that surprised actually. He's half in love with him. Sorry, that was bitchy.'

'Bitchy is fine, if there's truth to it. Neither Clara or Simon mentioned any of this to me.'

'They didn't really see the worst of it, or rather they weren't the ones being targeted. You know on my second day here, I'm in a meeting with Julian and some senior colleagues. Here I am, new to the post, still learning the ropes, and in a room full of some of the most senior civil servants in the country. I got a bit bored while they were talking about some dull white paper, and started to drift. I then became aware the whole room was silent, and they were staring at me. Because Julian was. He had stopped speaking to stare at me, and then he asked me what he had just been saying. I didn't have a clue. I tried to pretend, make something up, but he just berated me in front of everyone. It was humiliating.'

Zain didn't think that was particularly crushing, or a warrant for murder.

'And that was just the start. He had no qualms about shouting at people in public. He threw me out of so many meetings because he wasn't happy with some notes or some analysis. I don't even do the data analysis around here, but still he'd want me to go and fix it. After a while I just got used to it, we all did.'

'Was leaving not an option?'

'I started applying for jobs in my second week, but nothing came up. I was close to quitting so many times, but then Natalie was going through so much worse. And I need my salary; I'm saving up to get married and buy a place. Although the latter is pretty nigh on impossible.'

Zain didn't say anything about his own pad. He had been lucky, getting a key-worker flat in Waterloo.

'What sort of things was Natalie experiencing?' he asked.

'Oh it was horrendous. I don't know why he had it in for her; she never really said. But the amount of times she ended up crying after he had a go at her. I just remember having to pick up the pieces; there were days when she couldn't bear to come into the office. It was a crazy time. She lasted about four months, and then she left. But boy, she had the guts not to go quietly.'

'What do you mean?'

'She took him all the way to a tribunal. Through HR and the legal process. It was months of meetings, interviews, evidence gathering. Julian was put on suspended leave for a couple of weeks. The look on his face when he was told, that was a classic. He stormed into the office banging everything he could, grabbed his phone and just went home. Simon running after him like a fucking poodle, pardon my French. Nothing happened to Julian of course, he's too powerful and important. Still, after all of that, he became a much nicer person. Which isn't the sort of nice normal people are; he was still a twat, excuse my language, but just became more tolerable and tolerant.'

Zain was building a much more layered version of Julian Leakey now. And if there was a tribunal, there should be official case notes he could access. Just how nasty did it get?

'You don't know what the issue was, or what was discussed at the tribunal?'

'No, I really don't. Natalie wasn't here during the process, and she said she didn't want to say anything in case it harmed her case. She was a mess though. I saw her by chance once, she came in to see HR, I was coming back from lunch. I didn't recognise her at first. I mean she was wearing office clothes, but her hair was unwashed and all over the place, no make-up. She was trembling, literally shaking when she spoke to me. Poor cow.'

'Do you have contact details for Natalie now?'

'No. After the tribunal I lost touch. It didn't go well for her. I called her a few times, emailed. She went off social media, and I never knew where she lived. Then she changed her number, so my calls and texts didn't even get to her. I suppose she wanted a clean break from here.'

'What do you mean by it didn't go well for her?'

Emma took her glasses off again to clean them, before speaking to Zain.

'You'll probably find out anyway.' She sighed, as though it was difficult.

'Anything that might help us paint a picture of Julian is important at this stage, I can't emphasise this enough. Please, Emma, anything at all.'

'Natalie, well she ended up in hospital. Suicide attempt. And not just the once either, she attempted it a few times. Had to be put on suicide watch. And then that wasn't the end of it. She started sending Julian messages, threatening emails, and when her address was blocked, she started to send him texts and letters. It was really painful to watch.'

'How did Julian react?'

'Oh I didn't care about him, I mean it was sad to think Natalie was going through so much. Julian deserved everything she said and did, and more.' Emma stopped. 'I don't mean that. Sure I hated the bastard some days, but I wouldn't wish him dead.'

'I'm surprised the other two didn't mention any of this to me.'

'Well they have their reasons.'

'Simon and his affections. And Clara?'

'She's half in love with Simon. It's funny what infatuation can do.'

Zain knew how, closed up in a small space, infatuation could grow unfettered. Like fungus in the dark, until it took hold and did irreversible damage.

Kate flashed through his mind. He shifted her away, or tried to. He just hoped she was OK.

'You don't know what happened to Natalie, then?' he asked.

'No, she just disappeared. Clara once let something slip about a restraining order, but I think she was just being nasty.'

'So you have no way of contacting her?'

'No, sorry. HR might.'

'Have you still got her old number?' Zain could easily track her down with any information that Emma could provide. He didn't say this, no need to elaborate just how insecure and interconnected data was.

Emma sent him a contact card by text, which he forwarded on to Michelle.

'Is there anything else you can tell me about Julian Leakey's behaviour? How was he with other people he came across at work?'

'The same. He really didn't give a damn who he was speaking to. He would talk to government ministers like they were idiots, in a sneering and patronising tone. In meetings he was notorious for undermining the chair, and starting slanging matches for no reason. He was like an overgrown schoolboy, just causing trouble because people allowed him to get away with it and because he relished it.'

'How did he get away with it?'

'Men like that do. They are connected, and powerful, and they protect each other. It's a scandal, but it happens everywhere.'

Zain knew how that worked. Justin Hope was a prime example. Survival of the cruellest, Kate had called it once.

'The only time he showed any deference was when his wife came to see him for the odd lunch, or when his father-in-law would pop by. Then again, Lord Fox probably got Julian his job in the first place.'

'Lord Fox?'

'Oh, didn't you know? Anya, Julian's wife, her father is a peer?'

Zain hadn't realised, but then most of the bio he had was from Julian's HR file.

'Yes, she has a Danish mother. Julian hit the jackpot when he married her, she's stunning *and* connected. I still don't know why she married someone like him; she's absolutely lovely. Always so polite and funny when she comes in.'

'Did she make many visits?'

'No, not really. And, well, they were always impromptu really, never in his diary or planned. As though she was bored. Although Natalie had her own theory.'

'Which was?'

'She thought she was checking up on him, making sure he was at work. Silly really, all she had to do was call his private line and he would either pick up or not.'

Zain considered this possibility. Would Simon cover that private line, claim Julian was in a meeting if he wasn't available? Anya had assured Zain she was happily married to a wonderful man. That wonderful man was fast losing his halo, so maybe the marriage wasn't all that perfect either? Natalie and Anya: two women holding the keys to the inner sanctum of Julian Leakey's life, and a possible reason for his death.

Chapter Twenty-Seven

Michelle had worked fast to find Natalie Davies' current where-abouts. She sent them to Zain while he was still speaking to Emma. When he came out of the room it was to see thunder on Simon and Clara's faces. Zain wondered if they had been listening in somehow, or just guessed from the length of the conversation that Emma had been giving Zain the full low down. A version of their boss that they had both done their best to hide from him.

Natalie Davies was living in Southgate in North London, but when Zain called her she said she was on Oxford Street. Zain asked if he could meet her for coffee and discuss Julian Leakey. It was important. She seemed keen, and agreed to meet him at the PCC head office in St James's. They had interrogation and interview rooms which he could use when she arrived.

Zain checked in with Michelle and Rob back at the office.

'You look like you're the one in need of an autopsy,' said Rob.

'Thanks, do you mean it or are you just buttering?'

'Buttering?' asked Michelle.

'You don't know buttering?' said Zain. 'Means he's trying to make my day. Get with the slang, Cable.'

'You can keep it.'

'So what's the latest?'

'I'm bored as fuck. Looking at these videos, there is no one here who might be Julian Leakey. We've done a facial-recognition search, nothing at all. He was either already wearing his mask before he got on the Tube, or more likely he didn't use it at all. Can't find any vehicles registered to him in the area either, and his phone pretty much died as soon as he left his office.'

'His wife said she saw him yesterday morning, he should have been in the office most of the day. What time did he leave?'

'Not sure, but his phone died about six last night. After that, nada,' said Rob.

'His wife claims he didn't say anything to her about being home late, or going to spend the night at his club. He would normally inform her, but not always.'

'Night at the club?'

'You know, those gentlemen's clubs.'

'Strip joints?'

'Don't be a knob, the private members' clubs Leakey and his sort belong to.'

'Did no one raise the alarm, or think it was a cause of concern when he didn't come home?' asked Michelle.

'Apparently not. His wife assumed he just went off to his club and forgot to tell her.'

'Lucky man. He seemed to have a blank cheque to do what the hell he liked, if you ask me,' Rob said.

'Different world and different rules for these guys,' said Zain. 'They seem loaded to me. And I'm guessing it's Mrs Leakey's money. Sorry, Mrs Fox-Leakey, daughter of a peer.'

'Peerages are handed out like confectionary these days,' said Michelle. 'They don't come with money.'

'No, usually they come with a price tag; the rich adding another status symbol to their collection,' said Rob.

'So cynical for one so young,' Zain told him. 'Any word from DCI Riley?'

Michelle and Rob exchanged looks.

'What?'

'Nothing. There's a blackout. No one at the Royal Free is responding to us, not DCI Riley, not the doc and none of the medical team. I've tried everything barring going down in person.'

'Fuck, why does that send the panic up me?'

'It's meant to,' said Michelle.

'Well I think someone needs to get over there.'

'Stevie already is,' said Rob. 'I called her told her the beauty sleep was over.'

'You woke her up?'

'Judging by the coarse language I would say yes.'

Zain laughed. He could imagine Stevie first thing. She wouldn't be impressed by the wake-up call.

'What about PCC Hope? Has he been round?'

'Yes, just asking for updates. But, listen: I know this is your bag, the paranoia and all that, but there was someone with him. A guy with silver hair, panama hat, flasher coat. And when he walked past I swear he was looking for you or DCI Riley. He was clocking your chairs and computers, didn't really look at us.'

Silver hair, panama hat, flasher coat. Zain had a good idea who that was. DCI Raymond Cross. Question was, why was he here speaking to Hope already? Something was not right, and he needed to find out exactly what was going on. The mention of his old boss plunged Zain into the ice of his past.

Michelle's voice cut through his thoughts. 'Natalie Davies is here. Waiting for you in interview room four.'

Zain came to, pushing his past behind a mental barrier he knew wouldn't hold for long. It was time to see what Natalie Davies had to say.

Chapter Twenty-Eight

So many different responses to Julian Leakey's death. His wife had barely reacted, his PA had overreacted, and here was Natalie Davies. When Zain broke the news to her she clapped.

'Thank everything in the fucking universe. Finally.'

Natalie was wearing a beige coat with a collar he hoped was faux fur, in case Rob saw it. Her hair was plaited with coloured bands and when he shook her hand he picked up the smell of alcohol on her breath. It wasn't even midday yet. Zain did a double take. Today was interminable.

'I take it you're not a fan?'

'Come on, DS Harris, there's only one reason you would call me here. Because you know what that bastard did to me, and how much I hated him. And the fact you are questioning me: it's not good is it? I'm guessing it wasn't a natural death?'

'We are exploring all possible avenues at present Miss Davies . . .'

'Mrs. My husband did a runner of course, couldn't hack the stress of it all. Lightweight. Still, we're not divorced yet.'

'The stress?'

'You know what happened, surely it's why I'm here. And just so you know, I don't have a fucking alibi for last night.'

Zain didn't flinch, Natalie was obviously not well. Her hands were tapping on the table between them, her eyes darting around the room.

'What is it you do now? In terms of work?'

'Temp mainly. It was hard getting past what he did to me. Bastard. They wouldn't give me a reference. Not a proper one; it was going to come from HR. You know how that looks on a job application? Previous line manager won't give me a reference, so you have to go to fucking HR for one. Joke. The whole thing is a joke.'

'Do you need to be anywhere today?'

'I'm between contracts,' she said, her eyes boring into him, before carrying on their scan of the room. There wasn't much to see, just neutral greys and greens on the walls and the sofas they were sitting on. Natalie was leaning forward, as though gripping the table for support. Or to have easy access to it in case she needed a weapon.

Between contracts said enough to Zain. Natalie's life really had gone off kilter. Civil Service employees usually expected lengthy careers, unless they were let go, and the shock was sweetened by a redundancy package. Natalie felt she had no choice but to leave, it seemed, and he got the impression there had been no sweetener.

She scratched at her wrist, but Zain couldn't see signs of damage. The suicide attempts were probably tablet based. Shit, he was craving his own tablet hit.

'Can you tell me about your relationship with Julian Leakey?'

'What? Who the fuck told you about that? Was it that faggot, Simon? Or that fucking dumb bitch, Clara?'

Zain bristled at the onslaught, but was glad she had given herself away.

'Why don't you tell me, so I have the truth?'

'I knew they would. Fucking bastards. Trying to ruin me; it's all they're good for, those two.'

'Natalie, it would be good to hear it in your own words.'

'What do you want to know? I started working there, and things happened. We started seeing each other.'

'Who made the first move?'

'Him. Obviously. And me, like a fucking idiot, I just went along with it. I don't know what I was thinking. I wish to God I could go back and slap myself silly, stop myself doing that again. But back then, I fell for his bullshit. He was so charming, you know? So smooth, and I just fell for it. I was struggling with Dougie at home, we were trying for kids, there was no money, life is just crap sometimes. And then it just happens, you blink and you've lost your fucking mind.'

'How long did it last?'

'Oh, maybe a couple of months. I soon woke up to it. He was just using me, like he used everyone.'

'Using you?'

'Have you met his wife? Frigid cow. He obviously isn't getting any from his perfect little princess; she's too busy doing her make-up and furnishing their home. She makes me sick, always so nice. *Nobody* is that nice, DS Harris.'

Was this why Anya's reaction had been so muted? Was Natalie simply one of many? It had to be. Julian wouldn't have started something so close to home, with someone in his office, if it was his first time surely? There must be a sordid history? Had Anya finally snapped?

But the hatred coming from Natalie made him think that she was the one more likely to have crossed the line. And she had no alibi. Julian's manner of death and the time of infection might mean an alibi was needed for a few hours leading up to it.

Zain wiped his face with his hands, shaking off the pressure building in his thoughts. It just didn't feel right. How could Anya or Natalie get access to something that was being treated as a Category A viral infection and possible bioterrorism?

Natalie was slurping the coffee Zain had got her. It put him off drinking the one he had got for himself.

'Where did you carry out this . . . affair?' Zain asked.

'Cheap hotels, mainly. You know there's a website you can hire rooms by the hour? Sordid bollocks, isn't it? Julian would book us rooms and text me the address. We barely spoke in the office, he virtually ignored me, just so no one suspected anything. Which was crazy, because he treated everyone else like he'd just stepped in them.'

'So you think he's used this website before then?'

'I'm not an idiot. I mean I was a fool to get involved with him, but of course he did.'

'There will be a trace on his credit-card history?'

'I doubt it very much. He always paid in cash. I knew I wasn't his first, and I wouldn't be his last. But for the briefest moment, DS Harris, I actually thought we might have a future together.'

'And then you didn't?'

'No. I had a scare, I thought I was pregnant. It was a false alarm. Me and Dougie had been trying for ages, but it wasn't working. We'd stopped bothering by the time I started things with Julian. So I knew it was his. It was the slap I needed, and I stopped. I told Julian it was over and we couldn't do it again.'

'How did he take it?'

'Well, he said he understood, and it was fine. I think he was already shagging some other tart by then anyway.'

'How do you know?'

'His patterns. We would always meet during lunch, and he would always take a ninety-minute lunch. Give him enough time to get there and back. He was always fastidious about showering afterwards.'

'So he had quite a few of these ninety-minute lunches? And you weren't part of them?'

'Yes. Not a lot, but enough for me to realise. That also made me want to stop.'

'And so when you stopped, what happened?'

Natalie stilled her nervous behaviour, her tapping and shifting. She held on to the table in front of her, and glared at Zain. Her face reddened.

'He turned into a fucking psycho, that's what. Before that, he'd ignored me. Treated everyone else like crap, especially Emma. Did you meet her? She's about the only one I trusted. She's a good woman.'

Natalie paused, thinking about some happy times, Zain hoped.

'How did this change in behaviour show itself?'

'Oh, it was classic Julian. He did to me what he did to the others, only worse. He wouldn't just shout at me in meetings; he would properly call me out, calling me incompetent and telling everyone else there how you just couldn't get the staff. Stupid things like that. Then he would pick up on every little thing I would do. Change memos, complain about reports I produced, call me out if I was even five minutes late into work or coming back from lunch. It sounds so petty doesn't it, so small? But when you face these little things every day, every hour you are in the office . . . it just made me ill, I hated going in. Then bloody Simon got involved, probably jealous he wasn't the one Julian was screwing around with, and he started to do Julian's dirty work. Picking holes in everything I did. That I could take, but being abused in meetings? And when he wasn't happy, he wouldn't just say things to me, he would come up to me, and scream in my face, publicly. He didn't care who was watching. I would break down in tears, rush to the loo to calm down, and instead of showing me some sympathy, he would simply tell me I needed to make up my time because I had taken an unauthorised break. And in the end, I just had to leave. But I wasn't going to let that bastard get away with it.'

'So you took him to a tribunal?'

'Yes. That was a fucking joke and a half as well. HR were really on my side at first, encouraging me and asking me to tell them what had happened. So I explained it all, not about the affair of course. Just how he was treating me. And that was fine. Until he got involved and they asked him for his version of events.'

'What did he say?'

'He said I was a stalker of some sort, that I had fallen for him, and wouldn't leave him alone. His behaviour was challenged of course, and he was reprimanded for it. But he made me out to be obsessed with him, and then claimed I was a fantasist.'

'How did you respond? Did you tell them about the relationship?'

'No, of course not. I was still married; I didn't want that made public or put on record somewhere.'

'And you lost the tribunal!'

'Yes. They said his behaviour was something that needed improvement, but that it was consistently bad to everyone and I couldn't be singled out as having been particularly at the receiving end of it. Can you believe that? But that's the Civil Service for you. Don't pick on one person, but you can bully an entire department and get away with it. Fucked logic. But it was all a fix anyway. I didn't stand a chance against someone like that.'

'And afterwards?'

'There is no afterwards. Except my life falling apart bit by bit.'

Natalie had gone for a comfort break, while Zain checked in to see if Stevie had reported back from the Royal Free yet. She had arrived OK, but was then caught up in the same blackout as everyone else there. No communication at all.

Natalie seemed more relaxed when she was back, and Zain got the smell of spirits again. She was obviously carrying some flask or something on her. It wasn't an official interrogation, she wasn't under suspicion yet, so he couldn't really do much to stop her unless she drank in front of him.

'Dougie moved out. A week after I lost the tribunal. He said he'd had enough. And that's when I . . . well, the first time I tried to end it all. After that, I didn't know what was happening. I was broke, signing on, alone, messed up. I was in and out of hospital, trying to make it all stop. I wish they had just let me do it. Saved themselves the hassle and the cost. But they didn't. Stupid social workers actually doing their jobs and saving my life.'

'And how do you feel about that?'

'Great. Because then I got angry, and I realised that bastard had got away with it. And, well, I had nothing to lose. Dougie was gone, and he'd started divorce proceedings. Weak man, love of my life, but spineless. And with him gone, I sent a letter to HR telling them all about the affair and what had really gone on between Julian and me.'

'How did they respond?'

'A cold formal letter telling me they would not involve themselves in any further communication on the subject of me and Julian. Harsh and heartless. So then I started emailing Julian, telling him I was going to break it to his wife, to the press. He ignored me, and so I did. I wrote to his wife, I called her. She put the phone down on me. And next thing I know, your lot are at my door telling me to stay away or else.'

'Hang on, so his wife knew about your allegations?'

'Oh hell yes, she did. She didn't put that phone down until I'd told her that much at least. And unless he was tampering with her post, she got my letter as well.'

Anya's cool reaction was beginning to make a lot more sense to Zain now. Although Julian had been reckless to have an affair with someone on his staff, Natalie wasn't the first, and probably not the last, so it stood to reason that, if Anya knew about Natalie, she must have suspected others. Why did she put up with it? Or maybe she hadn't in the end?

'And I never got my life back. He was fine, kept his job, his perfect little wife and his fantastic life. Teflon Leakey, that's what people call him. And now I know why. And me? I just fell and I crashed, and the pieces can't ever be put back together again. So that's why I'm happy he's dead, and I hope it fucking hurt whatever happened to him.'

No alibi, plenty of motive and clearly enough pathology to be a credible perpetrator. But looking at the dishevelled woman, her life so badly damaged, Zain just couldn't figure out how she could possibly gain access to a deadly virus.

His phone buzzed. It was Michelle. Minutes later he was rushing to the Royal Free.

Chapter Twenty-Nine

Kate was in a familiar nightmare. She was in a New England forest, running through the changing seasons, leaves mulching underfoot. Her breath was caught in her throat, her heart beating so fast she thought it would punch through her ribcage. And fire. Everything was on fire, burning up around her. That was different, new; she hadn't experienced that before. And there he was, the man, out of nowhere. She saw the blade, and then felt the pain.

There was something else then. Another place, another time. It was her mother, she was lying still, sleeping. No, not sleeping, there was something wrong with the picture. She wasn't in bed, she was lying at the bottom of the stairs. Her face, it was covered in red, in blood, so was her body. Was she dead? No. Kate had found her like this, had dialled 911. And she had lived, she had survived.

Only she hadn't survived fully, not the same as before. She had lived, but there were parts missing. Her mother would never be the same again. And then there he was, the man who had caused it all, waiting in the background, getting closer.

Kate knew who he was, as he crept towards her slowly, weapon outstretched. Kate looked down, and saw her mother's face was covered in pustules. One of them burst, blood splattered over her face, she tasted the iron tang.

And then he was there, the man, standing right above her. He raised the blade and as it came down she looked into the man's eyes. Into her father's eyes.

Kate opened her eyes, and tried to move her body, but she couldn't. She thought the dream might be real, or was she still caught up in it? Unable to stop the past coming through, she let it engulf her.

Then slowly she heard the machines nearby, monitoring her, heard voices, muffled as though coming through a barrier of some sort. Her eyes focused, and she saw she was in a plastic bubble. There was a figure standing to her right on the other side of the pod, with her arms inside built-in sleeves and gloves that allowed her to touch Kate through the pod's wall.

She felt bile in her throat, but her mouth was too dry, she couldn't swallow it. She tried to move again, and felt herself able to. What was happening? Had she been infected, after all? She only remembered vomiting, and then she must have blacked out. She couldn't recall that part though, but somehow she must have been brought in to the hospital's isolation ward.

'Welcome back, DCI Riley.' It was Professor Gerard. 'You had us worried there for a while, as did Dr Kapoor. You are both OK, however. You started to show symptoms which caused us some concern, but they have subsided. Your temperature is lower, and there are still no antibodies or antigens in your blood.'

Kate wanted to speak, but her lips wouldn't move.

'Dr Kapoor has already been given the all clear, and I will be happy to do the same for you. It's good news DCI Riley, you aren't in danger.'

Kate closed her eyes, her body needed to sleep. She jerked awake again, remembering. Julian Leakey, the virus, the investigation. She didn't have time to sleep.

'Well if I'm not infectious, then get me the hell outta here.'

Chapter Thirty

The four hours were up, as the early afternoon hit London. There was no infection, not from a virus anyway. And definitely not from something they knew about. Kate called PCC Hope to inform him.

'You can let Public Health England and the Department for Communicable Diseases know that we aren't dealing with a Category A virus here, sir.'

'Then what the hell killed Leakey?'

What about, 'Are you OK?' or 'Well done?' At least half of London isn't infected with a virus that causes violent haemorrhaging.

'I'm just going into a conference with the medical team here to find out,' she told him.

Kate was allowed time to shower and change into clothes Stevie had picked up for her from outside the hospital. She was dressed in a maroon skirt and white blouse, with flowers and embroidery worthy of a woman in her eighties.

Stevie was waiting for her outside the conference room, and cracked up when she saw the outfit's effect on Kate.

'It seemed OK in the shop, boss, not much choice around here. So fucking good to see you're OK.'

Kate let her embarrassment at the outfit go; it was more schoolteacher than DCI. Stevie was wearing all black, including her mid-length leather jacket. She looked refreshed, signs of the explosion from the night before completely gone.

'How did you end up with shopping duty?'

'We couldn't get hold of you, and the tyrants on the switchboard wouldn't put us through. Literally no one was telling us anything.'

'I passed out, after vomiting. They thought they had misjudged the situation, their tests were mistaken, and we were about to start displaying some serious symptoms of a Category A. They panicked, rushed us into their isolation ward and started emergency procedures.'

'Yes, I got a sense of that when I got here. Security basically hauled me away and asked me to wait in a locked room. They had no idea why. No reception in there at all either. Until a nurse pops her head in saying you're OK and might need some clothes. Apparently they burnt the ones you came in with as a precaution.'

Kate could barely remember what she was wearing.

'I hope they kept the contents in an evidence bag.'

Stevie searched in one of her pockets and pulled out Kate's phone along with an eyeliner pencil, chewing gum, and a small card holder.

'That's all they saved.'

'That's all there was.'

Kate checked her phone but the battery was dead.

'So what do they think made you so ill?'

'I think that's what we're about to learn in there. What about back at HQ? What's the latest?'

'Zain is on his way here. I alerted him to what had happened and that you were about to leave quarantine. He's been interviewing the wife and an ex-lover, all a bit weird. We didn't think they could be involved when we thought it was a Cat A. Now though, depending what they tell us in there, both have some pretty legit reasons to bump off Leakey.'

Kate processed the information she was being given, but Stevie was right. Until they could determine a cause of death, they really couldn't even begin to identify who might be behind it.

'His DNA was fast tracked through, so we have a confirmation of that at least. They worked it up based on a unified number of genetic markers, but we should have full confirmation in another couple of hours at the most.'

'I thought it was a Cat A, you look like you need Gok Wan more than a doctor,' said Zain marching up to them, coffee in one hand. Kate looked at the scratches and scorch marks on his face, and the tears to his jacket. He had probably been rushing around all night. His eyes were bright though, blue against his olive skin.

'Here he is, no sleep and a near death experience, and still got attitude on him. I picked that out, so don't start,' said Stevie.

'For you,' he said, handing Kate the coffee. She had already had two cups along with some M&S croissants Stevie had also brought, but she took it anyway.

Professor Gerard asked them to step into the conference room, and the three of them filed in. Zain stopped her, letting Stevie go on ahead.

'Everything OK, DS Harris?'

His eyes looked into her, but she couldn't read the expression in them. He stared at her, making her uncomfortable. Had the events of the night triggered something in him? Was this how he would begin to breakdown on her?

'I'm just glad you made it,' he said, and then walked into the conference room.

Kate watched him for a beat. Was Zain someone else who had come to rely on her? She pushed the thought aside and followed him.

Dr Kapoor was waiting for them. They had managed to find her scrubs and a white medical coat, so she at least looked professional. Kate took a seat next to her. Stevie and Zain sat opposite them, with Professor Gerard seated at the head of the table. Once they were settled, he began explaining exactly what had happened to Julian Leakey.

Chapter Thirty-One

Kate listened patiently as Professor Gerard explained to Zain and Stevie how Cat A viruses worked, and how the symptoms Julian Leakey had displayed were synonymous with them. Then he explained about their contraction, through infected bodily fluids primarily, and their incubation and manifestation periods.

'So, not being funny, but could you be infected and it just not show up on blood tests?' said Zain. His blue eyes burned into hers as he spoke, and then he flushed. Guilt at the insinuation that she might be infected and not know?

'Yes. What wouldn't happen though, and to put your mind at ease, is that Julian Leakey's blood wouldn't show up as negative for antibodies if he had been infected. His bloods are clear of all known Cat A's, and there are no signs that there is any other sort of virus working in his system. Our bodies are trained to fight invasion; if there was the slightest hint of something untoward, his body would have begun that battle. The scars would be there in the tests we ran.'

'So if he's clear, then there's no chance anyone he came into contact with might be infected?'

'Precisely.'

'His body though, and I'm not questioning you here Professor Gerard, but it was an absolute mess. Was the 3D autopsy thorough enough?'

'It was probably more detailed and thorough than a physical one. The human eye, like anything that relies on people, is prone to error. We are all fallible. The 3D scan goes deep, and goes into great detail. It picks up things a pathologist couldn't.'

'Yes, it's true,' said Dr Kapoor. 'If there was scope for it in law, I would recommend its use on a common basis. Unfortunately, we don't have the test cases yet to back up any sort of evidence-based trial. Lawyers would have a picnic.'

'And then there's always hacking,' said Zain. 'Once a record or system relies on computers, it can be breached.'

'We have adequate security measures, DS Harris. These aren't things we take lightly, patient confidentiality is a priority.'

Zain didn't respond, and Kate could tell what was going on in his mind. The precariousness of modern technology and the idea that computer systems were safe. Even after some of the world's biggest firms had been hacked. She closed her mind to it; she didn't want to dwell on that as well.

'Ok fine I get it, it's not a virus, but then what did that to him? I mean we all saw it. His body was fucked up.'

'Pleasant turn of phrase,' said Professor Gerard. Kate immediately saw Zain's hackles rise at the patronising tone.

'If it wasn't a virus, then what are we looking at?' asked Stevie.

'Neurotoxins,' said Professor Gerard.

'What the what?'

Professor Gerard and Dr Kapoor gave Stevie the same background they had given Kate earlier about how neurotoxins worked.

'Our tests have come back, and we found high doses of neurotoxins in the blood taken from Julian Leakey's brain matter.'

'What does that mean?' said Stevie.

'His bloodstream was infected to lower levels, much lower levels, with the poisons we found in his brain.'

'Poisons?'

'That's essentially what neurotoxins are. They are poisons, most of them natural. In this case they breached the blood brain barrier, and entered the deceased's bloodstream directly into his brain tissue. That's where they remained, and did most of the damage.'

'I don't understand, how could something be so localised?' said Kate.

'The infection would have taken place via a nasal spray, or needle point, something very precise that would immediately attack the nervous system.'

'So it was deliberate?' confirmed Zain.

'Without doubt. Unless it was self-inflicted, maybe by error. I find that highly unlikely. And as a method of suicide, using a neurotoxin would be ineffectual in the short term and extremely painful in the medium to long term.'

'Murder then,' said Stevie.

'It's definitely looking that way,' Professor Gerard told her.

Chapter Thirty-Two

Kate felt she had done enough sitting that day, so walked around the table to stretch her legs. She drank the coffee that Zain had brought her, even though it tasted like cold milk.

'OK, so we have a poison, a neurotoxin, and somehow Leakey is infected. That's fine, but then why did DCI Riley and Dr Kapoor become so ill?' asked Zain.

'It was passive ingestion, I think. They must have had exposure to the poison during their examination of the body.'

'The thing that burst?' said Stevie.

'Yes, that seems the most probable cause. Direct exposure to the compound itself is necessary before it can have an effect, and definitely an effect that might cause harm or cause you to exhibit symptoms. The levels Dr Kapoor and DCI Riley were exposed to were small; it's why the effects were relatively slow in being realised, and why thankfully they were short lived and didn't lead to further complications.'

Kate let those words hang in her mind. Further complications. How close had she come to becoming a victim like Leakey? She didn't know how much life meant to her, until it was being threatened in this way. Her mother needed her, but she was also aware of the future with Eric that might have been lost. If that was her level of attachment to life, she could only begin to imagine what James Alliack had been feeling. The relief he must have felt when he was given the all clear. He hadn't been allowed to leave the Royal Free in case he let something ship during Kate's four-hour window. Now it was over she sent a message to Rob, to orchestrate his being allowed to go home to his family.

'Why was there so much confusion over the symptoms Leakey had? Aren't there obvious signs of neurotoxin being present in his body?' asked Zain.

Professor Gerard rubbed his eyes, his temples and then his neck. He looked across to Dr Kapoor. She smiled thinly, before taking up the explanation.

'Far from it. They cause internal damage mainly, paralysis, organ failure. Possibly haemorrhaging. Very rare though, and nothing to the severity that Julian Leakey exhibited. As for the skin lesions, nearly unheard of.'

'What are you saying then? That it wasn't a neurotoxin?'

'What I am saying is that this neurotoxin, whatever it is, was manifesting itself in a manner that is simply undocumented. It got into the brain, and aggressively attacked the nerves and the tissue, causing a complete breakdown in cell structure. In turn, it also panicked the brain and made it send signals to the skin, the largest organ in the body, and it ended up sending an alarm via the skin abnormalities we saw.'

'I've been looking at the chemical structure of the elements we have and there isn't a clear match, although it is closely related to a number of existing ones,' said Professor Gerard. 'My team aren't really experts on neurotoxins and we are using basic computer algorithms at the moment to do our match. We need specialist help, which we have resourced and we should be able to gain some more understanding about this substance.'

'It's just not something we've come across, and it's not matching anything we know might be available readily in this country at least,' Dr Kapoor said.

'What are you suggesting Dr Kapoor? That this was imported through some means from overseas?'

She nodded. 'I think it certainly appears that way. From initial investigation, I can't see how else it could have got into the country. It just doesn't tie up with any of the known substances we have available in the UK, or that have been used or manufactured here.'

'And the symptoms?'

'Again, nothing documented here. We are carrying out a wider search. Professor Gerard's team and my own back at UCH are trying to contact any institutions that might hold samples similar to this, and we are getting advice from leading experts from around the world.'

'Let me be clear on this,' said Kate. 'We are looking at an unknown neurotoxin, that is behaving and reacting in a way that is also undocumented? Doesn't it sound too elaborate a weapon to source to attack only one individual? Why go to so much effort?'

'Depends how much hatred was driving the person involved,' said Zain. 'When you're fucked off, you can pretty much stretch yourself to do anything.'

'True that,' agreed Stevie.

Kate's mind was reeling. She thought they had got past mysterious viruses and what they were capable of, but instead she was again faced with something unknown that reacted in a way nobody had seen before. And she didn't understand exactly who Julian Leakey had upset to the extent that they were willing to source a foreign toxin to annihilate him.

And then there was the question of the blood. The blood they had found that didn't belong to Leakey. Did it belong to the murderer? Had there been a struggle, had Leakey done some serious damage to whoever was behind this?

Whatever the truth, Kate needed to be back at HQ, and she needed to be on top of this investigation. Even if there wasn't a risk of infection, what exactly was stopping whoever did this from striking again and killing someone else?

The bitch had survived. The watcher saw her leave the hospital and head to a vehicle in the underground car park. She was flanked by two of her team. The butch one and the terrorist one. He didn't know much about them yet, but he would find out. He had plenty of time, to find out whatever he needed. Kate's father was paying him enough, and the desire for his own personal vengeance was burning him.

While Kate had been in hospital, the watcher had made contact with her mother, and she was running scared at least. Ready to do anything that was asked of her. The watcher had used a low trick, played on her maternal instincts, trapped the stupid bitch almost too easily. He felt he needed a challenge, a worthy adversary. And that would happen when he brought the DCI down, saw the look on her face when she realised it was time for retribution. He would savour that moment.

And then the games could really begin. Properly. And Winter Morgan or Kate Riley would truly know the meaning of the word suffering. She too would lose everything, just like he had.

Chapter Thirty-Three

It was nearly two o'clock by the time Kate was back at the Police Crime Commissioner's headquarters in St James's. It felt so good to step out of Zain's Audi and breathe in the air she was familiar with. She felt alive, despite the tiredness and stress, and told Zain she needed to clear her head. She took a walk through the park, passing familiar landmarks, until she reached the bridge. It was a favourite place of hers, somewhere she had brought Eric, where the two of them had strolled arm in arm in the darkness, with only a silver moon to guide them. She had been honest with him that night.

'I was only ever after fleeting moments of escape. I honestly never intended to allow any man into my life, and I don't even know if I'm ready.'

His hand had covered hers, as he touched her palm gently to his lips.

'You don't need to overthink this, Kate. I don't need an explanation. Right now this is what I want. Tomorrow we might not even wake up to see the sun rise.'

'I can't work out if you're being optimistic or not.'

'I think we're both mature enough not to raise our expectations too much.'

'Shoot, I better return the wedding dress then.'

He had moved closer to her, turning her around so her back was resting against his body, and had gently lifted her hair to kiss her neck. She didn't feel very mature, the thrill reminding her of the first time any boy had touched her.

'Let's not use words like everyone else. We don't have to label this. Lovers, friends. Who cares?'

'Are you psychoanalysing me or giving me advice as a professional, Dr Sandler?'

'I'm just laying it on thick so you let me do what I need to.'

She had gasped as his hands had moved between her legs, then to undo her belt, and pull her jeans down, before entering her from behind. In the dark, against the cold, she had felt so close to him as he made love to her, and yet she had allowed herself to feel just that. He understood her. And made her want to be ready for someone for the first time in her life.

Kate snapped away from that night and looked out towards Buckingham Palace. A swan glided by underneath. It was ethereal, not a part of her day, of the nightmare she had just been through.

Kate gripped the barriers of the bridge tightly, as people passed her unawares. And in that moment, when she was so invisible and so unimportant, Kate finally let herself break down.

Walking back, cleansed of the feelings she had wound up so tightly inside herself, Kate saw the debris from the previous night, lining the streets around St James's. It seemed so long ago, and yet it wasn't even twenty-four hours since the protests had begun, and even less since she had been called to the scene where Julian's body had been found.

When your life was hanging under such flimsy certainties, time really did slow down. She had felt it so acutely, and what was worse was the loneliness of the moment. Kate had always prided herself on being self-sufficient, on not needing anyone, able to walk away from everything she had known. She was the strength for those around her, protecting the vulnerable. Her mother's disability and her reliance on Kate were just extensions of Kate's natural bent. It was why she had taken to law enforcement, and why she was perfectly willing to inhabit a corner of the world where attachments were limited. Especially after those closest to her had betrayed her so badly.

And yet, when she feared that she was about to lose the relationships that she had kept close, her mother and now Eric, it was like her gut was being torn from her. How had she become this wax doll, from the ice maiden she had always striven to be? How had Winter become Kate? She didn't know, and she wasn't entirely sure she was happy it had happened.

She felt vulnerable, in danger, at risk from her own past. And though she was feeling weak, Kate knew it was her mother who was most at risk from that past.

Kate slowly closed the doors of doubt as she walked back to the office. She had to regroup mentally, and hoped she could over the next few hours. She had a killer to catch, one who was more sophisticated and dangerous than any she had known before.

Chapter Thirty-Four

The room was different to the one back in Victoria: all glass walls and inspirational words in white calligraphy across them. The outside world could look in, all emotions and conversations open to scrutiny. No room for secrets, or the worst behaviours that could go on in closed and opaque rooms.

It was a state-of-the-art conference room with linked slide panel screens, individual tablets, recording equipment seamlessly built-in to the ceiling. PCC Hope had asked for the best, and the most expensive, and had been given both.

Yet despite the new facilities, the team was the same. Her team, the men and women she had come to trust to do their best, for her, and for whatever they were working on. Special Operations Executive Unit 3.

Brennan, Pelt, Harris and Cable. Bad law firm. Phenomenal law enforcement.

They inspired confidence in her, and in return she gave them her trust and complete backing and support. The fact they chose to stay as part of Unit 3, despite PCC Hope's proclivities and seriously questionable connections and views, despite the pressurised work they were encountering regularly, convinced her of their loyalty to her. She had no doubt if she left, they would too. It wasn't arrogance. They had chemistry, and they worked well together.

And that was key. If Julian Leakey's killer was to be found, it was this team who would do it. She hoped so anyway, because she knew that whoever did this to Leakey would have no qualms about doing it to anybody else. And before that happened, she would make sure she found whoever was responsible.

There were images on the screen, graphic close-ups of Julian Leakey, the damage done to him. Beside his picture was one of his wife and another of Natalie Davies. There was a silhouette photo in the mix, and a postcard showing what they knew about the neurotoxin so far.

Kate was summarising the facts. They all knew them, but it helped focus the mind when it was so cluttered. Almost as though she was organising her own thoughts, sliding facts across a smooth surface, rearranging them until they made a shape she recognised.

'Julian Leakey, aged forty-seven, Permanent Under Secretary at the Department for International Development. One of the country's most powerful men, one of the faceless brokers that hold high offices across the Civil Service. Married for fifteen years to Anya Fox-Leakey, daughter of Lord Fox, member of the House of Lords.'

'Hereditary peer?' said Stevie.

'No, given the title as an independent. Lifelong diplomat, serving across a number of postings, ambassador to various Balkan states, just finished a post at the British Embassy in Moscow. What else do we know about Julian? Michelle?'

'He has a varied work history that's for sure. Started off working for HSBC, straight out of Cambridge, moved up the ranks there very quickly into senior managerial positions. Moved around the big hitters like Merrill Lynch, Barclays, Citibank. After a decade with the banks he jumped ship to the Civil Service, went straight in at Senior Executive Officer level, after a couple of years he rose up to head up a department at the Home Office, looking into terrorism policy. His move coincided with his marriage to Anya.'

'Nepotism at its finest,' muttered Rob.

'Leakey worked there for five years, before being seconded to the Ministry of Defence, where he stayed on for another six years.'

'MoD?' asked Rob. 'He involved in any sort of weapons testing?'

'Not that I can see, but his records there are very generic. A number of management posts, they don't divulge details. After that he did secondments as Assistant Under Secretary for various departments, including the National Health Service, the Foreign and Commonwealth Office, Department for Education, until he landed the top job at DFID three years ago.'

'It strikes me as relatively innocuous, but let's try and get access to any HR files or records that we can, or any work-related incidents or problems. There may be something in his work history that might allow us to explore an avenue we are yet to consider. And the MoD connection. I want to know if there's a link with any form of development and research into any sort of chemical or biological warfare preparation.'

'I don't think they just hand that sort of intel out,' said Zain.

'We need to get to the right people then. Any suggestions?'

Zain stayed quiet, but she hoped he was getting the message that he should use DCI Raymond Cross if necessary. He had helped them out before, without her approval, but at least this time she was tacitly giving it.

'Along with his postings he also held various executive offices, ma'am, so board member for a number of private sector companies. He seems to have done a few months in the public sector and then a few in the private of late. I haven't got much detail on the companies he worked for, often as a consultant, but they range from manufacturing firms to private healthcare bodies.'

'What the fuck?' said Stevie. 'He gets insider knowledge about how government departments work, then sells his secrets to the highest bidding private sector firms? I thought only wanker politicians did that.'

'It's far more widespread than you might think,' said Michelle.

'It's a joke, that's what it is.'

'His postings may explain his wealth,' said Kate. 'I can't imagine where else the money has come from. I thought it may belong to his wife, but I don't think career diplomats like her father would earn that much necessarily. Anya isn't working, so Julian must have made his money somehow.'

'As a consultant his rates were hitting over five thousand pounds a day, sometimes even more.'

'That's just ridiculous, no one is worth that much,' complained Stevie.

'A thorough check into his history would be useful. Let's see if any red flags pop up,' said Kate.

'Are we leaving behind the idea this might be an act of bioterrorism then?' asked Rob.

'I don't want it to distract us. While we thought this may be a virus, a Cat A one at that, then that risk was more acute. Now we suspect it to be a neurotoxin of some sort, a poison in essence, it changes things. It makes it personal, he wasn't randomly picked, and I believe he was the intended victim. I think we need to focus on the why, and hope it leads us to the who.'

'And if we're wrong?' said Rob. 'If he was just a coincidence, and this is some sort of mass attack?'

'We have to hope that the pathology of a neurotoxin means that we can contain the number of deaths. They don't work in the same catastrophic manner a Cat A would. Let's hope it buys us the time we need to find whoever is responsible, before they strike again.'

Chapter Thirty-Five

The screen was now showing images of the Leakeys. Julian, Anya, and their two teenage children, Ollie and Lucy, fifteen and thirteen, who were both away at boarding schools, expensive ones judging from the information that Michelle had gathered.

'The question of Leakey's finances keeps coming up,' said Kate. 'We need to get a handle on this. Stevie, can you get in touch with whoever you know at the HMRC? Let's see what he declared in terms of earnings, and use that to build a picture of what he might have been earning and how.'

'Yes, ma'am.'

'The marriage then. What do we know?'

'On the surface, and if you take Anya's view, then it's all pretty amazing. No problems or issues,' said Zain.

'And the reality?'

'Anything but. She didn't react when I said he might be dead; when she saw the 3D mock-up, again, she barely had a reaction. His PA was more cut up than she was.'

'What are you thinking?'

'I spoke to one of his staff and she gave me a version of Leakey that wasn't pleasant. She made him out to be a bully and a misogynist. This was corroborated by Natalie Davies, a former employee of Leakey. She took him to a formal tribunal for harassment, vindictive behaviour and bullying. HR released the files after a lot of convincing, and Natalie's permission. What is missing though, and which is key if it's true, is her allegation that she had an affair with Leakey for a couple of months.'

'Is there any corroborating evidence at all?'

'None that I can find yet. Nobody else has mentioned the affair. HR forwarded us the deranged emails she sent to them. She literally went into minute detail with them over it, even telling them what his favourite sexual positions were. She had by this point been left by her husband and attempted suicide at least twice.'

'Doesn't mean it's not true. Men are fucking pricks,' said Stevie.

'Really? You've never expressed that opinion before,' said Zain.

'And there you go. Point proven. Prick.'

'How did HR deal with the allegations?' asked Kate.

'They consulted Leakey, told him what Natalie was saying. They got the police involved after she started making threats, but Leakey decided not to pursue anything against her. At the time he told the investigating officer he felt sorry for her. Natalie was asked to stop contacting HR and him, so she went a step further. She contacted Anya directly.'

'Did Anya mention any of this to you?'

'No. We traced Natalie's emails to Leakey in which she threatened to tell his wife what they were up to. There isn't a response from him. Her emails were by this time being blocked and sent to a secure address. The police spoke to her again, but there was not much they could do. Especially as Leakey was so reluctant to do anything official.'

'We therefore only have Natalie's word that she spoke to Anya?'

'Yes, basically. Anya didn't let on when we asked about the state of her marriage. Then again, why would she? Her husband had just died: she wasn't about to say, "Yeah? Great. He was a cheating bastard anyway." I need to speak to her again. You see, I don't think Natalie was the first. I think there've been loads of others, and Anya for whatever reason was turning a blind eye to it all.'

'Perhaps she reached breaking point?'

'She's a diplomat's daughter, a Cambridge graduate. She's not stupid and she has the resources. She could easily plan something this elaborate. And Natalie, well, she's desperate enough and bitter enough to do the same.'

'Your doubts?'

Zain pushed back in his chair, putting his hands behind his head.

'It's the weapon used. How the hell would women like Anya and Natalie get hold of something like that? It just doesn't make sense.'

'I agree. So that's what we need to focus our investigation on.'

Chapter Thirty-Six

The day was fading when Kate finally got into her Ford Focus to head home. It had been nearly thirty-six hours since she had left, and it felt like an eternity. How her body was still able to function and drive, she had no idea.

The gates were closed when she arrived and the security guard, Charlie, looked her over. She smiled and waved as he opened the electric barricade to let her through. Kate wound her window down by the security booth.

'Hey Charlie, how are you?'

'All good, thank you, DCI Riley. Just saw PCC Hope on the news, said they found a body they believe to be some government top nob. You can imagine the buzz in here today.'

Kate nodded. Dolphin Square was full of politicians, civil servants and the bored, retired rich. It was also one of the most secure addresses she could find to live in.

'How is she?' said Kate, referring to her mother.

'Hasn't been out today, not even for her usual walk, or to eat lunch at the restaurant.'

Kate's face shadowed, as she headed to the underground car park. It was odd for her mother not to take her daily walk around the grounds; there were acres of landscaped gardens for her to explore; or she could have lunch at the onsite restaurant. There was even a shopping mall she could go to. Her walk often involved a trip down to the river, or to the Tate, nothing too far, and with a tracker on her wrist band and ever watchful security like Charlie around, Kate felt she could stop worrying. She didn't require the sort of intensive live-in help she had done when they lived in Highgate.

Sometimes she felt she might be taking her eye off the ball, be relaxing too much. That was always when the worst could happen, when she stopped watching for it. The past could surreptitiously cut through her fantastical existence, and she would be left destroyed for a second time.

Kate let the thoughts go, as she buzzed into the secure lift and then used her key card to enter her floor, then another code to enter the section of the floor she lived on. Finally she scanned her forefinger which allowed the keyholes to be opened on the front door. All done with CCTV watching her.

Once inside her flat, Kate shouted out to her mother, told her she was home. The flat was small, two bedrooms, and an open kitchen/diner/lounge. It meant she didn't have to wear silly wigs any more to stop her mother from freaking out. Her voice would announce her, and her mother would expect her. Plus she was used to the new haircut now. The brown hair down to her shoulders, replacing the blonde hair she used to have. It was enough, she hoped, to disguise her from a chance encounter with anyone from her past.

Jane was anxious, and hoped her face didn't give her away. Kate had showered then picked up takeaway from the restaurant for them. Kate was eating her usual grilled hake with vegetables, Jane was indulging in a spiced salmon burger. She had persuaded her daughter to share a chocolate brownie, said she needed the hit since she had been away from home for so long.

'Leave the diet, you have a man now,' Jane teased. She did a fake dance of joy, which made Kate laugh. Jane couldn't see the happiness in her daughter's eyes, but she could hear the sound of it, and it felt good. Kate hadn't laughed for too long.

'I keep healthy for myself, Mom, not some man. You should know me better than that by now. So how was your day?'

'The same, I suppose. Eric called. Just to see how I was. He's a good man. Please don't push him away.'

'Mother . . .'

'I know, you're old enough to know these things. I just don't want what happened to me to put you off, to scare you from taking the risk.'

'Nothing fazes me. I'm your daughter remember?'

Jane smiled, her pride unable to conceal itself. Whatever else she had or hadn't done, her daughter was an achievement she wanted to take the credit for. And yet, she wasn't her only child. There were her sons. She understood why they had behaved the way they did, while Kate never could. Jane had been terrorised by her husband for years, and when you were under that sort of fear and pressure, you sometimes felt unable to do anything except comply.

'Did you go for your walk?'

'Yes,' Jane said, again hoping the dishonesty wouldn't show on her features. 'It was very cold, so I didn't go far.'

'No?' said Kate. The word lingered. Jane kept her eyes on the TV. She couldn't recognise the people on screen, but she knew it was a *Dynasty* box set and she remembered who the characters were. Kate would suffer through re-runs forever with her. The stab of guilt again, the notion that her daughter would be better off without her.

'You should get an early night, I'm sure you'll be just as busy tomorrow.'

Kate yawned, kissed her goodnight and headed to her bedroom.

When she was gone, Jane took her phone from her dress pocket, and checked the messages again. Her heart was in her mouth, as the panic pricked at her skin. She remembered the phone calls earlier, the ones that had unsettled her, and upset her routine. She wiped her face, and typed a reply, before hiding the phone again.

She just hoped she could keep this from Kate. She had given her daughter enough to worry about, she didn't want to add to that list. Not just yet. She could deal with this on her own for now. She would have to.

The watcher was in his hire car. Had booked it under a false name. He was parked opposite one of the entrances to Dolphin Square. There was no way he could gain access to cruise the grounds or get any closer to Jane and Kate without being seen.

Still, he could intimidate the old woman from a distance. You didn't physically need to be present when you had access to someone's phone. The messages and the phone calls hit just the right balance. Abject terror but laced with a threat that things would end very badly for Kate if her mother didn't cooperate. And so far she seemed to be.

His phone buzzed. It was Jane. The watcher read her reply. And smiled.

Kate Riley's days were limited. He was sure of that.

Chapter Thirty-Seven

The city was baying, calling him in the form of screeching tyres and police sirens. Zain sat in the dark, naked except for his boxers, in front of his open window. He was burning up, sweat trickling down his back and his face. Was this withdrawal or the need for another fix?

He turned the silver foil over in his hands. There were no ingredients he recognised on the packaging; he had taken the pills on blind faith, purchasing them using the TOR browser for the dark web. TOR gave him the access and the anonymity he needed. He blocked out the thought that it also gave the same to the criminals he often found himself up against. Instead he focused on the pills. He wanted their effects. Help with his PTSD, anxiety, nightmares, insomnia.

Zain popped one of them out of its casing, and put it on his tongue. It was approaching zero outside, and despite the cold air coming through his window, he was still on fire. He lay down on his sofa, his skin sticking to the leather, making sucking noises as he settled himself, and closed his eyes, hoping sleep would come.

Zain was feeling refreshed by the time he got to the office. He had slept deeply, waking up to a frozen room, his skin goosed, his mind hazy on where he was. So much seemed to have happened. He could barely remember the explosion from two nights before.

In the mirror he could still see the scratches and scorch marks on his skin. They were superficial, or so he was told. He didn't need any more scars; he had enough already etched on his body.

The office was empty except for Michelle.

'Where are the others?'

'Out, working.'

'And DCI Riley?'

'She's giving PCC Hope a briefing.'

'It's nine-thirty, I thought I was early.'

'You are, comparatively.'

'Hey, what can I say? I work late to make up for it all.'

'And none of the rest of us do, of course,' said Michelle. She was in the zone, focusing intently on whatever was on her screen. Zain pulled up a chair next to her, and looked over her shoulder.

'What's the craic?'

'It's Natalie Davies' work history. I contacted the temping agencies she's been with.'

'Anything interesting?'

'I'm not sure. Yet. She's mainly done office-admin roles, didn't last long at any of them. Her temp agencies often let her go.'

'I'm not surprised. She must have been a crap employee with all her issues.'

'Yes, looks that way. Only, see here?' Michelle pointed to her screen, Zain followed with his eyes. 'Can you see?'

'Raxoman?'

'They're a pharmaceutical firm. She managed to stay with them for a few months.'

'Probably stealing the Prozac.'

'I've been trying to find out exactly what they produce.'

'And?'

'They're one of the leading providers of neurokine modulators in the country.'

'Yes . . . and?'

Michelle picked up her green tea, and took a swallow. She blinked and stretched, and started typing away at her screen.

'Neurokine modulators are used to treat rheumatic pain, I mean extreme rheumatic pain. They work by inhibiting the brain's synapses. They are formed from using neurotoxins.'

'*Fuck*,' said Zain. 'You think she was squirreling away the raw ingredients from the neurokine modulators? Or do you think Raxoman are secretly testing a messed-up version of a neurotoxin?'

'Only one way to find out.'

'Where are they based? Raxoman?'

'Industrial estate out past Romford in Essex.'

'I'll send Rob over to speak to them, shall I?'

'What are you going to do?' asked Michelle.

'Julian Leakey's laptop has been brought in. I'm going to crack the bastard.'

Michelle's eyes lit up at the prospect.

'Yeah, fine, you can help,' he said. She punched him on the arm. 'I'll need someone to watch Natalie as well. Make sure she doesn't do anything weird, especially if she's feeling panicked or worried at all.'

The laptop stared back at him. A Lenovo ThinkPad, secured with encryption panels on the edges. It was government standard issue, so Zain hoped it wasn't locked up as tightly as those used by the MoD. He switched it on, and immediately it asked for a Bitlocker code.

'Nice,' he said. 'We enter a wrong password here, it will lock the stupid fucker for an hour at least.'

'Any inkling what the password might be?' said Michelle.

Zain closed his eyes, drew down the facts about Julian Leakey that he knew. He tried combinations in his head for names of his family, dates of birth, work dates. He couldn't make them gel.

'It would be something before he got married, something from his childhood. Julian would think that was secure. In none of the conversations about him we've had is there any mention of his family. They haven't spoken to him in years, not properly. His parents are devastated but were honest enough to admit he hadn't seen them for close on two years. Christmas was only a phone call.'

'Heartless,' said Michelle.

'Just the reality of life. He lived and moved in different spheres to them. He was a genuine boy-done-good story. Working-class background, grammar school, Cambridge. Peer's daughter.'

'You sound like you admire him?'

'I admire what he managed to do. I don't know him enough to make any other decisions about his character yet.'

Zain opened his eyes and stared at the blinking cursor. What could it be? Names of his parents, siblings, a combination of names and dates? He could reboot and try his password-cracking software, but it would take a while to run. There must be an easier way? Zain took his phone out, and dialled Emma, back at Julian's office. She answered on his fourth attempt.

'DS Harris,' she said, very loudly, obviously trying to antagonise her colleagues. 'What can I do for you?'

'Emma, I'm trying to access Julian's laptop. There's a bitlocker password when I switch it on, do you know what the password is?'

There was shuffling at the other end, and Zain heard Emma's breathing, followed by a door closing.

'Sorry didn't want those two listening in. All our laptops use the same password for that bit. Leakey1st. I know, a bit rubbish, but there you go. I don't know his actual password, but Simon should if you need to access it?'

'No, that will do fine. We couldn't find a laptop at his home, only Anya's desktop. Do you know if he had a personal one?'

'I don't think so; he seemed to use the one you have most of the time.'

'Including his personal web surfing?'

'Yes, I think so.'

'Thank you,' said Zain. He ended the call and turned to Michelle. 'Ok we have the bitlocker password.' He typed it in and it started up his Windows, which then prompted him for the username and password to his system.

'Now what?'

'Now, I call Simon Wells and threaten to knock him into next week. In a nice way.'

Simon was less forthcoming, claiming he didn't know the password, but Zain did get the username from him. He then set his password-cracker software up to find whatever password Leakey had used.

It took an hour, but then it was done. Zain and Michelle were in, ready to comb through Julian Leakey's Internet history.

Chapter Thirty-Eight

The tinderbox of Julian Leakey's laptop opened up to Zain in minutes. The history wasn't deleted, Leakey assuming nobody would have access to his computer apart from him. Zain downloaded a snapshot as they found it, and Michelle got to work freezing it as evidence. Zain started to surf, like Leakey. The man had no awareness of security, not online at least. He had saved his passwords, his cookies, his form data. Every website Zain clicked through let him in, no questions asked. His security obsessed brain couldn't accept that somebody could be so careless.

'This just doesn't make sense. How can someone this important in a position that has access to the most sensitive data in our nation, who has *direct access* to the Prime Minister and Buckingham Palace, be so fucking stupid?'

'Come on, not everyone's a tech genius. Most people upload Norton and McAfee and then think they're covered; they stop protecting themselves with common sense.'

'It makes me angry. There is so much information out there, so many warnings about the risks. People need to get smarter. The criminals certainly are.'

Zain opened up private messages Leakey had sent online, even saved chat histories. The pictures were the most embarrassing. Selfies that would make a Kardashian blush.

'Fuck.'

'Just don't tell me it involves children, please.'

'No, thank God. This guy was shameless though. His wife must have known, there is no way he could carry on like this otherwise.'

'You would be surprised what husbands and wives hide from one another. I mean, mine is at home looking after the children. They're in nursery and school part of the day, so do I know what he's up to then?'

'Don't lie Cable. I so know you've got secret webcams all over the joint.'

Michelle blushed. 'I do not,' she said in a muted mumble. 'That's not the point though; he could be doing anything. Same for me. I say I'm going to work, I could easily pull a sickie, and how would he know?'

'Because I'd tell him.'

'Yeah well, what's that p-word Stevie used for you?'

'Are you being racist?'

'Prick,' said Michelle, blushing deeply again.

'If you can't take the heat, Cable, don't be using that language.'

Zain began saving more files and images, building up a picture of Leakey that conformed exactly to Natalie's allegations.

Zain cornered Kate after her meeting with PCC Hope to let her know what he had found. She looked like she normally did after any interaction with him. Her face was infused with anger, and she was banging at the keyboard on her desktop. He felt an urge to reassure her, touch her shoulder.

'That bad?'

'No, the usual. That man, I have never met a more patronising, selfish, narrow-minded . . .'

'Oh, hi, Commissioner . . .'

Kate looked over her shoulder.

'Not funny, Zain, not even remotely. And quite frankly, I would be glad to say all of these things to his face.'

'I'm sure you have, many times.'

'I believe in standards of professional behaviour, DS Harris. I will not fall to his level.'

'No, instead the hatred and anger can eat you alive.'

'What have you got for me?'

Zain told her what he'd found on Leakey's hard drive.

'Seems a little too easy?' she said.

'People are naive sometimes. I think he was too.'

'Still, surely you would expect a senior government employee at his level to have some sort of sophisticated security?'

Zain had just assumed Leakey was old school, didn't really care for security measures the way he did. Now Kate had said it, though, he was considering her words carefully. She was right, his IT department would have added a number of layers of security.

'I'll do a check with the DFID IT team, and have another look.'

Kate observed Zain. He felt her eyes on him, as her thought processes worked. She made a decision and told him. 'DCI Raymond Cross was here earlier.'

Zain nodded. He'd guessed as much from the description Rob had given of his panama hat earlier. 'He was assisting Hope, they needed SO15 involvement in case it was a terrorist attack, and to create a media blackout. I believe SO15 and MI5 may have been investigating parallel to ourselves.'

Having worked for both GCHQ and SO15, Zain wasn't surprised. He followed her reasoning through and came to the conclusion before she told him.

'Accessing Leakey's laptop is easy because someone has already been in and done the hard work. Fuck's sake: I am basically looking at the handiwork of some spook somewhere. Bastards.'

He saw the concern on her face, which stopped his outburst. He hated how immediately she could alter his state, but he couldn't help it.

'It saved us valuable time, Zain.'

'Why didn't they look into his private life, then?'

'I don't think adultery is their thing.'

'Since when is it ours?'

'Since it might be why a highly toxic weapon has been deployed on the streets of our city. And if it's been used once, you can bet your bottom dollar it will be used again.'

She was right. This was his existence now. For a moment he had thought he was about to chase terrorists again, and secretly still hoped there might be a link. Then he felt guilty. Millions at risk so he could get a thrill from his work? He shook his head and let the idea go.

His job now was to find out why Julian Leakey had been so hideously killed. And the women he had been cheating on his wife with might be the key.

'This one is particularly interesting,' said Zain, giving Kate a printout of a chat transcript between Leakey and a woman named Bianca. 'He is basically telling her to back off, and stay away from his wife. You see, she contacted Anya as well, just like Natalie. So Anya's version of the perfect marriage is beginning to unravel quite quickly.'

'I think you should speak to Mrs Fox-Leakey about these other women, and while you are doing that, it might be worth asking about an alibi.'

Zain smirked. 'Still doesn't explain how she got the neurotoxin.'

Michelle joined them. 'I might have an idea. Didn't Professor Gerard say there were rumours about the Russians carrying out tests on toxins prior to the fall of the Soviet Bloc?'

'Yes, they were only rumours though,' said Kate.

'Anya's father, Lord Fox, served as an ambassador and diplomat to a number of those nations after the fall of the Soviets. Before her marriage, Anya used to work for him. She would accompany him on his postings.'

'That would have been, what, fifteen or sixteen years ago now?' said Zain.

'Yes,' said Michelle. 'However, she still manages to accompany him for the odd holiday now and then. I checked both her and Julian's travel history. Most of those countries are not in the EU; you have to apply for visas to travel there. Julian has no history of accompanying his father-in-law, but Anya did, sometimes with the children, sometimes alone.'

'Something else we need to speak to Anya Fox-Leakey about,' said Kate. 'I think we should also speak to Lord Fox and some of his aides who were there at the same time as Anya. See if they can throw any light on exactly what she was doing out there.'

'Yeah, like Fox will just meet us,' said Zain. 'And if Hope finds out we're going after a peer, he'll be spitting.'

Kate smiled at them both.

'Yeah, OK I get it, win–win. He's going to tip off his daughter though if we speak to him.'

'Then focus on the aides,' said Kate.

'Lord Fox was recently out in Russia as part of a diplomatic mission,' said Michelle. 'They were negotiating with them over the conflict in the Ukraine.'

'Have you got his travel itinerary too?'

'No, I just Googled him.'

'Was Anya with him?'

'Yes.'

'How long ago?'

'Four months.'

'That should mean the staff he currently has were probably there with him. Can you check for me, and get me some names?'

Zain considered the figure that Anya Fox-Leakey was creating in his mind. She was far more complex than he had given her credit for, and if she was bitter about the affairs, then there was a reason why she might want to hurt Julian. And her trips might have been the way in which she had found how to deal with him, once and for all.

Chapter Thirty-Nine

The industrial estate was built off the M25, on a turning you would miss if you didn't know it was there. There were units for import/export companies, another under the management of a printing firm, and then there were a whole block of units used by the NHS. Some management arm no doubt, wasting money that could have been spent on front line nurses. Rob felt his indignation, which he proudly thought of as working-class and Northern, growing as he parked.

Raxoman had a separate block of units, made of glass and chrome, interspersed with patches of green lawn. He spotted a number of flash cars outside the pharmaceutical giant's offices, including a sleek green Porsche. He gave it a once over as he walked past, envy and curiosity mixing together.

He knew that no matter how wealthy he became, the boy born in inner-city Manchester just couldn't fork out that much for a car. The value of money was ingrained in him. Easy to say though when he was struggling on a public-sector salary in one of the most expensive cities in the world. He was looking at crossing thirty still sharing a flat with three other guys, all in the same position as him. Something had to give surely?

The receptionist was an older woman, who greeted him with a melodious Caribbean accent. He told her he was here to see George Sharp, Natalie's old boss. The woman placed a call and a few moments later Sharp was there, a man who looked to be in his forties, with hair greying at the temples, dressed in a smart blue suit.

'Sergeant, please follow me, I've got us a room at the back. And ordered fresh coffee.'

'Thank you,' said Rob, nodding at the receptionist who was now glued to a mobile.

The room had blinds on the glass walls, and a small table on which sat two cups of coffee. Rob took his black, Sharp added milk and sugar to his.

'What exactly can I help you with?' asked Sharp. 'You weren't too clear when you asked to meet.'

'I was after a lowdown on a former employee of yours. A Natalie Davies? She was a temp . . .'

'Yes, I remember Natalie. Is she in trouble with the law?'

'I'm just running a background check on her. How was she as an employee?'

'Natalie was fine. She had some issues, some serious issues.'

'And her work?'

'Hmmm . . .yes, OK. She wasn't the best by any means; I'm sure even she would admit that.'

Great, thought Rob, he was landed with Mr Nice.

'Doesn't surprise me though that she's in trouble. Lots of things happened to her. Always something to interfere with her work.'

'You kept her on for nearly six months?'

'Yes. She was having marriage problems, health issues. I just couldn't bring myself to fire her.'

'What was she doing for you?'

'Just basic admin. Taking meeting notes, writing memos, letters. Arranging conferences.'

'Doesn't sound like a lot you can get wrong?'

'She just kept making silly mistakes. On top of that she was coming in late all the time, disappearing for long lunches. I gave her verbal warnings so many times, but they fell on deaf ears, to be honest.'

'And yet you kept her on despite all of this? So what made you finally ask her to leave?'

'I'm sure it won't come as a surprise to you, but she ended up stealing from us. Not stationery, or money.'

'Then?'

'Drugs. She was caught stealing some of the pain-relief medication we were working on.'

Rob felt his heart rate pick up.

'Can you tell me about that?'

'Yes, of course. They were medicines we were testing for rheumatological pain, severe arthritis, dealing with recovery from complex surgery on the spine and other parts of the body that take a while to heal.'

'What were the drugs?'

'They were a form of neurokine modulator. A new form. Basically we were taking naturally occurring neurotoxins and using their destructive power to target specific areas of the neurology that sends pain signals to the body.'

Rob started messaging back to the office.

'Do you manufacture these on site?'

'Yes, we have laboratories here. It was why the theft was so serious. Natalie not only entered a secured area; she was potentially taking medicine that hadn't been tested and could possibly have serious side effects.'

'Why would she?'

Sharp took a sip of his own coffee.

'The drugs are pain relief. When the prescriptions run out, DS Pelt, I'm sure you can imagine those people that have come to rely on them will do anything to get their next fix.'

Natalie was dealing? In highly toxic untested medicines?

'You say she got caught – was it only the once that she took them?'

Sharp looked embarrassed, unable to meet Rob's eyes.

'We can't be sure. You see, we don't log the medicine that is created during the testing phase. Most of it is destroyed, but we don't really keep stringent records of quantities produced as such.'

'So she could have been stealing them for a while?'

'Unfortunately, yes.'

'Can you show me your labs, please.'

Chapter Forty

Rob looked over the laboratory where Raxoman were developing new medicines. It was sterile, although full of glass bottles and substances he didn't particularly want to come into contact with. Chemistry was not his strength at school, and he barely had a grasp on the things he had learned over the last couple of days.

There were CCTV cameras guarding the way in and out of the lab, and locks on most cupboards and glass cabinets. Rob heard screeching noises coming from somewhere. He felt sick. Images of large eyes, fur, trapped bodies. He had seen the evidence, the cruelty done to those without a voice, tested on for man's benefit. He tried to shut it down, he was on duty, he couldn't let his personal views interfere. But he couldn't help it, his skin was crawling, he wanted to free whatever was being held captive and punch the people doing the 'research'.

Sharp was staring at him. Rob became aware he hadn't spoken for a minute or two. He didn't trust himself, swallowed hard, looked away, before speaking.

'Everything seems secure. Tightly locked up. How did Natalie gain access?'

Sharp was fidgeting as he replied, and he'd been texting someone during the tour. They were probably trying to do some form of damage limitation. It made Rob's insides tighten more. These were the type of people he hated most.

'She was taking master keys from where security kept back-ups. I don't know how she knew about them.'

'And you never caught her on CCTV?'

'There was no need to check. We would only really play it back if we suspected something had happened. We had no reason to. None of the lab staff reported anything suspicious.'

'Why didn't you report it to the police?'

Sharp was red in the face when he replied. 'She begged me not to, said it was the only time. That she had enough problems and couldn't face any more.'

'And you just let her go?'

Sharp nodded.

Fucking incompetent, thought Rob.

'Can you tell me exactly what Natalie has done?'

Rob didn't explain, but asked him what sort of side effects the medicines they were producing at Raxoman might induce. Again, images of animals suffering during the testing process smacked him hard. He was feeling hot, and claustrophobic.

'They can vary, if neurotoxins are not tested properly. Side effects might be paralysis, vomiting, a breakdown of neuron responses.'

'Any type of haemorrhaging?'

'That would be rare from neurotoxins.'

'The modulated ones you are producing here, though?'

'You mean modified. And no. We are working with industry-standard chemicals, their effects are known. Our modifications would only work to enhance certain aspects of them, it would be unlikely they could cause a severe reaction.'

'You can't rule it out though?'

Sharp was quiet. He shook his head.

'Is it possible that these neurotoxins could have been modified to cause extreme adverse side effects? Even death?'

The colour drained from Sharp's face, as the implications of what Rob was saying started to hit home.

Natalie was happy. She couldn't help it. Julian Leakey was dead. Finally the fucking scumbag had met his end, and she hoped it was as painful and as dreadful as it could be. She should have been there though, she should have watched him suffer. It didn't feel enough to just know.

Her mood started to dip then. It didn't feel like closure. It should be. This is what she had fantasised about for so long, as her life broke down and her existence unravelled. Every cell that died chanted his name. Julian Leakey. The man that had taken her away from her life, and then dropped her from such a great height she had shattered. Every piece sharp and painful as she walked over them, trying to put herself back together.

Only she never could. And now he was gone. She wanted him to suffer, for every part of him to cry out in the pain she felt.

An anger tore through her and she screamed. Her voice bounced around her bedsit, and in that moment she didn't hear her door open, and didn't hear the footsteps behind her. When the hand covered her mouth, and the darkness overtook her, Natalie knew. Julian Leakey had come back from the dead to finish her off as well.

Chapter Forty-One

The interview with Lord Fox hadn't yielded anything significant. He was over seventy and his retirement was already late in coming. He had a gravitas about him, a charisma at least, and Zain could almost see the diplomatic life leaking from his every pore. He was polite, friendly, extremely well spoken, asked Zain about his own life, and yet when it came to answering questions about his daughter and son-in-law he was resolute and unyielding. That was the diplomat to the core, Zain thought.

His aides were just as opaque, not really revealing anything new except to confirm Anya's presence in Russia on numerous occasions and that she had in the past been on other trips to visit her father.

As with Julian Leakey's staff, Zain was convinced there would be a chink in the armour somewhere. One of them would be harbouring a resentment. It was finding the right person that was the problem.

Zain was walking back to the PCC HQ. Lord Fox's offices were in the Houses of Parliament, a stroll from Whitehall. Crowds were thronging the fences that looked into the heart of the British establishment, traffic jostling from all angles. Armed guards kept a watch on anything untoward.

He angled himself through people from across the globe, again lamenting the fact that he had London on his doorstep and barely took it in, when other people travelled thousands of miles for the experience.

He headed past the Cenotaph and on to the main stretch of Whitehall that led to St James's Palace and 10 Downing Street. It was then his phone rang, a number he didn't recognise.

'DS Harris? This is Mike Turner. We just spoke briefly? I work for Lord Fox?'

Zain remembered him, with sleeked-back black hair, gold-rimmed glasses and an earnestness in his tone. Zain had given all the aides his card when he left, hoping one of them would be willing to give him more details. And here he was, Mike Turner.

'How can I help you?'

'Firstly, I need to know that this will remain confidential. As in who the source of your information was.'

Zain threw out these assurances all the time, knowing full well he would ignore them if he needed to. I'll drag your ass into a dock if needs be, Mr Turner, but until then sure I'll give you false hope.

'Of course, anything you say will stay confidential.'

You don't have it in writing, so go ahead, do your worst.

'I didn't want to say this in front of the others, or in the hearing of Lord Fox. He is an exemplary man, and an extremely professional employer.'

'I have no doubts at all about that. Listen, Mike, would it be easier if we met somewhere? Did this face to face?'

There was silence on the line, but Zain's head was filled with the sounds of cars, buses, voices. London at one of its most famous crossing points. Eventually, Mike said he would like to meet, and gave Zain the location.

'It's a little alcove across the road from Parliament.'

'Yes, I know it well, we used to be based on Victoria Street and I went there a lot.'

The alcove was a garden in Westminster where the original Abbey buildings had once been. They arranged to meet there in fifteen minutes.

Zain hurried to where the garden was, retracing his steps past Parliament again.

Mike Turner was already there when Zain arrived, wrapped in a thick black coat, scarf and gloves. Zain took a seat on a bench opposite him.

They shook hands, Mike's soft and warm in his gloves. Zain put his in his pockets to try and heat them up.

'Thank you for meeting me, and sorry it's so clandestine,' Mike began.

'No problem. So what can I do for you?'

'It's more a case of what I know that might help you. We are obviously devastated by the news of Julian's death. He was a good man. Had his opinions, but carried himself with dignity at all times.' If only you knew, thought Zain. 'I don't know which direction your investigation is heading, but I can only assume your questioning of Lord Fox and my colleagues, means there may be something that doesn't sit right?'

'It is an investigation into an unlawful killing,' said Zain. He heard how he sounded. Whenever he met someone posh, he always ended up speaking like a twat. Still, Kate always did go on about mirroring people and the Reid technique.

'And the questions about Anya?'

'Just covering every angle.' Zain wanted to say 'innit' just to sound normal again.

'I may have some information which might be of assistance in that regard.'

The wind was biting, and Zain felt his nose begin to condense. He took a tissue from his pocket, wiped it. Mike watched, not speaking again until he had his full attention. Zain wanted him to just get on with it, hated protracted conversations. He bit the inside of his cheek, tasted the blood, tried to stay calm.

'Anything, no matter how innocuous or unrelated, could help. So please, go ahead.'

Mike glanced around again. Working for the FCO no doubt he had read enough le Carré novels to give him a sense of being wary of his surroundings.

'I can't really say if it happened in previous postings, I can only assume it has. While Anya was visiting us in Russia there was an incident. It meant that Lord Fox had to be rushed to a meeting with his Russian counterpart. The security vetted driving staff had to accompany her father, so I was left to take Anya to the airport. It was all quite smooth, the trip to the airport. Anya is pleasant enough, although she does have a habit of treating her father's staff as her own sometimes.'

There it was, the resentment that Zain had hoped for. Watch who you piss off, because if they ever get asked about you, their version will sting. Badly.

'At the airport, we were checking in her luggage. Everything was fine, apart from her not putting through one of her bags. She refused to, and the check-in desk staff were not impressed. On closer inspection though, I realised it wasn't just a normal bag. She had one of her father's diplomatic pouches with her.'

Zain understood, he knew how they worked. Diplomats used them mainly for sending confidential documents, with the guarantee that they would not be searched or checked leaving or entering a nation.

'Was that usual for her to do that?'

'I'm not sure. There were no special arrangements made, and she seemed to have acquired the pouch from somewhere. I asked the others afterwards but nobody admitted to having supplied her with one.'

'Her father possibly?'

'No, we hold his for him. He relies on us to keep them secure and use them when required.'

'That's odd. She may have brought it with her, possibly?'

'Yes, I'm pretty certain she did. I had none go missing while I was there.'

'What was in the pouch, do you know?'

'No. It wasn't documents, that much I can say. It felt like a box of some sort when I handled it.'

'Why did you?'

'She was worried security might confiscate it as she collected the rest of her bags after they had been scanned.'

'They let you just walk through?'

'I have diplomatic immunity; they don't really question my whereabouts.'

'Can you describe the box? How heavy was it? Could you tell what it was made from?'

Mike moved his eyes to the side, attempting to recall it. 'It didn't weigh more than a few grams, I don't think. It was sealed so I couldn't tell what it was made from, something solid though. It didn't feel like metal, so I can't say for sure.'

'How do you know it wasn't metal?'

'There was no metallic ring when I tapped it. Like I said, I really can't be sure, and the pouches are sealed securely.'

So, Anya had smuggled something back into the country then. Professor Gerard had said how lead boxes were the preferred way to transport toxic materials. Was Zain assuming too much? After all, Mike didn't actually see the contents.

He was thinking not only of what might have killed Julian, but also about the wealth that Anya and Julian seemed to possess. Was Anya doing this regularly? Is this where their income was coming from? Abusing her father's diplomatic privileges?

'Sorry, it doesn't seem like much does it? Only I thought it was important. It really bothered me that she had behaved that way. It's not something I can condone, and I thought it might help.'

'Could she have been bringing something back for her father?'

'Possibly. Only I can't say what. Unless it was so confidential, or so urgent, that he used her instead of waiting until we returned.'

'How are secure communications normally sent?'

'This isn't the Cold War anymore, DS Harris. We have emails now, encrypted methods of communicating via phone.'

'Is anything done over a network really secure? How was Anya's behaviour? Did she spend a lot of time alone while she was there?'

'Yes, of course. We were working during the days, and she would be left to her own wiles. In the evening she would join her father for dinner, or accompany us to a function or event. They are interminable really. I find them tedious. But they have to be done.'

Not only did Anya have the means to import something into the mainland UK without it being questioned, she also had the time to procure it. Zain thought this was enough. He called Kate, and let her know what had happened. She told him to bring Anya in for questioning.

'What about PCC Hope?'

'He can't know, not yet anyway.'

Was there warning, mistrust, accusation even in that sentence? Zain bit back the second guessing.

'He won't hear it from me.'

Chapter Forty-Two

Kate was trying to fit the pieces into place. She was in the conference room, the screen filled with images she was moving using her tablet.

Rob had told her about the Raxoman labs, about Natalie Davies stealing from them. Dr Kapoor thought it would be unlikely Raxoman would produce something so caustic and devastating, but she'd asked for their labs to be searched and for samples to be sent to her. She was still at the Royal Free with Professor Gerard, working on testing samples taken from Julian Leakey.

Kate had rushed through a warrant to take what they needed from Raxoman, and she asked for a patrol to tighten surveillance on Natalie Davies' flat. She hadn't left the bedsit she occupied in Southgate since they had put it in place. Kate had just been given a warrant to search her flat, which Stevie was on the way to enact.

Eric was sending her jokes on WhatsApp, but she ignored them. She felt as though she was neglecting him, but he would be there at the weekend. He understood how busy her life could become, and she in turn accepted his lifestyle. He had a small flat in Pimlico he had inherited, something he used when he was in London. It was on one of these trips that he had bumped into Kate. She had just moved in to Dolphin Square, and they ended up in the same deli. Coffee turned into dinner, as they reminisced about a case they had worked on together. Dinner turned into drinks, and then he told her his place was only a few minutes' walk away.

Was it love or convenience? Kate didn't know, and she didn't care. For the first time in a long while, she was feeling some semblance of normality. She was in a relationship, and it was working for her. It didn't get in the way of her mother or her job. And as much as she hated to admit it, his daily messages were becoming a habit and a need.

She turned back to the web page that Michelle had created for her, linking the people and places on her screen. It all seemed so plausible, and yet totally unreal. She could understand Natalie Davies and Anya Fox-Leakey. These were victims in a way, of Julian's selfishness and arrogance. Zain had showed Kate the adultery websites Julian had been on, the women he had met on there. Websites promoting themselves for married people looking for a hook-up. She couldn't really judge, she had done her own fair share, and the shame burned through her when confronted by it like this. She hadn't considered the other woman, not really. Ryan had been convenient; she had taken advantage of the situation. Chloe rarely encroached on her conscience. But here it was, her team calling out Julian Leakey for something she herself had done. Maybe not as much, or as blatantly, but it was about degrees on the same scale.

Anya had an obvious motive now, so did Natalie. It was the method, that's what didn't fit. Neurotoxins were poisons, the historical weapon of choice for women, but that was in the past; these days nothing was off limits. Still, she just couldn't make the leap from these wronged women, to what she saw on Julian's body. He had not only been poisoned, but it was done on the night of the Anonymous protests. It was pre-planned, carefully put together. Natalie seemed like too much of a mess to do that, and Anya, would she put her husband through that? Would she put her family through that? It was so public.

The thought hit Kate then. Unless they were working together? Anya the planner, Natalie the one that would get her hands dirty. No, she was being fanciful. She couldn't link the two women like that. And yet, they both had motive and possibly even means.

Natalie was stealing what they needed from Raxoman, or Anya was bringing it into the country from abroad. Either was a distinct possibility. Kate stared at the images as they blurred in front of her.

Michelle came in, interrupting her thoughts.

'Anya Fox-Leakey is here.'

'Thank you, I'll be down in a minute. And Michelle, can you have a look at Anya and Natalie's phone records. See if they've been in contact, or if their cell locations match at anytime?'

Too late she realised she'd slipped in her American 'cell' instead of using 'mobile'. Michelle didn't seem to notice. Kate's phone buzzed.

'Stevie. Are you with Natalie?'

'No,' said Stevie, sounding out of breath and anxious. 'She's gone, boss. I think she's done a runner.'

Chapter Forty-Three

Kate was trying not to think about the missing Natalie Davies as Anya Fox-Leakey sat calmly before her. She was an attractive woman, dressed smartly, and her lawyer was just as polished. Priya Shah was leaning forward, poised almost, deflecting Kate's questions as she put them to a non-committal Anya.

'Anya, we know a number of women have contacted you, including Natalie Davies, to inform you of your husband's infidelity. What did you make of the allegations when you heard them?'

She said nothing.

'Are allegations all you have, DCI Riley?' said Priya.

'I am asking your client these questions, Ms Shah.'

'She doesn't wish to answer your baseless accusations.'

Kate looked at Anya, who was trying to look bored but couldn't quite manage to keep her anxiety hidden. Her eyes kept darting to the floor.

'Did you begin to resent your husband? All the affairs, the humiliation? While you were keeping his home, raising his children?'

Again nothing, just the passive expressions she had kept throughout.

'Is that what drove you to decide to end his life?'

'Have you any evidence at all that my client was involved in the tragic and very sad death of her beloved husband?'

'Beloved husband. An extremely loaded word, *beloved*. It suggests some form of attachment, don't you think? And yet your reaction on hearing of the death of your husband was anything but full of emotion.'

'You're basing your assumptions on how my client reacted to such devastating news? Is there a guide to how people should react?'

'Anya, were you relieved that your husband was dead?'

Anya's mouth twitched, opened slightly. The slur was driving her past the instructions Priya had obviously given her. Still she maintained control, and repeated the only thing she had said throughout.

'No comment.'

'An aggrieved wife, taunted by the adulterous allegations of a husband who has neglected her, and more than that, humiliated her. How did you feel when Natalie and Bianca contacted you? Was there absolute rage inside you?'

Priya sighed, and rolled her eyes at Kate.

'When did you decide you were going to kill your husband?'

'No comment.'

'Was it after Natalie, or was there someone else? Is there another of his affairs that we are going to uncover, something worse? Did he threaten to leave you for one of these women? Is that what finally broke you?'

Kate was needling her, trying to break through the defence Anya had put up around herself.

Priya was looking at Kate as though she had just stepped on something, wrinkling her nose. There was real loathing there, and Kate wondered if it was directed towards her profession or if it was personal.

'DCI Riley, I don't think you have much to go on. You are simply obfuscating theories and trying to convert them into facts. What evidence do you have linking my client to the means of how her husband died? What exactly killed him? We are still unclear of the details.'

'That raises another issue. You see Anya, we think Julian was murdered using a highly toxic substance. Lethal, poisonous. Difficult to manufacture, difficult to procure. Unless you know the right people, and have the ability to move such things. Internationally move them, I mean.'

A flicker. There it was in the very corner of the eye. Everyone had these ticks, they betrayed people all the time. Kate just had to find the right buttons to push.

'We believe these substances are available in some parts of the world. After the fall of the Soviet Bloc, a lot of weapons programs passed into regional control. Some were lost entirely, the extremely sensitive and secret programs for example. There are a number of places where these things might surface on the illegal markets of the world, like Russia for instance.'

Anya looked away, her face giving away her emotions, as the colour crept into her cheeks.

'We know, Mrs Fox-Leakey, that you recently visited your father on his posting to Russia. And we know that, on your return, you brought back something using one of his diplomatic pouches. Is this true?'

Anya had lost her composure now, she was staring at Kate with steel in her eyes, rubbing her upper arms, self-comforting gestures, feeling the pressure of Kate's words.

'No comment,' she said, her voice devoid of its previous affected boredom.

'What was in that diplomatic pouch you brought with you?'

'No comment.'

'We are currently searching your apartment, Mrs Fox-Leakey.'

'Do you have a warrant for that?' said Priya.

'No, I just sent my team hoping that you wouldn't notice I was flouting the law so blatantly. Do I strike you as being so unprofessional?'

'I wouldn't like to say.'

'What will they find, Anya? Will they find something that might link you to Julian's death? Have you heard of Locard's principle? It's the theory that everything leaves its mark, anything that comes into contact with something will leave a trace of itself. We will find what you had hidden, and we will test that pouch. Do you still have nothing to say?'

Anya's eyes were ruinous as she bore into Kate, her words trembling.

'I did not do this,' she said. 'You are trying to frame me for something I had no part in.'

Paranoia? Kate hadn't expected that. She looked closely at Anya, and began to see something she hadn't noticed before. A defeated woman. Julian Leakey had not only treated his wife unkindly, he had chipped away at her sense of self. It was a form of abuse.

Before Kate could continue, the door to the interview room was banged open. Justin Hope was standing there, his eyes full of thunder.

'Interview terminated,' he said for the benefit of the recording equipment. 'I apologise, Mrs Fox-Leakey, you are free to go.'

Kate looked on as Anya and Priya left the interview room accompanied by the Police Crime Commissioner for Westminster. Her very core trembled with the anger she felt.

Kate drove home, too fast, and too angry. She beeped her horn for the smallest misdemeanour, and cursed under her breath anyone she perceived to have violated her space.

Charlie the security guard was surprised to see her, and only exchanged the barest of pleasantries with her, as Kate drove away hastily. She needed to get home, and then what? She parked in the underground car park, and put her head on the steering wheel. What had she done? She had let her emotions take over, and she had reacted. This was what she always worried Zain might do, his volatile and unpredictable nature always just under the surface of his calm obedience. And here she was, having done exactly the same, storming out of the office.

As the realisation came to calm her, she started to feel the prickling of guilt and embarrassment. And then she recalled what had happened. PCC Hope had stepped in, no he had stepped *on* her investigation, and totally discredited her. She could tolerate his meddling, and she knew if he had called her out of the interview, and asked her to terminate it, explaining why, she would have behaved differently.

He had made the choice to do it this way, to humiliate her so blatantly.

Kate felt the anger and rage pick at her again, reaching the corners of her mind she didn't control. The voices that were meant to soothe her were instead goading her, telling her how badly she had been treated, how she had done the right thing. How she needed to see him, tell him what she thought about him, and to leave Unit 3.

The same voices then started to echo from her past, until the past and her present were merged. She had fought powerful corrupt men like her father, men that had assumed she would behave a certain way, and she had won. Victory may have come at a price, and may have been hollow, but there wasn't a price to be put on doing the right thing. Justice was worth the pain, she'd always believed that. It's why she became a cop and why she still chose to be one, even when doing so was not the easy option. And when it meant moving her world so much.

Eric called. She told him what she had done. He started laughing.

'I can imagine.'

'I feel so unprofessional.'

'I wish I had seen you storm out. Well done, my love.'

There they were. Words that tripped off his tongue so easily. Words that instantly undid years of bitterness and hatred in her. Words she couldn't say back. Not yet at least.

'I feel like a fool. I should have reacted better.'

'You reacted the way you did. There is no wrong or right now.' That was his psychiatrist speak coming through. It irritated her. And was one of the reasons she knew he was right for her. If she couldn't see his faults, that's when she would know she was building him up to be something extraordinary. That's when there was a sucker punch just waiting to land, when reality came calling.

'I can't wait to see you,' she said.

'I'll come up tonight, start the weekend early. You sound like you need me.'

No, she didn't. She wouldn't allow herself to need anybody. Yet it felt good that he would do this for her.

'Don't stress yourself, whatever works for you.'

'This works for me,' he assured her.

Kate was oscillating between rage at PCC Hope, anger at herself and anxiety over Eric, when she got to her flat. She stood outside the door, looking for her keys, when she heard voices from inside. Raised, sharp, argumentative.

Kate felt her heart hammer inside her ribcage, and quickly opened the door, rushing in to defend her mother no matter who the intruder was.

'Mom?' she said, bursting into the lounge.

Her mother was standing in the middle of the room, phone to her ear, as she turned to look at Kate.

He had followed Kate Riley as she left her office, early, and from the look on her face, not under happy circumstances. His heart had picked up. Had her mother told her? Despite his threats? Was he now in a position to carry those out? He relished those moments.

Only, he was being held back. They wanted to know about her first, and they wanted to use her for their own purposes. He understood. But it was only a matter of time. When they had no more purpose for her, that's when he would step in.

He called her mother. He wanted her to be hysterical when Kate got home. He wanted Jane to confess, so that he could carry out his threats.

When he'd finished dismantling Kate Riley's life, she would pay in full for the sins of Winter Morgan.

Chapter Forty-Four

Stevie was at a loss. Natalie Davies lived in a bedsit, but on a residential street just off the main roundabout outside the Southgate Tube station. Areas like this didn't have the same sort of CCTV coverage she was used to in Central London. The Tube station was covered, and she had managed to access that. Natalie was seen at the bus station next to the Tube, getting off the bus, but that was all they could manage. And that was thirty-six hours ago already.

When Kate had asked for there to be a patrol to check on Natalie, the Southgate force had simply sent a car around while it was doing its rounds. No permanent lookout, no trace on her phone. She could have left anytime, and they wouldn't even know.

'The flat is a mess, but I'm not sure how much that is a cause for worry, and how much it's just neglect on her part. I've spoken to the owner; he's converted his home into a series of bedsits. He says Natalie is a bit errant, doesn't always pay the rent on time, but she's never so late that it goes into arrears.'

'Did the SOCOs find anything to worry about?' asked Zain.

'No, well, not in the amounts needed to raise a flag.'

'Anything that might provide a link to what killed Julian Leakey?'

'No. They couldn't find anything that she may have taken from Raxoman either. Which is odd, if she was stealing for a while.'

'What about the drug dealing?'

'I can't see any signs of her being a hardcore pusher.'

'How can you tell? Most of them live in big houses these days.'

'There are signs. And no phones. She has to have taken hers with her, but as per usual there's no signal. Whoever leaked the fact that taking the battery out stops us being able to trace it needs a fucking smack.'

'There are other ways to track phones now,' said Zain. 'Even with the battery removed.'

'Yeah well, unless your spook pals are willing to help us find a runaway woman who barely registers on the suspicion scale . . .'

'I think there's more to it. She may have been involved in the deployment of a bioweapon on British soil. That's how I'll spin it anyway.'

Stevie looked out at the still street. This was the suburbs. Stevie lived in a one-bedroom flat in Stepney Green, a council property she had been able to buy. Her past was not pleasant, and she had been forced to fend for herself early on in life. No education, no prospects: she had joined the police because even at eighteen she knew it would be better than the alternative she was being offered.

'Not to question you, but shouldn't those sorts of favours be kept for the really crucial stuff?' she asked.

'Yes, I guess.'

'Any word from the boss?'

'No.'

'So you call the shots while she's MIA?'

'Yes.'

Stevie didn't know how she felt about this. She had loathed Zain when he started. She had been a dead cert for Kate encouraging her to apply, even helping her with the forms. And then, PCC Hope had waltzed in with this twat. Zain was up himself, going on about his GCHQ and counter-terrorism background, unfriendly and interfering. He thought he knew best, broke rules at will and generally pissed everyone off.

Then things changed, and he proved himself. To a point. Stevie had thawed towards him, but still her allegiance was to someone else. She didn't like to think how much she only tolerated him for the sake of Kate. And if it came down to life or death, would she really have Zain's back?

Chapter Forty-Five

Rob was in the Leakey's bedroom. It was plush, expensive. He wasn't interested in the room so much though, more in Jessica. She was one of the SOCOs, one of his exes. He watched her observe the room in the way she did all rooms which she was asked to search as a SOCO. She looked at the layout, where the furniture was placed, what sort of furniture it was. Where people may in the course of their day put things, where someone under pressure might hide something. What sort of contact the dead may have had with each section of the space she was in, or what sort of intrusion was made by someone who wasn't meant to be there. Entrance and exit points. And clues to the lives that were led within the confines of the area she was asked to analyse. He remembered her telling him all this, the detail, the softness of her voice. Those intimate moments after making love, when he could pretend for a while she was the one. Before he shattered his own illusions.

'My favourite CSI,' he said.

Jessica didn't look at him, instead searching through the drawers one by one to the main dresser.

'How are you, Jess?'

Jessica had met him during a missing person's case for the PCC, and agreed to go on a date with him. It had led to a one night stand. She dated him once more, they went to bed again and then that was it.

Jess continued searching through the drawers without replying.

'Have you found anything?' he asked.

'No, nothing significant.'

Jessica moved next to the wardrobe that lined an entire wall. She opened it to reveal neat rows of clothes, separated by gender. Accessories like shoes and scarves all neatly lined up. Someone with too much time on their hands, or a SOCO. There were forensic levels of neatness here. Jessica started searching, but there was nothing. A small safe built in to the side, with a key panel on it.

'What time do you finish?' said Rob.

Jessica smiled, her mouth covered by her face mask, but her eyes, he remembered how they looked when she did. She was almost done with the wardrobe. She stood back, and checked the angles on the rear of it. She moved aside dresses, and had a closer look.

'Pass me my torch please,' she said to Rob. He brought it over, and stood close to her. 'I've told you before about leaving perfume traces at a crime scene.'

'It's not perfume, it's eau de Rob.'

She ignored him, and used her fingers to press the false backing. She checked the sides for a hinge, or a lock. Nothing was obvious. It must slide open, or click open somehow. And there must be a code.

'Can we get someone here to break into this?' she asked.

Rob got on his phone, and they had someone there within twenty minutes.

Twenty minutes during which Rob tried his hardest to get her to go on another date with him. Even he knew he was sounding desperate by the end.

'Why?' she said eventually, snapping. 'So you can put me down on a scoresheet again? Do you give yourself double points for a woman you've managed to re-seduce? Come on Rob, we all know your reputation. So do you.'

He felt the verbal punch. Harder for the truth behind it? He hated how people perceived him, and hated even more how he lived up to the perceptions.

'Doesn't mean I don't have feelings or a heart.'

'Honestly, I doubt you have either of those.'

'That's harsh.'

'Harsh is how you treat people.'

'They know what they're getting. I don't promise the world to anyone.'

'So it's their own fault then? You're not selling this to me.'

'I miss you.'

'I'm at work, maintain some professional standards, DS Pelt.'

He felt even more hurt, and left her alone until the safe cracker arrived. He was a man in his late fifties, neatly combed hair, a shirt and tie. He was wearing forensic boot covers and gloves, as he got to work.

'Piss easy,' he told them.

It still took him fifteen minutes to get in. Rob got a call.

'Balls,' he said when he was done. 'That was DS Harris, we don't have long. The owner is on their way back. They've been released without charge, our warrant to search the flat has been revoked.'

'I didn't hear that,' said Jessica. 'And you didn't tell me until after we're in.'

The safe door opened to reveal documents, jewellery, cash, passports. And on the side, another keypad.

'Double jeopardy,' said the safe cracker. It took him another twenty minutes to break the code. Twenty minutes when they were collectively watching and listening for the return of Anya Fox-Leakey. The rest of the team were already packed up, and loading up the vans in the underground car park.

When he entered the code for the side panel, Rob heard the mechanics start, and the back of the wardrobe slid open. Rob quickly ushered out the safe cracker, while Jessica started to explore what was behind it.

'What have you found?' asked Rob when he came back into the room.

She showed him.

'Fuck me.'

'Give it a rest, DS Pelt. It's not going to happen.'

They stared at the contents, and Jessica started cataloguing them. They heard raised voices, and knew Anya Fox-Leakey was back.

'You bag up all of these, and I'll stall her,' said Rob.

Chapter Forty-Six

Justin Hope was not moving. His fingers were steepled in front of his face, and his eyes were locked on to Zain's. Zain was trying to convince him, but the PCC was ignoring him and resolutely repeating the same mantra.

'DS Pelt has found a number of empty diplomatic pouches hidden away behind a false door. We found boxes in a few of them. They could have carried anything in them. I think Anya Fox-Leakey has been abusing her father's diplomatic immunity, possibly for years.'

'Have you anything more than your assumptions?'

'I need to ask her what was in them. I want her to explain what was in every single one of those pouches, and what she did with the contents.'

'They are carriers that have the protection of International Law; she really does not have to tell you.'

'She is not a diplomat.'

'Her father is, and they were issued under his name.'

'So these people can bring anything into this country then?'

'Unless there is cause for concern and a possible threat to national security, we do not check the contents of these things.'

'That's bullshit, sir, and you know it. She possibly brought in a bioweapon, and we aren't allowed to question her? There has to be a way.'

'Find me some evidence, DS Harris, and we will talk again. Right now, I will not drag the daughter of a peer and a UK ambassador through an interrogation based solely on your theories. You know how this works. You know the pressure this office can be placed under. I need something more, and then you will have my approval.'

Zain was fuming. They had the possible means of transportation for whatever killed Julian Leakey, and PCC Hope was preventing them from carrying out a proper investigation into it. The rich and powerful really did have different rules applied to them, he knew this, but it fucked him off every single time.

'I've given you approval to test the boxes you found. If anything comes up positive, then you let me know. Until then, nothing else will be asked of Anya Fox-Leakey. Do I make myself clear?'

'Yes, sir.'

'And why is DCI Riley not here making this request?'

Zain held his thoughts in check, unable to think quickly enough.

'Family emergency, her mother. She will be back shortly.'

It was better than the alternative, he thought. To tell him that she had just stormed off without a word and told them not to contact her.

The rest of the team were just as angry. They were gathered in the conference room, looking defeated.

'So what happens now?' asked Rob.

'We wait for the test results from the Royal Free. Has Dr Kapoor got back to you about the Raxoman results yet?'

'No, not yet.'

'What about Natalie Davies? Any sign at all?'

'Yeah, didn't I tell you?' said Stevie sarcastically.

'She didn't just disappear. We need to intensify our search for her.'

'There was no link between them I could find. No recent contact anyway. Natalie's phone provider only sent me her last six months' worth of data. We didn't get clearance for Anya's records.'

'What about Julian? Any calls between him and Natalie?'

'None that I could see,' said Michelle. 'There was the restraining order in place, so she probably didn't breach it. What I did find though were a number of unknown calls being made from and to Natalie's phone.'

'Evidence she was selling stuff then?' asked Zain.

'It looks like it. We are tracing the numbers and calling them back at the moment. Well I say we, but Leah and the admin staff are.'

'Would love to hear those conversations. Did you buy illegal substances from Natalie Davies?' said Rob.

'That's the problem, they're not exactly illegal. She wasn't selling anything recognised in law; the best we can do is get her on handling stolen goods or something. The serious stuff she's managed to avoid.'

'It's all such crap. Has anyone heard from DCI Riley?' said Stevie.

There was silence.

'What happens now?' asked Michelle.

'We wait,' said Zain. 'I suggest we call it an early night, and let's hope we get some test results back that might actually help us.'

And first thing in the morning he was hoping DCI Kate Riley would be back at her desk.

Chapter Forty-Seven

The evening was cool as they walked through the streets of Pimlico. They had eaten at a Turkish restaurant, Kate unsure whether her chicken was cooked through, but Eric seemed to think it was fine. She might have lost her sense of taste from the stress she was feeling.

She had demanded to know who Jane was arguing with on the phone, but her mother had refused to answer. And when Kate plied on the pressure, her mother had simply walked away, slamming the bedroom door behind her. Ryan used to call it the Norma Desmond act. Kate had picked up the same trait from her mother. She had behaved exactly the same at work, and now she was screening calls and emails, not communicating with any of her colleagues, while she weighed up her options.

In her head she rehearsed her resignation speech, while she tried to play grateful girlfriend to Eric.

He had made the journey from Cambridge especially for her. It was a gesture, one she wasn't used to. It felt good, and she resented the fact that it did. Why did she care so much, and since when had she become so reliant on someone else's response to her?

Eric laced his fingers into hers. She was jolted by it, the intimacy. It made her shy away, more than sex ever did. The physical act meant nothing, it was so primal. But this, the emotional side, the bits that mattered, the small gestures that said you were in love, they put terror into her. Kate felt guilty that while Eric was expressing his adoration in such intense ways, she was rehearsing her back-up non-resigning verbal assault on Hope. Which one she would deliver, she didn't yet know.

They were being watched. Kate and the lecturer, Eric. He had moved to hold her hand. It made the watcher cringe, such casual intimacy, PDAs. Not his thing. He looked away. It was an interesting development, one that needed to be reported.

'What is he like?' the man asked.

'Tall, Scandinavian looking. They seem to be getting along.'

'That's a shame.'

'Is it?'

'How are you getting on with her mother?'

'I've made contact, she is responding. Other than that, nothing concrete.'

'Keep picking away at her. She is weak, she will cave.'

The watcher doesn't understand what game is being played, but he knows it is a long-term one. Kate Riley is going to suffer, but when that happens is yet to be determined. For now, she will be observed and then slowly trapped.

Eric's flat was on a square around Pimlico market, the stalls all closed and packed away now, peaceful. It felt surreal. In the heart of London, and yet there was quiet. Just the two of them.

Kate stopped, and kissed Eric. It felt like adolescence, strange and embarrassing. And then, as he moved against her body, it felt right. There was nowhere else she wanted to be.

Her phone rang. She made a move to pick it up, but Eric grabbed her hand and wouldn't let her, his tongue exploring her mouth, as his body encompassed hers. She had to pull away, in case it was her mother, she needed to check. He kissed the back of her neck as she took out her cell and checked the display.

'Rani?' said Kate. It was nearly ten o'clock.

'Where are you, DCI Riley?'

'Just at home, why?'

'Can you meet me? I'm at the Royal Free. It's urgent.'

'What's wrong?'

'It's about Julian Leakey. I think you should come. Now. Please.'

Dr Kapoor ended the call. Kate didn't want to go; she should just let Zain handle it. Going would mean her choice was made. PCC Hope had undermined her, and yet she still stayed. She should just leave it alone, and resign. But the cop inside her wouldn't let that happen. She knew there wouldn't be much of a debate inside her head, as she dialled Zain and told him to pick her up.

Chapter Forty-Eight

Zain was driving, negotiating the traffic. He had picked Kate up on Vauxhall Bridge Road, then headed to the Royal Free.

They drove in silence, the brightness and noise of London filling her head. She didn't want any music on, and Zain didn't either. He had been at home when she called him, and she could smell the tangy citrus bodywash he used. It reminded her for a moment of a night in Winchester, when they had almost crossed the fragile barrier between personal and professional. She was glad that never happened. Never understood how she even got so close. Zain was a good officer, but he was also a loose cannon and a liability. Alcohol was involved, of course. And he was an attractive young man. Still, she couldn't imagine even touching him in an inappropriate manner at the moment.

'What does this mean, then? Have you decided to stay?' he asked.

'My mother used to say some people are so sharp they will cut themselves and their neighbours. Nothing gets past you.'

'I guessed when you stormed out, when I knew why, I thought that was it. You would leave. I hope things are different now?'

'I really don't think anything has changed in the last few hours. Dr Kapoor asked to see me, so I'm going.'

'I think you should come back. Forget Hope, he's a dick, we all know that. The rest of us need you.'

'You seem to be managing fine without me.'

'I think the rest of them are writing their resignations tonight, ready to leave if you do.'

Dr Kapoor looked exhausted when they met her. She was dressed in her normal clothes, but with a white medical coat over them. At least she wasn't in quarantine, and at least that wasn't the news she had for Kate. She still remembered the Ebola nurses finding latent strains behind their eyes and being readmitted. It had crossed her mind that the summons may have been to tell her they'd found something that meant she had to be back in isolation again.

They walked through empty corridors, following Dr Kapoor to the basement, where she said they had set up their labs. When they got to them, Kate was greeted by a woman who introduced herself as DS Joy Goldman.

'I'm part of the Kensington and Chelsea station,' she said. She was tall with dark blonde hair and black eyes. Well spoken, and smartly dressed.

Kate introduced herself and Zain.

'I wasn't expecting you at all,' said Kate. 'What's going on, Dr Kapoor?'

'Please sit,' she said. They all took an uncomfortable stool each. Kate smelled sulphur and acid, mixed with burning.

'Have you traced the Raxoman products yet?' Zain asked.

'Yes, I sent an email earlier. I don't think the Raxoman products could have been used in the Leakey case. We checked the chemistry and structure, and they don't match the neurotoxins used on Leakey at all. They also wouldn't result in the sort of symptoms we saw.'

Kate didn't think this could rule Natalie out completely. She may have got the toxins from somewhere else. Her motive was still strong, and under that sort of intense pressure, she may have been capable of anything.

'That's not why I called you here though. DS Goldman contacted me earlier today, and informed me of something quite startling. Do you want to fill DCI Riley in?'

DS Goldman nodded.

'Earlier this morning I was called out to an address in Earl's Court, on Cromwell Road. There was a strange smell coming from one of the flats in the building, so the landlord had gone in, in case it was gas, even though it smelt nothing like gas. The flat was unoccupied, so he didn't think anything of it. Only, it wasn't empty.'

Kate looked between the two women, but didn't understand how this was related to the Leakey case yet.

'What did he find?'

'It was the body of a young woman.'

Kate felt her eyes widen. Was it Natalie Davies?

'Did she have the same symptoms as Julian Leakey?' she asked, in a whisper.

'I'm not sure exactly what his symptoms were?'

'Pustules on the skin, haemorrhaging of the internal organs especially the brain.'

DS Goldman didn't flinch at the gory description, just shook her head.

'No, ma'am. What killed the young lady were multiple stab wounds. We found the knife used at the scene. It was a frenzied attack, the multiple wounds inflicted were done so within seconds of each other we think. We had a post-mortem carried out earlier today, and it was conclusive. She had been dead about forty-eight hours.'

Natalie was still alive in that time period. So it wasn't her.

'How is this linked then to our investigation?'

'We ran the girl's DNA through our database, but we didn't get a match on any known persons. Our tech guys ran another search, this time using broader criteria. And we got a hit to the Julian Leakey investigation.'

'That investigation is locked down, you can't access the details unless you are authorised,' said Zain.

'It was my team that were carrying out the autopsy,' Dr Kapoor said. 'When Joy's team were given the red flag that linked it to Julian, they contacted me and asked me to check what the flag was. It was connected to the tests we ran on Julian Leakey, so I was able to check.'

'What did you find?' asked Kate.

'Two things. Firstly, remember they found foreign blood on Julian Leakey's body that wasn't his? It was drenching his shirt?'

Kate nodded, finally understanding. Her heart had picked up.

'The blood and DNA we pulled from there, matched that of the young woman. Her blood essentially was what was soaking his shirt.'

'And the second thing?'

'We ran fingerprints and DNA on the knife used. Only two people's details were recovered from it. One was the young woman we found. The other, was Julian Leakey. I believe Julian Leakey may have murdered this woman, hours before he himself was killed.'

Chapter Forty-Nine

Cromwell Road divided into two parts. One side led to Glouces-
ter Road, and some of the most expensive postcodes in South
West London. The other side, split by Earl's Court Road running through it, led to a twenty-four-hour Tesco, and properties
that probably carried million pound tags but looked a bit more
rundown.

Zain parked outside an Easyhotel, and they walked to the
address DS Joy Goldman had given them. She was already
there, waiting. Zain could smell weed, and saw there was a
halfway house in one of the buildings they passed. A group of
young men were standing outside, relaxed and talking amongst
themselves. Zain nodded at them, but they ignored him.

Kate was walking quickly ahead of him, and despite her mis-
givings, she hadn't once said she wasn't part of this, and that she
was asking him to lead. He could tell she was back. At least mentally, and at least for now and this case. And it felt right. Being
by Kate's side, taking direction from her. It was clear to him that
she was the reason he was still on the force, or an early retirement and a different career would have been easier. He would
have missed working with her.

The building DS Goldman was standing outside looked der-
elict. The paint was peeling, there were boards over the ground-
floor windows, and rubbish bags on the stairs leading up to the
entrance. Zain caught the smells of cooking and decay in the air
as they approached the front door.

DS Goldman used a fob to unlock the main door, and they stepped inside. Newspapers and letters littered the small hallway, where a table with plastic flowers stood. A dismal projection of hope in the middle of the general wear and tear.

'Nice. And I bet the landlord charges full whack,' he said.

'The residents aren't much help. The lower floors are full of workers from Romania, sharing flats built for two between a dozen or so people. There's a family on the middle floor, council tenants housed under emergency conditions. Involves domestic abuse. Students in the other flat there. Top floor is empty.'

Zain knew there were places like this and worse all over London. Still, he hated the greedy landlords that preyed on the vulnerable. That was for another day, though.

They walked up unsteady stairs, and Zain smelt the rot, and something else. The smell of human decay and death was still there. Like rubbish that had been left out too long.

'The scene has been processed, and the cleaning team will be here in the morning. For now you can see how we found it.'

'And there's no ID at all for the young woman?' asked Kate.

'Nothing. No DNA match. We haven't found anything on her person and there's no reports of a missing person that might fit.'

They put on their plastic shoe covers and gloves. DS Goldman took keys from her pocket, and unlocked the flat door. They were greeted by the hum of flies, and the smell was overpowering inside. Zain didn't think it was all related to the dead woman. The flat wasn't anything more than a studio. The kitchen and bedroom were in one room, a door to the side leading off to a small shower room.

The bed was a sofa bed, covered in white sheets. They in turn were covered in blood. The red was smeared on the floor, scatter patterns of it on the walls, where it was black in places. There were footprints on the floor, again imprinted with the same crimson and maroon.

'We found her face down on the sofabed,' said DS Goldman. 'There isn't much else to see really. The flat is unoccupied, nothing in the cupboards or bathroom.'

'Why hasn't the top floor been rented out?' Kate asked. 'I'm sure there's demand, so the landlord could find someone without much difficulty?'

'They were both rented out to students until a few weeks ago, but they left without paying rent for a couple of months. The landlord has so many properties across London he hardly notices. The rent comes in, he's happy. It took him a couple of months to realise the students hadn't been paying. When he came to chase them, they were already gone.'

'He probably deserved it' said Zain. 'Keeping people in conditions like this.'

'They have hot water, electricity. I haven't seen signs of vermin. So I would say they are quite well off comparatively.'

'Comparatively, but you wouldn't put up with this sort of stuff if it wasn't London and everything wasn't so flaming expensive.'

'Supply and demand, simple economics,' said DS Goldman.

'Signs of a struggle?' cut in Kate.

'Not particularly. There were defence wounds on the victim, on her hands and arms, so she fought back. And we found skin and hair under her nails. Waiting for the DNA match on those, but I am sure they will belong to Julian Leakey.'

'Can we get a face fit of the victim?'

'Already done. Her face was relatively unscathed, so we have scene photos and a touched-up version run by our tech team.'

'If you can send those over to us, we can try showing them to Julian's staff, and his family. See if anybody can place the victim, make a connection.'

'Yes, ma'am.'

Zain looked around, but aside from the copious amounts of blood there was nothing else to indicate anything serious had happened here.

'I might go and question some of the neighbours,' he said.

'We tried. They didn't see anything.'

'They all say that. Let me stick the boot in.'

'We have tried.'

'No worries. Do you need a fob to get in?'

'Yes. In theory. There are only limited fobs though, so the ground floor residents often keep the main door on a latch. They also admitted that if you push, the door opens.'

'Any other way in?'

'There's an entrance leading out to a mess of a garden. But it's surrounded by a high wall, and full of nettles. Not sure anyone would risk coming in that way, but we have had forensics do an examination.'

'Let's get those images over to Anya, and Julian's staff. In the morning.'

'Yes, boss,' said Zain, smirking.

She was definitely back in charge.

Chapter Fifty

Zain was driving Kate back to Pimlico. 'What are you thinking?' he asked.

'We need to identify the woman.'

'You think it could be one of Leakey's lovers?'

'Possibly. Can you check on the women that were messaging him online? In case there's a match to one of their profiles?'

'Sure,' he said. 'Why would he kill her though? It really doesn't make sense. He has a great life. What did she know that made him feel that this was the only way? He must have known he wouldn't get away with it?'

'Possibly he was set up?'

'I don't know. Maybe. So Leakey's killer killed them both, but framed Leakey? And left no trace of themselves?'

'We don't know that for sure. Leakey's details raised a flag. If they're processing some unknown person's DNA, say the killer's, they won't get a match or a flag.'

'No, but they'll know someone else was there. They can build an unidentified DNA profile for them.'

'True.'

They were passing Abbey Road Studios, then Lord's Cricket Ground. Zain started humming a Beatles song.

'You seem happy?'

'Don't I always?' he said.

'Yes, of course.'

'So you're going to stay then?'

She looked out of the window, as they headed through the whitewash houses of Regents Park and Baker Street. It was the sanitised part of London, at least on the surface. He knew some of those expensive houses were just like the one they had left, with dozens of people crammed into small spaces not built for so many people.

Kate was still thinking, but Zain couldn't help feeling his mood being lifted. In a dangerous way.

Where would that lead exactly? She was with someone else; she was his boss. Kate Riley had shown him a kindness when so few others had bothered; it was just gratitude. His mind was trying to force her into another shape, another place.

Again that hurtful inner voice. *You are obsessed with her, admit it.*

No he was not.

'How are your family?' she asked.

'Fine. Mum is visiting soon. With her new husband.'

'What is he like?'

'No idea.'

'You didn't go home for the wedding?'

'No. Nobody did, not even my grandparents. She should get the message by now, she's turning into a joke.'

'Dr Kapoor said she was being called the Elizabeth Taylor of Mumbai?'

'It's funny, why do these pathologists read those stupid gossip magazines? Dr Mehta was the same.' Dr Mehta was in post before Dr Kapoor. 'My mum feeds tabloid gossip, that's all. She married a Bollywood producer as husband number two, since then she's a Z-list celebrity over there.'

'Rani showed me her picture. She is a very beautiful woman.'

'She's my mother, she doesn't have to be beautiful. You know she's threatening to do their version of *Strictly* and *Dancing with the Stars*?'

Zain held back his resentment. His mother had focused on him after divorcing his father, making sure Zain was her priority. Until he turned eighteen and then left home for university. Correction, *he* didn't leave home. Despite living in London, she made him go and stay in the halls of residence at SOAS. And then she had begun her own odyssey of marriage and divorce. He found out more about her daily pursuits from online columnists and bloggers than from her.

Still, she did message him every day and call regularly.

But he had been through too much without her; too much pain had entered his life and his body; he just didn't know how to tell her. The words they exchanged were hollow, empty. Instead, it was his father who Zain had turned to. A man who hadn't been there much after the divorce, who had his own new family. When Zain was in hospital the first time, recovering from the ordeal of being held captive and tortured, it was his father who had stepped up. A military man, he had held his son's hands, and told him to wear the scars of war with pride.

It was a different type of war Zain had fought. On paper it seemed simple. In reality, he was completely lost. He hankered for that sense of belonging and purpose again. He couldn't explain to anyone how on any given day he felt as though he had been pushed off a ravine, and was waiting for the ground to smack into him.

Kate Riley understood. She had been through her own version of hell, in which she too had lost everything that she knew, everything that anchored her. Betrayed by her own father, she had stuck to her internal moral compass, and she had fought him. That took guts, to put your own father away because you knew what he was doing was wrong.

Yet what had her reward been? In revenge her father had had her mother attacked, and Kate had moved from America to London. Why did it feel as though fighting for justice, against evil, seemed to end up destroying your life?

Zain was following the river now, heading towards Pimlico. It was lit brightly, the yellow flares and artificial lights bobbing in the gently moving water. All an illusion, just like the city.

Chapter Fifty-One

They were in the conference room, it was approaching lunch-time, and they were all on edge. Zain had told them that Kate would be back today, had filled them in on the trip to Earl's Court and the dead woman who had been found there.

'I saw Anya Fox-Leakey this morning,' said Rob. 'She didn't recognise the woman, but then again she's not exactly the paragon of truth.'

'Still, if anyone was going to charm her, it would be you right?' teased Stevie.

'I do my best. Anyway she had her lawyer woman there, so I didn't really get much of a chance to be honest. I also took the e-fit to Leakey's staff, but none of them recognised her either.'

'I think I may have another angle on Anya Fox-Leakey,' said Michelle. 'I started to look at the money trail. Their flat is worth a cool two million, and they bought it six years ago, mainly using a cash payment. I calculated Julian's salary based on his HMRC returns, and there is no way he could afford to pay for something like that.'

'And what about his wife?' asked Zain.

'She inherited a small amount from her grandparents, but nothing to that value. And there is nothing in her normal account suggesting an income of that size.'

Zain couldn't help but grin at her. The words normal account indicated Michelle was about to drop something.

'Tell me,' he said.

'She has a shell account, in Panama. She was named in the leak, but her name got hidden among all the high-profile ones, because it's under her maiden name.'

'Do we have details of it yet? Any transactions?'

'Not yet, but that got me to thinking. Anya must be smuggling something in those diplomatic pouches. And she must need help offloading it. So I checked her phone records more thoroughly. And I may have something. A Vince Hopper. He specialises in precious gems. Anya seems to call him whenever she's back from one of her trips.'

'And there's your explanation for the money,' said Zain. 'What about the dead woman? Can we widen the search?'

'I put an alert out,' said Michelle. 'The woman's image is currently being circulated through various media channels and online. Hopefully somebody will recognise her and come forward.'

'Somebody must know who she is,' said Rob.

'You sure you haven't slept with her?' asked Stevie.

'Ouch!'

'Where is DCI Riley?' said Stevie, ignoring him.

'I'm guessing she decided not to come back after all,' said Michelle. She turned to Zain, and it was a touching gesture on her part. 'What happens now DS Harris? Where do we go from here?'

'We need to keep looking for Natalie. Find out who this dead woman is and what relationship she had with Julian. I've looked through the Internet chats and adultery websites he was on, but nothing has been a match so far. He may have met her some-where else; after all, he met Natalie in real life, not online. And the rest, we really need Dr Kapoor to get us some . . .'

Zain stopped. Kate was walking across the office, with Dr Rani Kapoor in tow. The women had serious expressions on their faces, and were walking with purpose. Kate met his eyes, nodded briefly to him, through the glass walls. She opened the door, and let Dr Kapoor take a seat.

'Apologies for being late, everyone, I got an urgent call from Dr Kapoor this morning so was up at the Royal Free. Zain, please continue with your briefing.'

'Erm, I think I'm done, boss. We were just saying how we need Dr Kapoor to get us some test results on what killed Leakey.'

'That was why she called me this morning. I believe we may have some answers to that part at least.'

Zain sat down, as Dr Kapoor began her explanation.

'Apologies everyone, especially if I get technical now.'

'No worries. How come it took so long to get these results through?'

'You have to understand, DS Harris, testing for neurotoxins is not a simple task. There is no key test that will identify their use. I think I've explained before: if you're infected with something like Lymes disease, for example, the symptoms take time to show, and it is difficult to really pinpoint them. They could be related to a number of other illnesses. Yet, if you are bitten by a snake, immediate action can be taken. Most neurotoxins don't enter the body quite so dramatically though.'

'Snakes?'

'Snake venom is a form of neurotoxin, Zain.'

'Didn't know that.'

'There are hundreds of neurotoxins, as you know. Tests are developed for some of the major ones, the ones that occur quite regularly. We can match samples of code in bloods, but the tests are not universal. The test that might pick up one neurotoxin is only specific to that particular one. It won't work on any others. And for the majority, tests don't exist.'

'So what have you been doing exactly if there aren't any tests?' said Zain.

'We ran tests sequentially, testing for the known neurotoxins. And then checked the structure of what infected Julian Leakey to see if we got a close match. We did, eventually. But we went about it the wrong way. It's partly my fault.'

'Not at all, Dr Kapoor; we are not placing blame in any of this. We are all trying to find out the same answers,' Kate assured her.

Let's see, thought Zain. He wasn't beyond placing blame on anyone.

'I asked Professor Gerard to focus on the blood fluids I had taken at the crime scene. I was blindsided, convinced that was where we would find the answers we needed.'

'It wasn't?'

'No. You see, the neurotoxin found in Julian Leakey has very low levels of presence in the plasma of the human body. A urine sample is much more effective. And that's where we found what we were looking for.'

Kate was tapping on her tablet, and brought up an image on the screen from Google.

'This is our killer,' said Dr Kapoor.

Zain looked at the innocuous picture on screen.

'It's a fish?' he said.

'Yes. It's a member of the Tetraodontidae family.'

'In English?'

'It's a puffer fish. The most famous one is called Takifugu. Often eaten as fugu.'

'That's the Japanese delicacy?' said Zain. 'I remember. The fish carries poison in its liver, but is eaten as a challenge almost. They had to close down that Japanese restaurant in Mayfair because it wasn't handled properly and a customer was poisoned.'

'Yeah, I remember that,' said Rob. 'But that's quite common. Loads of people in Japan get poisoned all the time eating this stuff.'

'Yes. The puffer fish carries a toxin called Tetrodotoxin, or TTX, and we tested for this early on when we suspected a neurotoxin. As I said, we found no match in the blood, but the urine sample showed something that was a close match.'

'A close match?' asked Zain.

'Yes. We know the structure of the neurotoxin the Tetraodontidae carry. It's ten thousand times more powerful than cyanide as a poison, but the substance we found was only a 70 per cent match to TTX. And in the blood, there was none.'

'So what exactly have you found?' Zain massaged his temples. He barely had a grasp on what Dr Kapoor was telling them. He understood binary code and information security, but the complexities of science were always hard to follow.

'As I said, the variant of TTX had a partial match with the Tetraodontidae, DS Harris. It wasn't a full match. It's basically been doctored, heavily. You're looking at a new generation of biological weapon, jumping from a toxic poison to incorporate elements of a Cat A virus. It's like loading a cluster bomb with radioactive material. I hope you understand that analogy?'

'Yes.' *Fuck*. Yes he did. 'Who would know how to do that?'

Dr Kapoor looked embarrassed now.

'TTX mutations are being trialled at a number of institutions around the world,' said Kate. 'Commercially there's a possibility they can lead to breaking down brain tumours, without the need for operating.'

Zain looked at Dr Kapoor, who still couldn't meet his eyes.

'Name some of these academic institutions.'

'Zain,' warned Kate.

'Let me guess. The leading institution for testing this stupid bloody toxin in the UK is University College London? Is that right? Your own *fucking university*, Dr Kapoor?'

'DS Harris, I suggest you go outside and cool down. And that's an order.'

Zain left the conference room, banging the door behind him.

What the hell had Dr Kapoor been doing these last few days? She was playing test tube at the Royal Free, when the actual place she should have been looking was in her own backyard, at her own university.

Kate found him half an hour later, sitting in the faith room. It was an empty room with a cupboard full of materials used by various religions when they prayed there. He was sitting cross legged on a prayer mat, trying to calm himself down.

'This is the male prayer room,' he said. 'You're supposed to be next door.'

'Depends which faith you believe in. I don't have an affiliation so I'll stick to my own rules of free movement.' She sat down next to him.

'That was not professional, Zain.'

'Really? How else should I deal with dumb doctors?'

'Unfair and harsh. How could she know?'

'You know what the PCC is doing.'

'Have you any idea how big UCL is? Thousands of students, lecturers, researchers. There is no way anyone can know everything that's happening there. Dr Kapoor is a pathologist; she is the PCC pathologist. You will not behave like that towards her again, do you understand? You will apologise to her.'

'Whatever.' He guessed he was being unfair, when he thought about it. UCL was a massive campus, and Kate was right. How could Dr Kapoor know what everyone was doing?

'As soon as she discovered the toxin, and its origin, she started an online search. And she found UCL. It doesn't mean there's a link; it's just a source of the raw materials.'

'The only source?'

'The likely source. TTX is manufactured synthetically for testing purposes by a number of institutions, UCL is one of those places, but not the only one in the world. We can't assume.'

Zain breathed out, hoping some of his anger would go with it. 'It's been a long few days,' he said.

'Yes. It has. Don't forget Rani has been at the very heart of the pressure throughout.'

He breathed out. 'I'll think about an apology.'

'Good. My primary focus though is to go and find out who at UCL had access to the TTX neurotoxin, and the ability to mutate it.'

Chapter Fifty-Two

University College London was based in Bloomsbury close to a number of other universities including SOAS and Birkbeck. It was associated with the central dome structure that filled its main courtyard, but the actual academic buildings and institutions were spread out across the area.

Kate had parked on Gower Street, and walked the rest of the way on foot. The building she needed was close to the British Museum and Senate House, and looked more like a house than a lab. It was accessed by broad stone steps, and was made from the same light stone of the museum.

There was a security guard at the entrance, who was suspicious but not probing. He said she wouldn't be allowed in unless accompanied by one of the staff. Kate saw CCTV, plus a number of locks on the main entrance door, but it didn't seem very robust or secure.

She was greeted a few moments after signing in by a Professor Bernhard Keller. He was an attractive man, in his early thirties she guessed, tall and well built. He was wearing jeans, trainers and a T-shirt, despite the cold, and didn't strike her as being particularly academic. His accent was Germanic, or Swiss maybe.

'Dr Kapoor called and told me you would be coming. Please follow me.'

Kate was more assured by the secure fob he needed to get through the main doors.

'I believe you are interested in our TTX?' he said.

She nodded, and he led her to a basement and into a corridor lined with foil-covered pipes that was obviously a dumping ground for laboratory equipment and boxes of paperwork.

There were a number of doors leading off this main artery, all of which looked heavy and which had secure locks built into them.

Keller used his fob on one of them, and then put his eye close for a retina scan. It was safe, as safe as something like this could be.

Behind the door was what looked like a student common room. Low chairs, tables, a soda machine and a vending machine full of snacks. None of them healthy. Copies of *New Scientist* and *National Geographic* were on the tables.

Keller invited her to take a seat on one of the chairs. 'Can I get you a drink?' he asked.

'No, thank you.'

'So how can I help?'

'Professor Keller—'

'Please call me Bernhard.'

'Bernhard, I need to understand your research in more detail. I believe Dr Kapoor has spoken to you about what we found, a potential victim of TTX, and she thinks it's from a strain that you are working on?'

'Yes, she did. We have about a dozen puffer fish in tanks on the UCL main campus, that we use for our source of TTX. I had a check and they are all accounted for.'

'What about previous specimens?'

'We normally dispose of the ones we use. We extract the Tetrodotoxin from their organs, and keep it stored safely. All of it is monitored and logged.'

'Who has access to it?'

'I have a number of PhD students who have access to the laboratory. To the actual TTX that we are working on, only myself and two other staff. Both are researchers.'

'I will need to speak to them. Have you a record of how much TTX you have in storage? Did you do a preliminary check on whether any is missing?'

'I did, and it is all accounted for.'

Kate was losing hope now. Nothing had gone astray. Unless of course Bernhard was lying to her, either to cover up a mishap like the one that had happened at Raxoman, or because he was involved in some way? It was still quite a leap from the lab at UCL to Julian Leakey. That was the part that Kate didn't understand.

'Dr Kapoor said you use the TTX to try and eliminate brain tumours?'

'Yes we do. We are trying to manipulate the TTX, to change its code. The idea is that we bind the changed TTX toxin to a brain tumour, and it literally burns it, melts it away. It does so in a targeted fashion, so there is no peripheral damage to any of the surrounding tissue or nerves. You can imagine the risks involved in brain surgery, and cutting tumours in that area is especially problematic. If it could be done without an invasive procedure, it would be revolutionary.'

Kate could understand that. What she was really interested in was what the process did to the tumour.

'And the tumour, the melted part I mean, how would that be extracted?'

'We would hope the bloodstream would carry it away as natural waste, or we would have to find a mechanism for drainage. We believe we can disintegrate it to extremely small amounts.'

'How are your experiments going?'

'Still going, as they say,' he said laughing. 'We have a research grant for five years, so we are still very much in the testing stage.'

'And what do you test on?'

'Mice, generally,' he said. Kate would have to keep Rob away. He detested animal testing in any form. 'We also have synthetic tests that we are developing, so we can see the effects on tumour tissue. That can be through human organ donation. Luckily we don't have much need for brain transplants, so anybody giving up their organs, well the brain is usually not utilised except for research such as ours.'

'And what about those unsuccessful experiments? What sort of side effects have you observed?'

'Plenty. And yes, DCI Riley, I checked the sort of symptoms your victim was displaying. We have had reactions similar to that.'

Chapter Fifty-Three

Kate asked for a drink after all. She had a feeling she was going to be there a while. Bernhard brought her a weak vending-machine coffee. She took a sip, then put it down.

'Sorry, you get used to the substandard taste when you're in academia. No budget for luxuries like decent coffee.'

'It's fine, thank you. You were saying about the reactions you had? In your experiments?'

'Yes. So we test tissue samples and we also test live subjects. The neurotoxin TTX is very powerful, so we obviously cannot inject this straight into humans. It would mean death. Usually symptoms take twenty minutes or so to start, but death can take anything up to four hours. It is not pleasant.'

'How do you prevent that?'

'We haven't yet. What we are doing though is synthetically altering the TTX, which allows us to crack its structure more easily, and make additions and changes to it.'

'And you've already begun these?'

'Yes, we have. We have performed experiments where we saw, for example, that instead of just melting the tumour, the TTX2 as we call it, also melted the brain tissue. It broke it down, and I believe this is what happened to your victim?'

'Yes. And the TTX2 used in those experiments, where is it now?'

'We destroy most of it, but keep smaller amounts with a detailed structure graph, to make sure we don't repeat the same mistakes. It's a delicate process.'

'Sounds more like trial and error?' said Kate, taking another sip of coffee.

'In a way all science is. Very few eureka moments, lots of painful failed ones.'

'And the small amounts you keep? Are they secure? Can you vouch for the integrity of your colleagues who have access to them?'

'Yes.'

'What about the haemorrhaging and the skin lesions?'

'We have performed experiments where both have happened.'

Kate imagined the mice that were being tested on, writhing around in agony and pain. Rob was definitely not coming here.

'At the same time?'

Bernhard looked at Kate intently.

'No, not at the same time. However, we would keep records of the effects with each mutation we did.'

'It's not beyond the realms of possibility then that someone could make a combination of those batches?'

'Technically, no. In reality, the process is so precise it would be difficult to. And there is no guarantee that you would get a similar result. It's the realm of science-fiction rather than science-fact, I think.'

'And yet, I have a body infected with the toxin you are working with, displaying all these symptoms that you have described.'

This was it, Kate could sense it. She had found where the toxin had come from. Now she needed to work out who could have administered it.

Kate took her phone out and showed Bernhard images of Julian Leakey and Natalie Davies.

'Do you recognise either of them?'

'No. I mean I recognise him from the news reports. Is he the one you found with these symptoms?'

Kate didn't answer. Bernhard seemed genuine, and she didn't really understand how the link could be made between his research and the two people on her phone.

'You said two of your colleagues had access to the toxins? Are they here?'

'Yes. Emeka Benson is, he's one of my PhD students. But the other, Mark Lynch, is away on leave.'

'When is he due back?'

'Not until next week. He's taken a month off.'

'Has he gone travelling?'

'No, he needed some time out. Rather, I asked him to take some time out.'

'Any particular reason?'

'It's how we work. We are so engrossed in what we do, holidays become interruptions. I am guilty of this myself also, and my annual leave builds up. It's HR policy, use it or lose it, as they say.'

'You have his details though? I can contact him?'

'Yes of course.'

'And Emeka?'

'He's here, I'll get him for you.'

Kate messaged Zain while Bernhard went to get his colleague.

Emeka was polite, with a very broad smile. He didn't recognise either Julian or Natalie. Kate asked for all their details, including the names and contact details of the other PhD students that worked in the lab.

She sent them to Michelle to begin an electronic search, to try and identify any links that might exist between them and Julian Leakey.

Chapter Fifty-Four

Mark Lynch hadn't responded to the messages that Kate had left him, so she sent Stevie out to check on him. Mark lived in a studio in West Brompton, opposite the cemetery. Cemeteries creeped Stevie out at the best of times, and with the day fading into evening, she wasn't best pleased to be anywhere near the place. She wasn't afraid of anything she could see – she could kick the shit out of most tangible things – but all that invisible poltergeist stuff really freaked her out.

Stevie avoided looking at the gate to the cemetery as she rang the bell to flat three, where Mark Lynch lived. It was on the first floor, and she could see a light was on. Maybe he just left it on for security while he went out? She continued to buzz but there was still no response.

Stevie called Kate.

'Nothing boss, he's not answering.'

'Can you let yourself in, have a look around? See if knocking will make him open up? Or check with the neighbours if they've seen him leave?'

'Will do. He might have gone away after all?'

'Possibly. Strange he's not replying to any of my messages though. If the police called, you would get in touch. If you had nothing to hide.'

'Maybe. Then again, we don't think like the other side.'

'Don't we? I thought that's what keeps us alive, being one step ahead?'

Stevie laughed. She buzzed one of the other flats, and checked with the neighbours. They said they hadn't seen Mark for a few days, weren't sure when they had last. It wasn't one of those love-thy-neighbour situations. That was London for you. Welcome to the busiest city in the world, also the emptiest and loneliest.

Stevie checked Mark's post-box, opening it with a tool on her key ring. It was piled quite high, and hadn't been emptied. He was definitely gone.

She decided to go back and knock again, calling his name. No response. She was about to leave, when she heard something. A faint hum. She leaned in closer, put her ear to the door. She heard it again. There was also a distinct odour. She would have put it down to *male, alone*, only it had a tinge to it.

'Boss, I'm going to go in,' she said, calling Kate. 'Is that OK?'

'If you have immediate cause for concern, then yes.'

Stevie pushed the door gently, felt its shape and weight, examined the locks on it. Stevie leaned back and kicked. It didn't budge. She kicked again. A small break, and it dented inwards. She then put her weight to it, using her shoulder. It opened further. After another couple of kicks it gave way.

The smell hit her hard, and she choked. She could hear the incessant humming of insects now. What the hell? She moved in quickly, covering her mouth and nose with her sleeve. It was a one-bed flat, the kitchen and lounge one small room. She checked they were clear, and then went towards the bedroom. The smell and sounds grew thicker, and she gagged as she opened the door, and saw him. Mark Lynch was on the bed, flies swarming around him and on him. Stevie went to turn the lights on, only she smelt something else. It was there lingering over the smell of death and putrification.

Gas.

'Fuck,' she said, dialling 999.

She then started banging on all the neighbour's doors, telling them to get out of the building. One by one the residents started to evacuate, slowly, dazed.

'Get a fucking move on before you're blown to pieces,' she yelled.

'No need for language like that,' one man said sullenly.

'Fine you stay and get fucking well burnt alive,' she shouted back. 'Hurry up. Leave your fucking coat, and your laptop. What is wrong with you all?'

It took about ten minutes for everyone to be gone, and she still couldn't be sure someone wasn't inside. The fire brigade hadn't turned up either.

'Shit,' she said. She just hoped they got there before the place went up. They needed Mark Lynch's dead body in one piece, or whatever state it was in. He was now key evidence to this case.

Chapter Fifty-Five

It took nearly half an hour for the gas to be switched off and the building ventilated fully. Stevie got the all clear from the fire brigade, went back up to secure flat three, and waited for Kate and Dr Kapoor.

They took another twenty minutes to get there, by which time half the block were harassing Stevie, who was standing outside the entrance to the flat, asking her what was going on.

'Go back to your own apartments please, this is now police business.'

She sounded like a fifties copper in her head, and really wanted to tear the residents to shreds. She kept her tongue in check though, didn't give in to her anger.

Kate arrived breathless, with Dr Kapoor.

'Had to park miles away,' said Kate, zipping into a forensic suit. Dr Kapoor did the same, and gave Stevie one.

'Well this feels familiar,' Dr Kapoor said.

'Public Health England are on their way, they've asked us to wait. In case Mark Lynch's been infected with whatever Julian had.'

'It's a neurotoxin. It will only infect us if we ingest it,' Dr Kapoor told her.

She handed Kate and Stevie hoods, with respirators built into them.

'Now it feels like déjà vu,' said Kate.

The three woman walked slowly into flat three, Stevie leading the way into the bedroom.

Dr Kapoor set up lamps against a wall, which cast eerie shadows on the walls. The blinds were open, and Stevie could see the cemetery in the background. Not freaked out at all, she told herself.

Mark Lynch was lying on the bed, his arms out to the sides, his legs apart. The insect buzz was still strong, as they picked at the dried blood that was all over the sheets and body. Stevie moved in closer and could see this wasn't the same MO as Julian Leakey.

'Cut to the carotid artery,' said Dr Kapoor.

Someone had simply hacked through his throat, and let the blood stream freely. It was spattered on the walls, the bedside table, the carpet. His clothes were drenched in it, as was the bedsheet he was lying on.

Dr Kapoor was taking photos, and examining the victim's hands.

'There are no defensive wounds,' she said. 'No struggle. He doesn't seem to have fought back at all. More than that though, look at his hands. They are relatively clean. He didn't try to stop the blood flow, or protect his throat.'

'Maybe his wrists were tied?' said Kate.

Dr Kapoor had a look, and saw nothing that suggested he was being restrained.

'You mean he just let someone cut his throat, and didn't react?' asked Kate incredulously.

'Didn't react, or couldn't react?' said Stevie.

'His eyes are open,' said Dr Kapoor. 'And yet everything else seems so . . . still?' She examined a glass on the bedside table which was spattered with blood too. She bagged it. 'There's something odd about the splatter on that wall.'

They all turned to look at the wall facing Mark Lynch's bed. Stevie couldn't see what Dr Kapoor was pointing out.

'Turn the lamp that way will you, towards the wall,' she said. Stevie did so, but she still couldn't see properly. 'The pattern: look where it's the strongest.'

Stevie looked, and then began to see. There was a definite gap in the spatter, a space that was less covered in the deep brown spots.

'What does it mean?'

'I think,' said Dr Kapoor, 'that someone was blocking the blood spatter. The murderer was standing or sitting here, cutting his throat. Sorry. I shouldn't speculate, it's not my job to.'

Stevie could see it clearly now. The question was why didn't Mark Lynch do anything to stop his throat being cut, or try to stop himself bleeding out?

Chapter Fifty-Six

Professor Bernhard Keller was clearly shaken up, his eyes red, watery. He was an academic, looked normal, but still part of a rare breed. A cocooned breed, protected from the real world by their passions and their pursuits.

Zain felt for the guy as he spoke to him, telling him about the death of his colleague. This was the real world at its worst, crashing into the unreal set-up they had at UCL. Kate had been there the day before to ask him about Julian Leakey. And now he was there to discuss Mark Lynch.

What the link was, Zain couldn't say. But it was too much of a coincidence not to have one.

'Can you tell me anything about Mark that might help? His background, where he was from?'

'I think the Midlands somewhere, near Birmingham?' Keller pronounced the 'h' thickly. 'I think he was an only child, or if he had siblings he didn't mention them. His parents, he spoke of them, but again, I don't know the details. He went to visit them regularly. I thought when you couldn't contact him he had gone there, maybe.'

'What about friends?'

'Ah, well I don't think he had many. It's a very lonely and intense experience sometimes, doing a PhD. His social life was built around his work; we tended to go out on Fridays. I can't remember him doing much else. The only thing he did regularly was attend a war-games society in Covent Garden. '

'Where was that?'

'A community centre, oh, where was it? . . . Seven Dials, yes, there.'

'Thank you, I'll check it out. So no girlfriend? No other associates?'

'None that I can think of. And no, there was no girlfriend.'

'Boyfriend?'

'No, nothing like that. Our work is very immersive, detective. It takes over, leaves very little time for other pursuits. And remember, Mark was also conducting research into his own PhD as well as working here as a researcher. From the outside, academia looks like an easy option. But in truth it is quite the opposite.'

Yeah, tell that to someone who wakes up at four o'clock everyday to clean offices or the public toilets. There's difficult jobs and then there's *difficult* jobs. Where would he class his own? Zain didn't know. To him it sometimes felt like torture, but in reality? He was lucky, wasn't he?

'When did you last see him?'

'Three weeks now. He took a month off. I asked him to, and told him he could use the time to work on his own research. He was due back next week. I can't believe this. He was so gifted.'

'I don't think death discriminates like that. Professsor, what part of the research was he involved in particularly?'

'He worked closely with me on the modification elements. We are working with nanotechnology, really breaking down the minutiae of code that sits on TTX2. It requires fine attention to detail, and patience. Not easy to come by.'

'He was at the heart of the research then? If anyone knew how these modifications worked, apart from yourself, it would be Mark?'

'Yes, without doubt.'

'And are you sure there is nothing missing? None of the previous substances you produced? You know the ones that went wrong?'

'I told your boss. We track everything, and all of those were destroyed.'

'When you say tracked and logged, who did that?'

'Myself and . . . well . . .'

Zain watched Professor Keller's expression run the gauntlet. It was his favourite thing to see, people's faces go through the spectrum from firm belief to being unsure to realising that actually they werc wrong.

'Let me guess, yourself and Mark Lynch?'

Keller nodded, and put his face in his hands. 'Come with me, DS Harris,' he said, taking his hands away. 'Let's go and have a look at exactly what's been happening.'

Chapter Fifty-Seven

It was painstaking work. Zain was wearing latex gloves, along with Bernhard and his other PhD researcher, Emeka Benson. They were going through the electronic database, checking for stored TTX2. Emeka was reading out the container numbers, and the expected weight. It was recorded down to the milligram. Keller was then weighing up each container, making sure the two matched.

'Once they are weighed, they are locked away. There shouldn't be any change.'

'Unless somebody took something after the fact?'

'Yes, unless somebody did that. Or unless the initial figures were incorrect.'

They continued weighing and reading out, until finally they started seeing discrepancies.

'There are four milligrams of TTX2 missing from here,' said Keller.

'Is that bad?'

'Twice the amount needed for a lethal dose.'

'Fuck,' said Zain. 'Let's see exactly how much you've misplaced.'

They found in total nearly twenty milligrams missing from a number of containers. With each discrepancy the tension in the room mounted, as did the temperature. Bernhard was struggling after the last container had been checked, his face red and sweat rolling down it. He rubbed at his eyes. Zain was surprised at the emotional response. Then again this was an absolute betrayal of everything he lived for.

Betrayals like that could erode your trust forever. Zain knew how that worked.

'Why do you need so many containers in the first place?' Zain asked. He hoped his irritation wasn't too palpable.

'We don't like to keep that much toxin in one container just in case. This way if someone took one, the impact could be minimised.'

'I see. Because someone with access would only ever take one container. I think it was reckless not to destroy the samples completely. At least we know there's TTX2 missing. Question is, what else would Mark Lynch have needed to modify it?'

'He had everything here,' said Emeka. 'We have protected time to do our research in the lab. If he did take it, then he could have done it here?'

'Yes,' agreed Bernhard.

'You said you kept notes on the experiments that went wrong? They're electronically stored, I'm guessing?'

'Yes, we have a database for them,' said Bernhard.

'A database that logs who opened the file last?' This was more Zain's territory.

'It should. Emeka can you please bring it up for DS Harris?'

Emeka logged into a terminal that was sitting on one of the work benches in the lab. Zain saw there were cages with white mice in them on a shelf. Rob was so not coming here, he thought. He would probably free them, and punch the staff so they knew what it felt like.

Once logged in, Bernhard started to click through files until he had the relevant ones open for Zain.

'These are the ones that have videos of what happened to our test subjects, the date we ran the experiment, and what modifications were done to achieve that particular formula.'

Zain sorted them by date modified, and checked for the username. He saw MLynch had opened and modified a number of them in the days leading up to his leave. Zain started to bring them up. The files were essentially zip drives, containing everything related to that experiment.

There was one particular file that had been accessed on the very last day Mark was in the lab. Zain wanted to know if they could tell how many times a file had been opened by someone easily.

'No, I don't think so,' said Bernhard.

Zain said he would have to use some code to find out, if they gave him permission. They didn't refuse, so he rebooted, and ran the code he needed to, checking it on his phone first. He had logged in to the secure area at work where he kept his files.

With the additional programing entered, he was able to check a log that showed which files had been accessed, by whom and how many times. He couldn't access the files without an authenticated username, but he checked the files that Mark had looked at the most.

'This one, what is it?' he asked.

'I can't say for sure, it was one of Mark's experiments,' said Emeka.

He logged back in on a different terminal, and opened the file Zain had highlighted. There was a video, and a report detailing what had happened to a mouse it was tested on. Emeka played the video, and Zain watched, transfixed but also horrified by what he was seeing.

'Fuck me,' he said when it was done, holding back the urge to throw up. This was it, he could feel it. This was the breakthrough. They had found the weapon used to kill Julian Leakey.

Chapter Fifty-Eight

Zain was driving through Central London, heading to the club in Seven Dials. Kate was on loudspeaker, having just watched the video he had seen earlier.

'Do *not* show that to Rob,' Zain told her.

'Quite. I wish you hadn't insisted I see it.'

The video was like a horror movie. A small white mouse was infected with a modified version of TTX2. At first nothing had happened, and then the video was sped up, to show the effects on the poor creature. It had started convulsing, retching, its eyes bulging. It had died horrendously, and most tellingly, there were skin lesions on it and blood from haemorrhaging.

'It's fucking sick and cruel,' said Zain. 'I'm joining Rob next time he goes on one of his hunt sabotages.'

'I don't think I'm meant to know about those. Not officially.'

She was right. It wouldn't sit well if a cop was known to be a hunt saboteur and passionate animal rights activist. Rob kept it quiet from most people outside their immediate team.

'And Bernhard couldn't remember the experiment?'

'No. Neither could Emeka Benson.'

'Mark did some private work then.'

'Yes. That mouse basically showed us what Julian Leakey went through. Forty minutes of intense agony, and then a painful death. Bernhard said the body shuts down because sodium intake is inhibited, and the neurons stop transmitting. But you can still feel it, and sense it.'

'So we have our weapon.'

'Yes. Mark Lynch created a bioweapon. How it was used on Julian Leakey and why, I have no idea. And how it relates to the dead woman, and to Mark's own death: again, no idea. But I don't think you need a PhD to realise we are looking for another person behind it all. You think Natalie Davies is capable of doing all this? Or Anya Fox-Leakey?'

'Let's not jump to any conclusions yet, but I think anybody is capable of anything,' said Kate.

'Michelle is still looking into the gem smuggling by Mrs Fox-Leakey. She could have paid Mark.'

'Possibly. The question is: how do we tie all these pieces together, and follow that link to the source?'

'I'm only a humble DS, boss. You get paid the big bucks to figure shite like that out. Was there anything from Mark's post-mortem?'

'No. His toxicology tests are still not back, but Dr Kapoor did some rapid tests on a urine sample for TTX. Nothing showed up. She does think he was drugged though. There were physical symptoms of some type of anaesthetic. Where are you going now?'

'There's a war-games club on tonight that Mark used to frequent. I'm going to talk to the person who runs it, see if they can give us any more background. Let us know who Mark Lynch was away from the lab.'

'War games? Isn't that for well . . .'

'Hey, I used to be into it at school.'

Kate choked on the line. 'Sorry. Really?'

'Yeah, it's a lot of fun if you know what you're doing.'

'I'm sure. I just can't imagine you being a part of something like that.'

'Yeah, well.'

'How did you leave them back at UCL, anyway?'

'Professor Keller is in shock, I think. He doesn't have a clue what to do next.'

'He has his work, I'm sure he will be OK.'

'Is that what people say about us?'

'There is truth in it.'

She was right. For all the trauma Zain had been brought by his work, it was also the only place he felt some sense of belonging and purpose. The job kicks you in the stomach and then gives you the cure. Nothing else would ever come close. It was in his blood.

The war games society was held twice a week on the second floor of the Seven Dials club, opposite the Donmar Theatre in Covent Garden. It was a community centre, rumoured to be owned by a philanthropic billionaire, which was why it was so cheaply available and able to thrive in the middle of Covent Garden.

Zain didn't think it looked like any community centre he'd ever been to, with its exposed brick walls, polished wood floors and art deco wall paintings. There was a main room with a bar, a library, and a large room at the back where the war gamers were holding court. Or battle.

The members were mainly men, with a few women. They were of varying ages and attire, from casual to smart city types. People on the outside never really understood the appeal. Zain felt the urge to join in, seeing the tables with green felt cloth on them to act as grass, the miniature plastic armies all lined up in battalions. Tape measures and manuals out, to orchestrate what would be a game of skill and chance.

'DS Harris!'

The young woman running the club, Yvonne Hall, held out her hand to him. He shook it, and she directed him to the library to talk. It was empty, so it was just the two of them, sitting on a sofa that sank too low with their weight, surrounded by books. Zain spotted everything from Jilly Cooper to Dostoevsky.

Yvonne was probably early twenties, straight black hair, and dressed in a Metallica T-shirt.

'It's not mine, it's my brother's. I picked it up in haste while getting ready.'

'I wasn't judging. They're pretty cool,' he said. He must have sounded like a dick. You didn't say cool to young people, you just didn't. 'Thank you for speaking to me.'

'You wanted to know about Mark?'

'Yes. Did you know him well?'

'Not really. We all meet here, we go to war, we don't really talk about our personal lives if you know what I mean. It's not the place, really.'

'For forming friendships?'

'Those things happen outside of here. There are much easier ways now to do that. We have a WhatsApp group for example, Facebook and Twitter. Here, we focus and we use our skills.'

'I understand. Was he particularly close to any of the others?'

'We all get on, we're here for a shared purpose, Detective.' Yvonne had that conviction of 'I know it all' that only the young can carry off. Zain was too burned out to even fake that sort of optimism.

'Yes, but did he spend time with any of them in particular?'

'I can't say, not any one person. No, I can't think of anyone.'

'How was he when battling? Did he show any signs of being over competitive?'

'Yes, then again everybody does. When defeat is biting you in the ass, or when you smell victory. Everyone gets passionate.'

'Yes, I remember that thrill.'

'You battle?'

'Used to, haven't for a while. Well not these sorts of battles anyway. Plenty of others though.'

Yvonne stared at him. She wasn't his therapist, she probably wasn't interested in his dramas.

'Did he ever get into arguments with anybody? Heated ones?'

'We keep our violence for the theatre of war. The aggression stays there.'

'So nothing odd about Mark then?'

'Not really. He was extremely clever, you could tell by the things he knew. He could give you precise measurements without even using the tapes or rulers we have. He could calculate the casualty rates, the strengths and weaknesses of formations. It was a bit off-putting actually, made it difficult for the less experienced members to spar with him.'

'Was he controlling at all? Show any signs of wanting to dominate conversations or activities?'

'No, not at all. He was the opposite, quite shy. We went out for drinks occasionally, and he would always be quiet.'

There were shouts from the next door room, and some applause. A battle well fought had just finished.

'Was there anything unusual about him of late? Did his behaviour change in any way?'

Yvonne considered his question before replying. 'Not his behaviour as such. But he did change, in subtle ways. I don't think the others noticed but I did. He changed the way he dressed, became a bit smarter. Started wearing aftershave, putting product in his hair. Stopped going out with us.'

'Do you know what brought about these changes? Was there someone in the group he was trying to impress?'

'No, not in the group. It all happened when he got a girlfriend.'

Zain tasted breakthrough. A piece of Mark Lynch's life that no one had yet mentioned.

Chapter Fifty-Nine

Zain bought Yvonne a latte. It was the least he could do after her help. He got himself a Red Bull, his teeth protesting as the sugar coated them. It tasted like vomit, he thought. Still, he gulped it down. It didn't provide the kick his tablets gave him, but it was something, and he needed to cut down on the pills.

'When did Mark start seeing her?'

'Maybe three or four months ago. It might have been longer; that was just when she started coming here.'

'She was part of war games?'

'No, but she would meet Mark after we finished, and they would sit in the bar room next door. That was him keeping himself to himself, or rather staying in his couple unit.'

'Can you describe her? Do you have a name?'

'I never met her. She would text him when she got here, and then he would leave pretty quickly and join her in the bar. I saw them when I was walking past to go home.'

'How do you know she wasn't just a friend?'

'He had his arms around her once. I don't know, it seemed very intimate.'

'Can you describe her to me?'

'Hard to say. She had a long coat, black or navy, her hair was always falling into her face, and she wore sunglasses often.'

Zain could recognise a disguise when one was described to him.

'Hair colour?'

'Blonde. I didn't get a look at her eyes, and can't really tell you more.'

'When was the last time she was here?'

'She was here with Mark last week. She joined him after we'd finished gaming.'

'How were they? Was their behaviour odd in any way?'

'No, not at all. They were their normal clingy selves.'

'Did you never ask him about his new acquaintance?'

'Why would I? Our personal lives stay private, generally.'

Zain appreciated adherence to information governance and data protection and rules that kept people safe, but he didn't think there was the need to guard your personal space with so much force.

'Is there anything else you can tell me about her?'

'No. But the bar staff or manager may know more?'

The staff didn't really remember Mark Lynch or his girlfriend. They were just customers, and the club had plenty of regulars. A couple that generally kept to themselves weren't going to raise an alarm.

Zain asked if he could access the CCTV to the club, but it only covered the entrance, not the main rooms. Zain looked through footage of the war-games evenings for the last month, and asked Yvonne if she could identify the woman that might have been Mark's girlfriend.

'That's odd,' she said, as they sat in a backroom off the library, where the club manager had his office. 'Her hair, coat, sunglasses. They are so distinctive. If she came in through the front door, wearing all that, I would spot her on the CCTV.'

Zain checked to see if there was another way in at all, but the club team assured him the only entrance was via the front. Whoever Mark's girlfriend was, she was coming in to the club wearing something totally different, or she had discovered another way in.

Zain asked for the CCTV to be sent over to Unit 3, and asked Michelle to have it analysed. Anyone who fit the visual description and arrived alone would be a potential suspect. The fact was, nobody at UCL had mentioned a girlfriend. Mark's next of kin was also a mystery. UCL's HR files had no one listed, not even his parents or siblings. A Midlands address was only found when they managed to access his undergraduate application to Imperial College, but that property had changed hands twice since Mark had last lived there.

Michelle was carrying out a deeper dive to try and identify contact details for Mark's parents, but nothing had come up so far.

'What about medical records? Can we get access to those?'

'I'm on the case,' Michelle told him, when Zain called her on his way back to his car.

'It's late. Why don't you go home?'

'DCI Riley is still here, briefing PCC Hope. I'll wait until she leaves.'

'OK. I'm heading home, I need some sleep. I think tomorrow's going to be a long day.'

Zain sped towards Waterloo, thinking about the mystery woman. That night, his dreams were plagued by visions of her, but her face was always obscured and out of reach. When he finally managed to grab hold of her, he removed the glasses only to see her face was Kate Riley's.

Chapter Sixty

Kate was at home, stirring hot chocolate, watching her mother and thinking about work. It was a ritual she tried to maintain if she could, sharing drinks before bed with Jane. It was a moment in the day when the two of them could come together, and Kate could be herself.

Her mother was used to calling her Kate now, but in these moments at night, Jane would drop the pretence and use her birth name. It felt good to be Winter again, even despite the baggage and vandalised history that came with it.

Yet these last few nights, Jane had been off key. She wouldn't make eye contact with Kate, barely spoke to her.

Her mother was staring in the direction of the TV but didn't appear to be watching it. What was she thinking?

'Mom, is everything OK?' she asked tentatively.

Jane didn't hear her. Kate asked again.

'Yes, all just fine. You?'

'Yes. Is there anything you want to tell me?'

Jane looked at her, her mouth open. Kate knew this was one of the effects of prosopagnosia. Kate's face would be invisible to her mother for the rest of her life. It hurt to think that, and yet what was the point on dwelling on something that couldn't change?

In those seconds though, it felt as though her mother was shocked. Did she think Kate knew what was going on? That just worried Kate more. What was her mother so concerned about?

'Tell me, what's wrong?'

'Nothing.'

'Mom . . .'

'I'm not a child. Leave me be. If I need your assistance I will ask for it. I can't breathe sometimes in this place.'

There was another sign. Her mother only got into a bad mood when she was under pressure, or seriously worried about something.

Kate picked up the cups of hot chocolate and took them over to the sofa, giving her mother one.

'This is a very small flat, Mom. There is nowhere to hide. Tell me, what's happened?'

She hated buried secrets. Her father had plenty of those, and he had ended up destroying them all because of them.

Jane looked at her, and Kate saw in her eyes the effort again to try and focus and put her features into place. To once again see her daughter completely. It wasn't going to happen, and Jane's shoulders sagged. A regular defeat that happened every day.

Jane took her phone from inside her dressing gown. She unlocked it, and handed it to Kate, who started to scroll through her mother's message history. There were texts, WhatsApp messages. All from the same number.

Kate read them, her blood heating with each one. She was shaking with rage when she had read them all.

'What did you do?' she said, her voice more steady than she felt.

'I'm sorry my darling,' said her mother. 'How can I refuse?'

'You can refuse, because that bastard nearly destroyed us. Because look at you, what he did to you. Mother, what the hell have you done?'

Jane started to cry, and Kate knew then, her world had just been tilted off its orbit. The past was going to burn her again, and she didn't know if she had the strength to survive it this time.

Zain was sprawled on his sofa, naked. He had been practising his Krav Maga and then started using his weights, trying to tire himself out. It was his usual one o'clock wake-up, the insomnia kicking in. Having worked out, he had showered, and then lain down on his towel in the lounge to dry and try to relax. Sleep had overtaken him eventually, and he was awake now, frozen and aching.

He checked the display on his TV. It was six-thirty. He had managed a good few hours at least. He got up to take himself to bed, and checked his phone. There were two missed calls, both within minutes of each other. That's what had woken him up, he realised. Then it rang again.

'Stevie,' he said. At least in his head. His voice was thick with sleep, and his dry mouth meant all he had managed was a mumble. He repeated her name again.

'Wake up pretty boy. We've found Natalie.'

Zain listened, dressed, and rushed to the address.

Chapter Sixty-One

There was a row of houses boarded up just off Victoria Street, terraces all waiting to be remodelled or demolished: either way they'd been sold off for a vast fortune. This was prime Westminster property right in the heart of Belgravia, close to Victoria Station.

No door was apparent as he walked to where Stevie had told him to go, the plasterboard intact as far as he could see. He called her, and watched as one of the boards was lifted, to reveal her standing in the doorway of one of the houses.

She was dressed in a forensic suit.

'I guess I know what that means,' he said. Stevie nodded and threw him a suit to put on before gesturing for him to follow her in.

Dr Kapoor had already processed the scene by the time he got to her. There was a brief moment of awkwardness, but it passed quickly. Zain had apologised to her for his outburst, but embarrassment remained on both their parts.

'What happened?' he asked. She moved out of the way, and he saw for himself. Natalie Davies' throat had been slit.

'She struggled, tried to escape. I found bits of wood and brick under her broken nails.'

'Who found her?'

'Building inspectors. They check regularly in case squatters have moved in, and for gas leaks and the like. This is going to be millionaires' row soon enough.'

'My new place then,' he quipped.

'You wish,' Stevie told him. 'Unless you mean they're hiring cleaners? Or gigolos?'

'My jeans aren't that tight.' He had slipped on the first pair that came to hand, a pair that had shrunk a bit in the wash.

'Poor cow,' said Stevie.

Natalie's face was contorted in horror. It seemed unfair to Zain that she had been through so much, and that her last moments were just as violent and painful. And why her? She had been destroyed by Julian Leakey, so whoever had got rid of him should have been on the same side as Natalie, *if* it was personal.

And then he thought about Anya Fox-Leakey. There was a woman who would gladly have killed both Julian and Natalie. But how did she connect to Mark Lynch, and how did she connect to the dead woman they had found? The one that Julian had killed.

Zain couldn't make sense of it. There had to be a link somewhere, and when that final piece fell into place, the whole thing would become clear. Until it did? There was a killer somewhere in London armed with a weapon Unit 3 couldn't stop or control.

Chapter Sixty-Two

Kate was still fuming from the night before. How could her mother have done what she did? After the sacrifices that Kate had made, the effort she had put in to moving them to a new place, a safer place. Her mother had jeopardised all of that in a moment of weakness. Deliberately making contact with Kate's brothers, and worse than that, agreeing to help the man who had destroyed their lives. To help reduce her father's sentence. The very idea sent fire through Kate. She had to physically swallow the anger back each time she thought about her mother's reckless actions. And for what? Sons that had done nothing for her. Sons who had taken the side of her monster husband, who had carried on living their lives in the corrupt safety he had built for them. They were still there in New England, still in the police force, and no doubt spending their father's cash, waiting for his return. With no thought for their mother. Did Kate not mean anything to her?

'They can share the burden with you, don't you see? To care for me?'

'And what about the evil son of a bitch you are helping to free in return? He will be out immediately if you do this; the case you helped build against him will collapse.'

'You won't understand. You don't have children.'

That hurt. It was partly to care for her mother that she hadn't allowed herself to even contemplate a family of her own. Eric had dropped plenty of hints that he really didn't care too much about kids, and although they hadn't been together long enough, at least she knew they were on the same page on this, that he wouldn't get the urge and leave her for a younger woman who would give him children.

Kate had ignored her mother every time she tried to speak to her. Now, sitting at her desk, she was beginning to feel guilt replace the anger. Jane wouldn't see anyone all day, apart from Charlie, or other strangers. And she would dwell on their fight, and worry about what she had done, while Kate would be distracted and occupied by work.

She needed to call and say it was OK, open up communication channels at least. Even though it wasn't OK. Kate breathed in. She couldn't let her past and her own drama interfere with what they were doing. She had four dead bodies, a toxic poison no one had come across before, and no motive or link between any of them. Except for Julian Leakey, who had had an affair with one of the deceased, was possibly involved in the murder of a second and was probably killed using the poison developed by the third.

Zain was convinced that Anya Fox-Leakey tied it all together, and was now working the angle that Mark Lynch's mysterious girlfriend might have been her. Rob had questioned Vince Hopper who Anya had called, but the man also ran a legal jewellery business, and explained that this was why she had been in communication with him. PCC Hope was still adamant that without any actual evidence they were not permitted to go near her. Her father and the Foreign Secretary, and by association the PM, were all protecting her.

What was Kate left with then?

Her phone rang, interrupting her thoughts.

'DCI Riley, this is DS Joy Goldman. We've identified the dead woman. Her sister came forward.'

Selena Cowan was still in shock when Kate met her. They were in the Kensington and Chelsea police station, where DS Joy Goldman was stationed.

She didn't look older than forty, but people were experts at taking care of themselves, or letting themselves go. She would now only judge someone's age from an official ID.

There were tracks down Selena's face, where mascara had mixed with her tears.

'I should have known something was wrong. She didn't come home, and she wasn't answering her phone. But I thought: no, she's a grown-up.'

'Had she disappeared before in a similar manner?'

'No, not like this, anyway.'

'And the last time you spoke to her?'

'It was on Bonfire Night. She said she was going to a party, that she would call me when she had time.'

'She didn't arrange a specific time to call?'

'No.' Tears were falling over her face again. 'I should have looked for her sooner, raised the alarm. She might still be OK then.'

'Do you know why your sister might have been in the Earl's Court area? Did she have friends there, or any work connections?'

'Not that I know of. She was working at Great Ormond Street.'

'Doing what exactly?'

'She was a pharmacist there.'

Kate nodded. A pharmacist may have understood the chemistry behind what Mark Lynch had created at least. But how that connection then led to Julian Leakey, and Natalie's violent murder, Kate just couldn't understand.

She tapped her netbook, and brought up pictures of Julian.

'Do you recognise this man at all?'

Selena shook her head. 'Is he involved? Did he do this?'

'We found his body the same day we believe your sister was killed. Are you sure you don't recognise him?'

Selena shook her head again.

'Did you and your sister speak openly about her life? Would you know about her relationships for example?'

'Yes, I think so.'

'What if she wasn't particularly comfortable about the nature of one? Would she speak to you about that?'

'I'm not sure I understand?'

'We are just exploring all possibilities here, so please don't take this as an accusation or get upset. Do you think if your sister was having an affair with a married man, she would tell you?'

Silence, as Selena thought about it. 'No, I don't think she would to be honest.'

'Has your sister been worried by anything recently? Any threats, or any concerns that she's shared with you?'

'No, she hasn't mentioned anything. Oh God, I really wish I had acted more quickly. I can't believe I let it get this far. I could have saved her!'

'What about ex-boyfriends? Have there been any that you were particularly worried about?'

'There have been some I loathed, but none that I think could be capable of something like this.'

'And her work, has she ever mentioned to you anything that she was concerned about?'

'We don't discuss her work. I just don't get it, I'm not really into science. So we don't talk about it, unless I get prescribed something by my GP. I tend to ask her to check the ingredients and the side effects. That sort of stuff.'

'She wasn't particularly preoccupied when you last spoke to her, or saw her?'

'I don't think so. I honestly can't remember. I should have called sooner, I can't believe I waited. I could have saved her.' Again the self-blame, the guilt that she would probably always carry with her.

'Please, Mrs Cowan,' said Kate. 'There is nothing you could have done. Your sister was probably murdered on the night of the fifth itself. Raising the alarm wouldn't have helped her, I'm afraid.'

Selena Cowan started to cry loudly, while Kate tried to comfort her.

But at least they had a name for the dead woman they had found in Earls Court.

'Freya Rice,' Kate said later to Michelle. 'I need you to find out everything you can about her, and most of all any link she may have had with Julian Leakey.'

Chapter Sixty-Three

Zain was mining Mark Lynch's laptops and phone. He was using the Police Technical Operations software he was officially allowed to, instead of the sophisticated stuff he had 'borrowed' from his previous employers. He needed to get those upgraded anyway, they were probably out of date by now.

Mark's computer hard drives weren't giving up much. He had an Internet history which wasn't surprising. Lots of links and page downloads from science websites, journals, articles. There was a lack of porn though. He loved his classical music and his heavy metal, so there were lots of YouTube videos in his watched list.

'I can't really see anything that screams out to me,' he told Michelle. She was looking into Mark's phone history, trying to track numbers that might be of interest.

'He must have kept all his workings at the lab,' she said.

'That's odd though. That was a database that anyone could access; if he was carrying out all these dodgy experiments, why wouldn't he keep private records?'

'Sometimes things are safer where everyone can see them. Who would check up on his work at the lab? Who would suspect anything?'

'True.'

'He may have been a creature of habit as well. Do an experiment, write up the notes. I don't think he was thinking very far ahead, or logically.'

Zain continued flicking through the files he had recovered. There was nothing else of interest, even in the deleted files he had managed to restore.

'I can't find anything that might indicate a girlfriend,' he said.

'Neither can I. There are no consistently rung mobile numbers, apart from his colleagues. There are plenty of calls he's received from withheld numbers, though.'

'You think she was calling him? Maybe she's married? They can release those numbers to you, anyway.'

'The phone company is playing hardball. They said there are issues of data protection.'

'Punch them with a warrant then.'

'I already have. Their lawyers are looking over it now.'

'Arseholes.'

'Quite. There is this one, though,' she said, typing it into Google. 'See.'

Zain came over and had a look at the address details Michelle had picked up.

'I'd better go and check it out,' he said.

The offices were located off Westminster Bridge Road, part of Guy's and St Thomas' Hospital. The blue NHS hoardings guided Zain to where he was meant to be going, a small building to the side of the main hospital. It looked more like a Portakabin than a hospital department, but the signs on the outside were clear.

Zain pressed an intercom, and, after showing his badge, he was let in. The receptionist asked him to wait while she placed a call to let her boss know he had arrived. He read posters on the wall, warning of the crisis in the NHS, offering a whole series of numbers for helplines that were available to those in need.

'DS Harris?'

'Dr Stevenage?'

Dr Philip Stevenage was a portly man, who looked as though he was in his fifties, with grey hair like a halo. Zain followed him down corridors that were free of the lino that he had seen in most hospitals. These had brown carpets and lined wallpaper. It looked like a seventies drawing room from an ad he had seen on TV once. How we used to live.

Dr Stevenage's office was past a series of communal rooms, which mainly had chairs laid out in circles. There was a relaxing atmosphere in the building, although it still felt sanitised and clinical. The office itself looked quite informal. There was no desk, just a low table, a sofa and a 'client' chair which was offered to Zain. He had flashbacks to the copious amounts of therapy he had undergone over the years, feeling strangely anxious as he sat down.

'How can I help you?'

'Firstly, did you get the warrant I faxed over?'

'Yes I did. I am aware of the circumstances of the case, and yes I am happy to comply. Mark Lynch's death is a shock, and while I am not sure how I can help, I will do my best.'

'So you're OK discussing his medical notes with me?'

'I only have his therapy notes. I treat patients here using CBT mainly, cognitive behavioural therapy? It's a talking therapy.'

Zain knew what it was, he'd had enough himself. Didn't work as well as his green pills, but he didn't say that.

'Those notes might be more useful than anything an actual medical file might contain anyway,' said Zain.

'What do you want to know?'

'How long was Mark Lynch a patient here?'

'For the last seven years. He came to us when he moved to London, after a referral from his GP and therapist in Birmingham. I believe it coincided with the start of his course at UCL.'

'Were you treating him?'

'No. I run the centre, but his actual therapist is a psychologist called Brid Hearne. She's away at the moment at a conference in Edinburgh, so asked me to meet with you and discuss his notes.'

'You spoke to her? She gave you permission?'

Zain was now worried about anyone involved in the case that might be on leave or 'away'. Both Mark Lynch and Freya Rice had been missing, or 'on leave'.

'Yes.'

'Can you tell me what his issues were?'

'Yes, of course. Mark started therapy quite early on in life; he was fifteen I believe. We don't have those notes, because when he turned nineteen any of his previous notes were destroyed. It's to protect the young.'

'He was a legal minor until nineteen?'

'For our clinical purposes that is the cut-off age. He transitioned from Great Ormond Street's mental health services to us.'

'How long was he at Great Ormond Street?' said Zain. Freya Rice was working there before she died. Was there a link?

'A matter of months, just while he was formally transferred to the adult services we offer.'

'What did those services involve in terms of treating him?'

'Mark lost his mother as a teenager.'

'How?'

'To an aggressive form of brain cancer. She had tumours that couldn't be removed or treated. I believe from diagnosis to death it was a matter of weeks.'

Brain tumours? And Mark had ended up working on something that might be able to remove tumours without surgery, to save other lives. To do for others what he hadn't been able to do for his own mother.

To Zain that felt noble. So why exactly had he ended up creating a neurotoxin that did anything but save lives?

'How did the death affect him?'

'He was a vulnerable teenager and had a particularly negative reaction to it. Depression at first, which became severe and debilitating. A fear of death, and he was worried about his father all the time. He thought if he couldn't see him, it meant his father would die.'

'How do you know this if his notes are no longer available?'

'There is a summary at the start of his adult notes. So no detailed sessions, but we have the general gist of what was discussed.'

'And yet he managed to get into UCL? That's not easy?'

'No. He was given special measures for his exams, extra support. But yes, quite an achievement considering how severe his illness was. However, that was the illness at its most intense. He was treated and cured partially for years before he applied for university.'

'If he's still coming here, how effective was the treatment?'

'Mental illness isn't something that can be switched off, DS Harris.'

'I am aware of that.' Fuck, was he aware of that.

'Part of Mark's issues were dealt with, but other aspects of his condition needed constant support. Especially when he lost his father.'

Shit, thought Zain. Talk about life kicking you fucking hard when you were lying on the ground bleeding already. He had been there. Degrees on the same scale maybe; he couldn't imagine what losing both your parents would feel like.

'It caused a relapse?'

'Yes.'

'How old was he?'

'His father passed away last year.'

'And before that, what was he being treated for?'

'He hadn't healed properly; he was holding on to a lot of resentment and blame from when his mother passed away. I was trying to fix the teenager inside him that was broken. His symptoms were a lot milder, of course.'

'Was he on any medication?'

'When he was younger, yes. But by the time he came to us, he was managing through the therapy. He was prescribed Prozac and sleeping tablets last year after his father died.'

Zain thought about how crap Natalie's life had been leading up to her death, and now here was Mark, suffering for years, and in the end meeting a terrible death. Dr Kapoor had confirmed the use of anaesthesia from Mark's toxicology tests. He hadn't been able to move and he wasn't awake when he had been killed. The open eyes were a reflex, she thought.

It shouldn't matter. Murder wasn't nice and shouldn't happen to anyone. But when people had shit lives, it felt worse. His grandfather always reminded him that a traumatic death was a way to have your sins forgiven. Zain couldn't see into a parallel existence, or a future like that. He had to deal with what was tangible to him. Maybe he needed to let go, follow his grandfather's route a bit more? Get down with the Sufis.

'His therapy was all done through CBT then?'

'Yes. He had weekly sessions, and he attended a support group once a month after his father's death. It was a bereavement network, where we put those who have lost loved ones together, hoping they can help each other heal.'

'The sessions took place here?'

'Yes.'

Zain studied the doctor carefully. Would he comply with Zain's next request? It wasn't normal procedure, and would be flouting a number of data protection edicts. Still he had to ask.

'Is it possible to access the records of everyone who attended the support group? And what their medical histories are?'

Dr Stevenage smiled, but he was displaying his teeth in a fixed grin. Kate had told him once that was a warning in nature.

'What do you think my answer to that request is going to be, DS Harris?'

Chapter Sixty-Four

Michelle was furiously building up profiles on Mark Lynch and Freya Rice. She had as much data on them as she could get hold of electronically, from various HR databases, HMRC, the DVLA and the passport office. Anything where they had filled out an electronic form. She had their personal files from their hard drives, their private phone messages. The only number she was still trying to access was that of Mark Lynch's mysterious withheld-number caller. But sifting through everything she could, there was nothing that helped her work out a link between them, or with the other two victims.

'I can't see anything,' she said to Rob, who was scanning CCTV taken from vantage points where the victims might have been. 'No crossed work histories, no contact. There is no intersection between their lives.'

'Keep looking, they must have had some moment when they got together somewhere.'

'I am, it's just frustrating. I've tried running algorithms, I've tried manually. Nothing is getting me a hit.'

'Here!' said Rob. He tapped his screen. 'I got them.'

Michelle came over and looked at the image on his screen. She saw two blurred shapes, captured at night, under the glow of street lamps and shop signs. It was raining, so the image was smudged slightly.

'That's Mark Lynch, and here we go. The mystery woman he's been dating.' Rob zoomed in, but she was indistinguishable to the description they already had from the war games organiser Yvonne. The shades, the fringe in her face, and the dark coat.

'Well, at least we know she's real, and not some made up person.'

'Shame she doesn't take the shades off somewhere,' said Michelle.

'I shall follow her home, see where she boards public transport, and see where she might have ended up.'

'Probably in zone six somewhere, where they don't have any CCTV. So yeah, good luck with that.'

'Oh ye of little faith.'

Michelle went back to her own search.

'How is Jessica by the way?' Michelle said carefully. 'I heard you and her . . .'

Michelle stopped, she heard the noises coming from Rob's machine. She got up quickly and made to shut down the video he was watching.

'Don't look at that, Rob,' she said quietly.

Rob was staring, the anger clearly written all over his face.

'I hope that little fucker Mark Lynch suffered worse than this. *Bastard.*'

Rob got up abruptly and left.

Michelle thought about going after him, but decided to let him cool off first. Frustrated with her own search, she decided to put the names randomly into different search engines she could access across government databases. She got garbled hits, but decided to plough through the returned search pages anyway.

On page forty-seven of one search engine she got a hit. She'd found the link between Julian Leakey and Freya Rice.

Chapter Sixty-Five

They were in the conference room, all of them dragged back to base by Kate. Even Rob who wanted to be taken off the case for ethical reasons.

'I really don't give a shit what happened to some fucking animal torturer.'

'It's about more than that now, Rob. You have a duty to serve, and be part of this until we find out who is behind the deaths. And until they are stopped. Surely you have to believe in the sanctity of life? All life, even human?'

'Not so sure about that.'

He was there though, sullen but present. It felt familiar to Kate, in a good way. There was a breakthrough and her team had got closer to understanding what had happened to Julian Leakey and the others.

Kate was seated next to Rob, Stevie and Zain opposite. She looked into their faces, the circles around their eyes, their drained complexions. They were dishevelled, tired, pushed to their limits, yet they were here. Her team, fighting for their shared beliefs. She felt a moment of contentment looking at them. And then remembered why they were there.

'Michelle, the floor is yours.'

Michelle stood up, tablet in her hands, while the wall-mounted screen reflected what she was looking at. 'So I was trying everything I could, all these different complicated searches involving all the data that we managed to collect. It was a pain, but I ran them through everything I could think of. Only, nothing came up, nothing was connecting. It all felt so disparate. And that's because it was.'

'What do you mean?' asked Kate.

'The data I was feeding into my programs, it was separate. I was putting through isolated work histories, personal details, soft intelligence. There was no overlap between our four victims.'

'Apart from Julian and Natalie, I assume?'

'Yes. We know their link. I mean with the others. There is no overlap on any of the official paperwork I've seen. That's because the files I've been looking at deal with logic, and compare like with like, or at least contrast similar pieces of information.'

'Squares and squares,' said Zain.

'Precisely. Only, the link between Julian and Freya isn't that straightforward.'

'What did Freya do exactly?' asked Zain.

'She was a pharmacist. Worked for Boots for a while, and then she joined the NHS, became an embedded pharmacist at a number of trusts. She worked for Barts, Chelsea and Westminster, North Middlesex. And finally, she ended up at Great Ormond Street Hospital.'

'So she's never worked for the government, or the Civil Service?'

'No.'

'Let me guess, she was on one of the adultery websites? Did I miss her in my search? Shit. Nicely played, Cable.'

'No, that wasn't it.'

'What did you do?'

'I went back to basics. I put their names into every search engine I could, and checked where there was a link. I used the common ones first, and then started to look on any of the official government ones.'

'That must have taken forever.'

'It wasn't easy, but sometimes you just have to put in the legwork.'

'Where did you find the link?' asked Kate.

Michelle brought up the images on screen. It was a repository of official documents going back many years, to when the Primary Care Trusts and Foundation Trusts still existed. Before the re-organisation of the system by the current government.

'This is a list of PDFs, official releases and archived documents. And here, can you see? There is a panel where both Julian Leakey and Freya Rice were signatories.'

Kate saw their names in bold onscreen, surrounded by other names.

'What are the details of the panel?'

'This is a mistake. The names should not be there. The robots picked them up and highlighted them, but the names are contained in archived and secret documents.'

'Documents to do with what?'

'These are documents where the NHS have commissioned trials on drugs, ones that are yet to come onto the market.'

The team were sitting to attention, taking in what Michelle was saying. She explained how when a patient was sick, so sick that their treatment was rare and only available through experimental drugs, it was up to the drug companies themselves to make the decision whether or not they would fund the treatment.

'The reason why I couldn't find a link is because when Julian and Freya worked together, they didn't work for the same organisation. Freya was a pharmacist in the private sector, but at the same time she freelanced for other companies. Julian was doing one of his private-sector consultant roles at the time. This is going back five years now.'

'What was the company?'

'It was a firm called AREL, a pharmaceutical company that no longer exists. They were bought out by one of the major brands. But at the time they were producing cutting-edge medicine, drugs to treat rare conditions. Things that might affect only a handful of people.'

'I'm guessing that means expensive drugs, that they could charge a fortune for?' said Rob. 'After testing them on innocent fucking animals, no doubt.'

'I can think of some humans that they could be tested on,' said Stevie.

'Don't look at me!' cried Zain.

'Once they had approval, as in they had tested their drugs and were allowed to sell them, they usually did to the NHS. That is the biggest prescribing body in the country, so no surprise there. What is more complex is what happened when they were still developing their drugs. When they made the decision to treat or not.'

'What was the criteria?' asked Kate. 'How did they decide which patients to treat?'

'It was done on clinical need apparently. Would the drug be likely to be successful or not?'

'So you mean money?' spat Rob. 'If they thought the drug would work they would be willing to take the financial hit, and if they thought it wouldn't, then fuck it?'

'In a way. These firms often do trials in clinical settings for free. And I mean, supply drugs for months, costing thousands, without expecting compensation.'

'That comes when they sell their drugs in bulk to the health service,' said Rob.

'They need money for research,' Michelle said, but it was a mumble.

'Yeah, I know what they do their research on.'

'Tell me then about AREL. How are Julian and Freya involved?' Kate cut in.

'Well, for a period of about six months, Julian was chair of the committee that signed off on who would receive free treatment for test drugs.'

'And Freya?'

'She was one of the contracted pharmacists testing the drugs, and providing clinical approval or denial. So between them they basically decided who would get treatment and who wouldn't.'

'What you're saying is they in essence controlled who might live, and who might die?' Kate thought it sounded over-dramatic in her head, but when Michelle didn't respond she knew that's exactly what had happened.

'How many cases are we looking at? Were Julian and Freya responsible for making every decision?'

'I don't know,' said Michelle. 'The problem is accessing the records. They no longer exist, as AREL is gone.'

'I'll speak to PCC Hope. We can get the warrants we need . . .'

'It's more that they might not physically exist anywhere.'

'You said you found these in an archived database?' said Zain.

'Yes, but it was an error. I shouldn't even have found these.'

'Yes, but you did. It means there is a directory somewhere that holds these cases. Leave it with me.'

Kate knew what that meant; he was going to call in a favour. She didn't care though: what she needed to know was exactly who out there had a grudge against Julian and Freya. Enough to not only kill Julian mercilessly, but also Mark Lynch and Natalie Davies. How Mark and Natalie were linked, Kate was yet to discover. And how had Freya really died? She didn't know if she thought Julian capable of murder anymore.

Chapter Sixty-Six

The day was cold, but there was no rain, just a light fog. Zain was waiting by the entrance to Westminster Cathedral, watching throngs of tourists go in and out of the building. It was a different time of day to the last time this meeting had taken place.

DCI Raymond Cross loped across the courtyard leading to the cathedral in easy strides, covering the distance quickly. He had his panama hat on and his coat was hanging open. Zain walked towards him when he spotted him, and they shook hands, before moving past the cathedral into the heart of Belgravia.

'How have you been, Zain?'

'Great.'

'That good?'

'I'm fine. Sir.'

'You don't look it.'

'It's been a tough few days. You know what's it like when you're on the front line. You get burned, quite literally in my case, tired, battered and function on adrenaline. I'm under pressure.'

'I get it. You're wondering why I didn't just tell you this by email?'

'The thought had crossed my mind, sir.'

Zain had sent the directory link to DCI Cross. He had the resources that would crack it a lot more quickly than Zain or Michelle could. But he'd insisted on meeting in person to deliver the results.

'I wanted to see you,' said DCI Cross. 'Is that so bad? After all we've been through together?'

'You make us sound like lovers, sir.'

'The bonds we share are stronger, don't you think? We really did risk life and death for each other.'

'Possibly. More for the country though.'

'I don't believe that, neither do you.'

He was right. When Zain had been a teenager on the brink of carrying out a suicide mission, DCI Cross had saved him. He had asked him to betray the cell he was part of, and instead work for the British government. What had followed was years of being bankrolled by the state. His Arabic studies at SOAS, his training in cyber-security, joining up with GCHQ and then ending up where Raymond Cross had always wanted him. In counter-terrorism, SO15, he put everything he had learned to its most effective use.

Until it all went horribly wrong. Zain had got back on track with DCI Cross there to support him. Those bonds were indelible, bonds that even family members couldn't share.

Zain still hadn't recovered fully. His time with DCI Kate Riley was meant to be a form of rehab, or some sort of golden goodbye: he wasn't sure which. It hadn't worked out like either. He was convinced he would get hurt no matter who he worked for.

'Loyalty isn't something you lose, not easily. Of course, I feel that sense of loyalty to yourself, sir.'

'I'm glad to hear it.'

They slowed their walk as they entered a quiet street behind the cathedral. They were alone, and unobserved, as far as they could see.

'I worked with Justin Hope at the beginning of this whole case,' DCI Cross said carefully. 'He is quite something.'

'He's paid his dues. Maybe he's allowed to be?'

'Yes. Possibly. It made me more determined anyway.'

'For what?'

'I want you to come back. I want you to leave Unit 3, and come back to SO15. I think you've more than proved yourself. It's time Zain. I think you're ready.'

Zain felt a mix of elation – this was what he had secretly hankered after for a long time – and resentment. He wasn't a dog, DCI Cross couldn't just whistle and expect him to come running.

'That's quite an offer,' he finally said.

'I thought you'd bite my hand off.'

Was DCI Cross taking the piss? Was that some sort of thinly veiled canine analogy? Fuck that. And then that unbidden voice. That DCI Kate Riley needed him, that the loyalty he felt nowadays was not to DCI Cross, but to her. Not seeing her on a daily basis, he didn't know if he could cope with that. He let the thoughts wash over him and go, not letting them drown him by struggling against them. It was a classic CBT response.

'It's very generous of you, sir . . .'

'Think about it Zain. Carefully. I may not ask again.'

'I will . . . Did you break into the directory?'

'Of course. We found about thirty case files that Leakey and Rice were involved in. Details have been emailed to you just now. We also managed to track down contact details for the others involved in the decisions. Good luck.'

'Thank you, sir. Another thing. Anya Fox-Leakey. I believe she may be hoarding money in an account in Panama.'

Zain wasn't entirely convinced now that she was involved in her husband's death, but he liked the idea of presenting her head on a platter in a way to Kate.

'I see. I can ask the right people to look into this. But you know how closely MI6 and the Foreign Office work together. Leave it with me. And please Zain, think about my offer. And hopefully see you soon?'

'Yes, sir. Thank you.'

Zain didn't know what to think. When faced with such a dilemma, he did what he always did. Focused on what was in front of him, which was finding Julian Leakey's killer.

Chapter Sixty-Seven

The case files were sad to read. People in dire need, turning to AREL for their last bid at life and health. Cases where parents were desperate to save their children, where men and women were desperate to save themselves for their children.

Each case was backed up by clinical need, with predictability of success and what the results would mean. It was horrific to read in parts. If this man, aged thirty-seven, was successfully treated with a new drug that dealt with a neuron dysfunction that would slowly paralyse his body, then the benefits would be realised in quite a significant population. If this two-month-old baby was given the same, given the extreme rarity of a two-month-year-old needing it, it just wouldn't have the same impact.

'Julian and his team made these decisions, usually in favour of the company. They needed to realise the most impact. If that baby was presented when there were no other cases, they approved the drug being given. Put the two-month up against the thirty-seven-year-old, and no chance.'

Zain was trying not to sound angry, as he presented what the files had shown him to Kate and the others. They were back in the conference room again, trying to formulate a way forward.

'How many of these thirty cases did they reject?' asked Kate.

'Thirteen.'

'That's quite a lot of people.'

'Yep. They basically signed the death warrants for the thirteen patients they rejected.'

'That's unfair isn't it? I mean there was no alternative, the patients were going to die anyway? The drug was still in its testing phase?' Michelle was trying to be reasonable.

'They had a choice, *they* were the alternative. They decided not to go ahead with it though.'

'So we have thirteen cases where possibly there is someone with a grudge against two of the deceased?' said Kate.

'Yes.'

'Then that's where we start.'

'It still doesn't connect to Mark and Natalie though,' he told her. It was true.

Kate ran her fingers through her hair, and then across her jaw.

'I've been thinking about both those cases. And I think the link may be collateral.'

'What do you mean?' said Stevie. 'That sounds pretty harsh.'

'I'm thinking that whoever is behind this, they may have been targeting Julian and Freya. Julian was killed using the toxin that Mark produced. Mark was killed to protect the murderer's identity. Freya was probably a set-up, Julian was framed for it I think. I can't believe he would kill her so coldly. And Natalie . . . well think about it. While she was missing, we thought she might be behind it all. So possibly she was deflection?'

'Why kill her though?'

'I know, it doesn't make complete sense. But remember, we aren't dealing with someone who is thinking logically. Things are messy and complicated, that's what happens, even with ample planning.'

'Collateral damage,' whispered Zain.

'I don't know, these are just theories. Until we know for sure what we are dealing with, *who* we are dealing with, it's all just my interpretation.'

'It's one that makes sense,' said Stevie.

'So I guess, we start exploring the cases Julian Leakey and Freya Rice rejected.'

Zain stared hard at Kate, as his mind started working, making maps in his head of links that might exist.

'I have an idea. It's crazy, and probably jumping way ahead of anything we've found out so far, but I think I might know how Mark really links in to all of this. And I think I know where contact was made with him.'

Chapter Sixty-Eight

Dr Stevenage was again adamant on the phone that he would not release the medical notes for those that were involved in the support group that Mark Lynch had attended at Guy's and St Thomas' Hospital. They were alive and their confidentiality had to be protected.

Zain drove down again to confront the man face to face. Only this time he took reinforcements with him.

Dr Rani Kapoor was already waiting for him outside the mental-health unit. She was still a little nervous when greeting him. He hated that he had this effect on her, hated the side of himself she reflected back.

'Shall we go in then?'

'I'm hoping you'll be the key. Or the hammer,' he told her.

But Dr Stevenage remained unmoved. He let them into his office but refused to give them access to his records. He handed over Mark Lynch's file to Dr Kapoor, and she pored over the notes. She wasn't a psychiatrist, but he obviously accepted her as one of his own. Zain just needed to manipulate him a bit more.

'I don't think you understand, Doctor. It's so important that we know everyone Mark may have formed an attachment to. And the group could help us. We're trying to track down one person in particular, someone Mark was close to. We've explored other aspects of his life, his few friends, work colleagues. This group is the last avenue for us. *Please.*'

It was true. They had run traces on everyone they had managed to associate with Mark, Julian and Freya through the files they had been given by DCI Cross. Even Natalie's associates had been run through it. There was no hit.

Zain knew the bereavement group might be important. Whoever was behind the murders had a warped pathology, and bereavement was one of the most powerful mind-altering experiences an individual could go through. And even if the group didn't yield any results, at least he could tick it off his list.

'I can assure you of my professional and ethical responsibility to your patients, Dr Stevenage,' said Dr Kapoor. 'I don't need to know case details, just contact details of members of the group.'

'They will all be unfairly targeted. I do not want them connected to a police investigation. Unless you can give me specific cause for concern, I just can't betray their trust in such a manner.'

'And what if one of them is behind these murders? And goes on to kill again?' asked Zain.

'Which one? You tell me which of these patients is of interest, and I will help. Not a blanket handover though.'

'We're looking for a female in particular.' Zain showed the doctor pictures of Mark's girlfriend. There was no recognition, not surprising since she was so obviously disguised.

'I have an idea,' said Dr Kapoor. 'We are trying to match your list to ours. What if we release our list to you? The names that are of interest to us? Could you verify those against your group members?'

Zain didn't feel comfortable doing that. He had similar confidentiality issues to the doctor.

'I can supervise the process,' said Dr Kapoor. 'That way we have a level of protection for all involved. What do you say, DS Harris?'

Zain was reluctant, but he had to trust Dr Kapoor, and it seemed this might be the only way.

'I'll get Michelle to email them to you, Dr Kapoor. You share them one at a time, and the details are not transmitted to Dr Stevenage or to anybody else. Is that OK?'

'Of course.'

'Thank you, Dr Kapoor.'

She shrugged it off, as Zain called Michelle and had the details emailed over. Michelle had created a safe landing page on the PCC infrastructure. It would mean that Dr Kapoor could access records in a rich text format, but not download or copy them. Names, dates of birth, last known addresses, contact numbers.

Michelle sent the link to the secured page to Dr Kapoor with a password. She opened it, and together she and Dr Stevenage began comparing the bereavement group to the details they had of failed cases that AREL had refused to fund.

Zain hoped somewhere on the two lists there would be a match.

Chapter Sixty-Nine

Kate was trying to stay calm. She was in PCC Hope's office, this side of his steepled fingers. Her anger at his treatment of her in front of Anya Fox-Leakey and her lawyer was still bubbling away inside her. But Kate was an expert at staying calm. It was probably why her tantrum had upset her so much. She was glad that Hope hadn't seen her in that state.

'I was right then, looks like Anya Fox-Leakey isn't involved. We don't have an irate peer after us, at least.'

'She's not in the clear yet, sir. She still has the right motive, and access to the neurotoxins.'

'She's hardly capable of multiple homicide.'

'There is a lot more to investigate with her, I think. And there is no evidence yet that she *isn't* behind these deaths.'

'I'm sure you know what you're doing. I wouldn't have hired you otherwise.'

She still couldn't work PCC Hope out. She didn't kowtow to him, she knew things about him that would embarrass him if she ever repeated them, and she was generally a strong-willed woman who ran her team the way she wanted to. He could only be making false platitudes, but for what reason she wasn't sure. He enjoyed trying to keep her on her toes.

What Kate needed to do after this case was figure out exactly what she wanted to do next, and where she could go that would allow her to be safe once more . Because her mother's actions had put her at risk in a way that she hoped she never would be again.

The watcher was seething. He had done his part. He had acted on behalf of Hilary Morgan, Kate's father, and his associates. He had done their bidding.

When Morgan had been put behind bars, the evidence had landed his right-hand men in prison with him. Or on the run. Except the watcher. He had been away for a few months.

Trailer trash. That's what Jane Morgan had called him once. She was sharp. Before he had battered her, and thrown her down the stairs. Because she had helped expunge the only light he ever had.

The sort of upbringing he'd had, he hadn't done anything in his life that was good. He knew that. Except for one thing. His daughter. He hadn't stayed with her mother more than a few months, but he had made this miracle with her. Ashton. His lifeblood.

Even now, hearing her name in his head . . . his heart ached. She had been everything to him, he had even contemplated giving up his work for Morgan for her. Until one day, when she got sick. So sick that she was given up on. Just like the children of those with nothing are.

And then Morgan had stepped in, had provided the funds to save Ashton. And so the watcher had left to see her treatment through.

Until Kate Riley and her mother had brought everything crashing down. And with Morgan gone, so was his money. And without the money, Ashton was once again a child with nothing.

The watcher let the tears flow.

Hilary Morgan may have achieved his ends through the watcher's threats to his ex-wife and her pathetic need to see her sons again. But it would not end there. Both mother and daughter would suffer. They had hidden well, and it had taken the watcher years to find them. But now, it was just a matter of waiting. Kate Riley's sins would come back to burn her. And he would be the one carrying the torch.

Chapter Seventy

Zain watched as the two doctors compared lists. Dr Stevenage was reading from his iPad, and Dr Kapoor from her phone.

'My eyes are beginning to feel the strain,' said Dr Kapoor, laughing as she did so.

'Would you like to take a break?' said Dr Stevenage.

Zain held his breath. The psychiatrist had played into his hands a bit too easily.

'I'm all right for the moment. We must crack on; this is important to complete.'

There was more tapping of the screen, followed by name checks.

'Actually, sorry Dr Stevenage, my eyes must be feeling the strain of the last few days. I will need to take a break from this.'

'We don't have time,' Zain told them. 'We need this done urgently.' He checked his phone, looked at them both. 'Lives are at risk. Don't you both have Hippocratic oaths or something?'

'Please don't patronise me,' said Dr Kapoor. 'I'm not one of your criminals.'

She sighed, rubbed her eyes, then rolled them and shrugged her shoulders at Dr Stevenage. All that Bollywood movie watching hadn't been wasted on her.

'What do you suggest we do?' she said finally.

'Finish?' said Zain. 'Now.'

'I really don't appreciate your tone, DS Harris. Do you want our help or not?'

Zain didn't reply. Dr Kapoor looked around the office and then at Dr Stevenage.

'Dr Stevenage, I saw a break-out room earlier. It had views across London? The light in there might be just what I need? Is that possible?'

'Yes of course, we can take some refreshments in there too,' he said, giving Zain a withering look.

'Thank you. DS Harris. I will contact you once we are finished. I'm sure you have much-more-important things to do than watch us.'

Dr Stevenage locked his office door, taking Dr Kapoor with him, while Zain headed out of the hospital.

Zain walked around the building to the rear, which was up against another hospital building. There was hardly room to walk through the narrow gap between walls, and no CCTV. He counted the windows, and came to the one he had fixed earlier. He pushed, and it opened up easily. While in Dr Stevenage's office before, he had surreptitiously opened one of the windows. The building wouldn't be alarmed until night, so he was sure it would remain unnoticed. He slid in, quickly making his way to Dr Stevenage's computer.

While Dr Kapoor had distracted him, her professional status like nectar to the doctor, Zain had been observing his keystrokes. The doctor wasn't the quickest typist, and while Dr Kapoor made a big show about looking away when he typed in his password on his iPad, Zain had zeroed in on exactly which keys he had pressed.

He had a vague idea, and if that failed he could use other ways to crack the computer. Although they would be slower. Dr Kapoor had just told him that she would text him as soon as they were done, giving him plenty of escape time.

Zain flexed his fingers, cracked his knuckles, stretched his neck and sat down, like a concert pianist about to begin playing. He thought of what he did as an art in itself, albeit a bit different and definitely illegal in the wrong hands.

Zain typed in the doctor's password from the iPad into the desktop, but was denied access. He looked over the keys, and changed the middle keystroke, which got him the right password and access to the doctor's computer and files. He did a quick search trying to identify where the confidential information would be, using bereavement as his key word. It was too big, returning too may files, so he looked at the installed programs instead. One was a patient database, but when he opened it, he saw each patient had their own separate record: there were no group lists.

He checked his phone, hoping Dr Kapoor and her pretend eye-strain was still keeping him. He needed to work faster though, and come up with a list. A new email arrived, the envelope symbol diverting his eyes to the corner of the screen. A list. If patients were all individually stored, he doubted the busy doctor would spend time compiling a list of those that attended sessions of the bereavement group. No, he would get someone else to do it. Zain opened the doctor's Outlook. It asked for a password before it updated with any new emails, but the one Zain had seen earlier didn't work on it. It didn't matter though. Dr Stevenage's old emails were available to view, and there was one from his assistant already opened with the list of patients. Zain pulled their IDs, and opened the patient database. There was a search facility by patient ID, which allowed multiple criteria to be used in the search term. Zain pasted in the list of patient IDs, and hit search.

He watched as the timer started to churn, looking at his phone for the warning text from Dr Kapoor. He felt his heart race; he needed to download the list and get out of the room before they came back.

'Come on,' he said, tapping the side of the machine. It was running far too slowly for him, and then froze. Zain breathed deeply; he would have to shut the whole thing down if he ran out of time. The program started up again, and the list was onscreen. Files of the bereavement group patients, not just the names Dr Stevenage's assistant had put together, but complete records. Zain hit download to Excel, waited again, before putting in his USB stick. He started to transfer files when his phone buzzed. They were heading his way.

Zain texted Dr Kapoor, 'NO'. He heard their voices in the corridor. *Shit*, this was not good, he felt panic, the files were still transferring. The voices grew louder, and then Dr Kapoor's voice, her laughter. Was it to tell him she couldn't stall anymore? They were outside the door, the files still not on his USB.

'Oh, Dr Stevenage, I am so sorry. I left my phone back in the break-out room.'

The voices began to retreat. Zain had about two minutes. The files finished, and as he heard the voices get louder as the doctors were coming back again, he forced shutdown of the desktop computer and hurled himself out of the window, crashing to the ground outside.

Rob was only half watching the TV, his mind still replaying the video he had seen. The experiments Mark Lynch had carried out. The experiments that would still go on.

He turned his attention back to the screen, the volume on low. He was in the break-out room at the PCC HQ, guzzling diet Pepsi, and trying to clear his head. He needed to separate his feelings for Mark Lynch and remember the poor bastard had been killed brutally. And so had three other people.

It was one stray word that caught his attention.

'Pharmacist.'

He turned the volume up and listened. It was too random, maybe a coincidence. But he didn't believe in coincidences. He rushed back to his desk. Michelle was at her computer.

'Leanne Birch,' he said. 'The last anyone heard from her was 4 November. She's a pharmacist. I'm contacting Sussex now, will get you more information, but see if you can start a search. Her details must be in SHERLOCK or some other database.'

It might not be relevant, but there was no harm in checking.

Chapter Seventy-One

They were gathered in the conference room, a frenetic energy running around them. Kate could feel it, every member of her team on edge, excited. Things were starting to fall into place at last. It was the usual mix. Chance, perseverance and just hunting down every last clue and piece of evidence until it proved worthless. Or became invaluable.

She had already bawled Zain out for what he had done back at Dr Stevenage's clinic; embroiling Dr Kapoor in his game had just made it worse.

'You really think Dr Kapoor would involve herself in something like this?' he said. 'She's far too up herself to do anything questionable. I just asked her to text me when she was done, that's all. I wanted to touch base with her.'

'Why did she leave Dr Stevenage's office?'

'That was not my doing. She had eyestrain.'

Kate didn't know if she believed him, and she wasn't about to accuse Dr Kapoor of being complicit in a crime. At the very least she would insult her and make things awkward between them. At worst she would end up reporting Zain and what would that do?

Why did he insist on pushing back all the time? Yes he got her results, but at what cost? Once you started picking apart the moral framework they worked in, you didn't stop.

'I have a list anyway, names, numbers, addresses. Everyone in the bereavement support group. Let's see what we can do with it.'

'Did Dr Kapoor find a match?'

'Of course not. But she was reading names off a list. We need algorithms and deeper checks than that. We are linking historical records to this current list. What if someone changed their name and number for the group? We need to trace that number, it will give us a link to their previous identity, which will give us an in to the trials that AREL ran.'

'There must have been another way. A legal way, one that means we can use the evidence you found?'

'My way was the only one I could do in the time we have to stop this person, before someone else dies. And it's only patient details, an expanded list.'

Rob had tracked down Leanne Birch in a much more organic way. He had seen her sister's press conference on BBC News, and immediately linked in to Sussex Police to get more background. Leanne Birch was a pharmacist, but more than that she was a consultant pharmacist for hire. She provided the neutral expert advice often sought out to give approval and sign off on drugs or policy. And her disappearance at the time everything else was happening was too much of a coincidence not to be connected.

And yet, the first of them to die hadn't been Julian or Freya. Dr Kapoor had confirmed that Mark Lynch had died at least twelve hours before Freya had been killed. Would they find Leanne's body, and what state would it be in by the time they did? Kate dreaded to think.

Michelle had control of the main screen, bringing up various files for them to look at.

'You were so right to check this, Rob,' she said. 'I did a trace on Leanne through the files from AREL, and she was there. She was part of the cases that rejected the trial requests with Julian Leakey and Freya Rice.'

'How many cases did they overlap on?' asked Kate.

'Five of the rejected ones.'

'That narrows it down. We start with those. I think we've done enough virtual checking. I want to trace the families involved in these rejected cases. And I want to know anyone who might be holding enough hatred to carry out something like this.'

'I also have details of the bereavement group. I'll feed the details into your database, Michelle,' said Zain. 'We need to start building a complex file that traces through multiple identities. If someone has orchestrated this whole thing, you can bet they've gone to the effort of changing their personal details.'

'We'd better check who's faking it as well,' said Stevie. 'The bereavement group members, I mean. Finding out who doesn't exist will help us work out who's lying.'

'Good point,' said Zain.

'Where are the five families that AREL rejected?' Kate said. 'Any of them in London?'

Michelle clicked and brought up the list onscreen.

'At the time of treatment none of them were. Since the rejection, two families have moved here. I have to warn you, all five cases didn't end well. The rejected patients all died.'

There was silence in the room. That was the reality of this whole thing, the links they had found. Death was the beginning and the end for all those involved in this whole mess.

Kate just hoped there wouldn't be more death before the day was done.

'I'll get local forces to contact the families outside of London. Stevie, can you contact the two in London?' Kate asked Michelle to send the details of both families to her. 'Who else was involved? In the five cases we know Leanne worked on with Julian and Freya? Was anyone else making the decisions?'

Michelle scanned through file notes, checking minutes and sign-offs. 'Three of the cases were signed off by a Dr David Milne, and two by a Dr Sue Knight.'

'Get me contact details for them as quickly as you can please, Michelle. I need to speak to both doctors. Can you also coordinate the national contacts for the rejected families?'

Kate just hoped the doctors were still alive.

Chapter Seventy-Two

Stevie read through the notes again, before getting out of her car. She was in Stepney Green, East London, close to her own place. The flat she was looking at was in the middle floor of a converted terrace, with trees lining the street, surrounding a small park. You could see Canary Wharf in the background, as though you might be able to touch it.

Stevie had spoken to Esther Lake earlier, and told her she would be coming to visit. When Stevie explained why, Lake had been hesitant. She said AREL was history, a past she didn't want to rake up, but Stevie had told her that they just needed details on the company and those involved in the funding requests that they had received. She didn't mention Julian or Freya or Leanne, and insinuated that it was some type of fraud investigation.

Esther was in her late twenties, attractive, in shape. Yet she was dressed as though she couldn't be bothered, in a loose grey sweater that covered her knees, and black joggers. She showed Stevie into an impeccable lounge, with nothing out of place. There was an almost OCD level of cleanliness. Stevie had a similar level of fastidiousness in her own home. Esther's eyes were moving across surfaces and spaces; she was skittish, looking for something. Stevie declined the tea that was offered.

'I know this is going to be painful,' she began. 'And I'm sorry, I really am. I am going to ask you to go over what happened with

AREL. And please, take your time, and tell me as much as you are comfortable with.'

Esther looked as though she hadn't heard, her eyes looking behind Stevie, then around the room, and then finally focusing on Stevie.

'I'm not comfortable with any of this.' Esther, sat back on the sofa, pulling her legs under her and holding one of the cushions close. She rested her chin on it, looking heartbreakingly vulnerable for a moment. Then the wandering eyes were back. 'What do you want to know?'

'Can you tell me about your son? What made you approach AREL in the first place?'

Esther froze, her eyes staring straight ahead. Her lips didn't move. Stevie decided to ask about the husband instead, ease Esther into talking about her son.

'How did you meet your husband? Nathan?'

'We met at university. I went to Newcastle to study biochemistry.'

Stevie let that sink in, and felt her instincts rise. That would give Esther enough scientific background to understand the TTX stuff. Stevie barely understood it, just accepted what DCI Riley and Dr Kapoor had been saying.

'Was he on your course?'

'No he was a builder. I met him at a student bar; one of his friends was on our course. We were very different: he was working-class, I was a privileged Home Counties girl.'

'Opposites attract.'

'Yes, I know. Maybe it was his accent, maybe it was him. He was one of the most moral people I ever met. I felt so safe around him. As though nothing could harm me when I was in his arms. Isn't that funny? When you think about what happened?'

Stevie nodded. Esther stared into the space between them, her memories anchoring her to the past, and stopping her from feeling anxious about the situation they were in.

'We married straight after graduation, and then started planning a family.'

'That was a bit sudden.'

'Nathan was so keen. He wanted more than anything to be married and to have a family. He had his own reasons, I guess. And he was earning a good wage by then, more than I would get as a graduate starting out. And so we started trying.'

'How long before you fell pregnant?'

'Eighteen months. And we were really trying. But it happened, and since then I've met so many women who take years to conceive. Some who I think would make amazing mothers, but never do. Life just really knows how to punch you in the gut sometimes, doesn't it?'

'Yes, I suppose it does.' Life had certainly given Stevie a good old kicking, but she had learned how to punch back. 'And the pregnancy? Were there any problems?'

'No. I know friends who have had horrendous first pregnancies, who are literally laid up in bed, chronically ill. Mine was fine. I had some morning sickness, but that didn't last long. Nothing else. Everything was fine, the baby was growing ...' Esther stopped, clutching the cushion tighter to her torso. Her breathing became irregular. 'He was fine. His heart was strong, and I watched him at each scan, watched him become who he was. I always knew I wanted to call him Robert, after my father. It was incredible, and Nathan was just as excited. He was an only child, and wanted a huge family.'

'Do you have siblings?'

'Yes. I'm one of three.'

'So there were no signs at all that anything was wrong?'

'No, nothing. He was perfect. And when he was born, again it was so easy. My waters broke at home, and he was almost breaching by the time we got to the hospital. And then he was there, and it was so ...' Esther's eyes hardened, her jaw set. Anger was in her voice. 'It was meant to be my happy ending. Life was going to be perfect, because I had him.'

'When did you realise something was wrong?' Stevie was trying to read Esther. The woman had done every emotional cartwheel possible. Almost as though she was acting each one.

'It wasn't like that. It wasn't a sudden realisation.' There was the same hardness to Esther's voice. 'He was perfect, growing up, healthy. None of the staff were concerned about anything. I've met people that have kids with hearing or sight issues. And they don't know, but they see things, small signs. And they ignore them, hoping they don't mean anything. And then there comes a point when they can no longer do that, and they take the child in for tests.'

'Is that what happened with Robert?'

'No. I was a good mother. I used to worry about every little illness, made sure my baby got properly checked out. He got jaundice once and his temperature was so high, I was a wreck, screaming at the doctors and nurses. I grabbed one of the doctors at one point, he was about to stick a needle into Robert. They called security, and Nathan had to control me. I spent so much time worrying about all the small things. And something so much worse was just waiting to happen.'

Stevie, didn't know how to ask what that was. But she had to.

Chapter Seventy-Three

Both doctors were proving difficult to track down. Sue Knight had gone to Africa to work with Médecins Sans Frontières after her time with AREL. She had been working in the Congo, in the forgotten war, helping rescue child soldiers and their victims. After that she had transferred to Australia. Finding her current location was proving to be difficult.

'She must register with the General Medical Council, or she loses her right to practise here. I've had a look at their website and she is a current member. I can try to speak to one of my contacts there, get you some details?'

Dr Kapoor was proving much more helpful than any pathologist Kate had previously worked with.

'What about Dr Milne?' she asked Michelle.

'He's a consultant working at King's College Hospital. I've asked his office to get him to call me, but they said he's on leave.'

'Leave where?'

'They said he's got a place in the Lake District, up north somewhere. They won't give me any of his contact details, so I guess we wait?'

Waiting felt like the wrong option. But until they could verify which of the doctors were missing, there was no way to narrow down the cases they were investigating. The local police forces Michelle had contacted had reported similar stories. Devastated people left behind after a rare illness. They could all have the motive to do this. Kate didn't want to waste resources tracking where everyone was, not until she had confirmed the doctors were still alive. Then they could start looking at signal bounce-back from mobile phone masts, and check CCTV.

They still hadn't managed to work out Julian Leakey's last movements. He wasn't seen anywhere in Earl's Court or St James's Park, not prior to wearing the Anonymous outfit. After that he would have blended in with the crowds. Freya Rice was also invisible. CCTV was still being checked, but so far they hadn't managed to trace her.

It was frustrating, and Kate just couldn't work out how Natalie Davies fit into all of this. Kate had a theory that would link Julian, Freya and even Mark Lynch. But Natalie? What was her role? And where exactly were the missing Leanne Birch, and the two doctors?

She checked her phone. Stevie was in Stepney Green with the mother of one of the people who AREL had refused to treat. Rob was on his way to check in on a second family.

Kate thought about the threads she was following. Lots of people lost their loved ones, they didn't then seek revenge in such elaborate ways. The person behind this must have been pushed over an edge they were already leaning over. Existing problems accentuated and exacerbated by some new trauma.

Her phone rang. It was Dr Kapoor.

'What have you got for me?'

'Dr Sue Knight's details. I hope you're sitting down.'

'Go on.'

'She was found dead two days ago.'

Kate rolled her chair over, and sat down heavily.

'Where?'

'She was in London, came back for a birthday trip. She had been planning it for a while apparently, just her and her husband.'

'I don't understand, why didn't she show up in any of our searches?'

'Because she changed her name. She's now Dr Sue Lewis, married in Australia to a fellow medic she met in the Democratic Republic of Congo.'

'How did she die?'

'Her body was found in her hotel room, drowned in the bath.'

'Where was she staying?'

'The Ritz.'

'That's a bit plush.'

'It was a special birthday. Her fiftieth.'

'Thank you.'

Kate asked Michelle to check the Met's database and bring up Dr Sue Lewis's details. The report suspected a suicide attempt. A tox report had been ordered, which would give a clearer picture.

'Her husband said she had been diagnosed with terminal cancer last year. It's why the trip meant so much,' said Michelle. 'It wasn't just for her birthday; I think it was her last goodbye to a city she had spent so much time in.'

'They still haven't processed the toxicology,' Kate said. She forgot how things worked in the real world sometimes. Budgets, priorities, lack of resources. Things took time, and in a suspected suicide, they wouldn't rush the results. 'Get those samples sent to Dr Kapoor. I want them analysed quickly. And I want a positive ID on Dr Milne. Get the local force to check his Lake District retreat as a matter of urgency.'

Kate looked through the notes and could see the lead officer had barely done an investigation. There was no CCTV check, and only a couple of staff had been questioned. The husband was in Selfridges buying his wife a special birthday present at the time. They had presumed suicide because of her terminal diagnosis and speaking to her husband, and then everything had pretty much stalled. The killer move for any cop to do: make your assumptions and then make the evidence fit.

Kate made some assumptions of her own. Dr Lewis had been murdered. Once Michelle confirmed that Dr Milne was very much alive and well and on holiday, it meant there were now two families they could focus on. Families that were broken, full of pain. And anger. Stevie was already with one. Kate messaged Rob and sent him to Rochester where the second family were.

Esther brought drinks. A glass of water for Stevie, and a tea for herself.

'I hate to ask about the details, but are you OK to elaborate?' said Stevie.

There was a sound from somewhere in the flat. Esther's eyes darted around the room, then looked at Stevie, then down into her cup. She drank her tea, her lips curled as the hot liquid burnt them, but her eyes remained steady. She put her cup down, and pulled her cushion close again.

'You said it was sudden?' prompted Stevie.

Esther looked confused, as though unsure of whom Stevie was speaking to.

'Yes,' she said eventually. 'He was absolutely fine, and then one day he started to choke. I thought maybe he had swallowed something, and tried to get it out. But there was nothing and he was crying and really struggling to breathe . . . it was horrible, coming out in long drawn out gasps. I didn't know what to do, I was panicking, calling 999, trying to get him to tell me what was wrong, trying to help him. The ambulance took twenty minutes to arrive, and I don't think I've ever experienced anything like that. I felt every second, every bit of pain my baby was in. I can still hear him . . .' The hardness was back in her voice. 'I just wanted him to be OK. And he wasn't. I kept screaming at him. And I . . . I was so confused, so scared. I slapped him. I still feel the sting in my hands sometimes. I wanted him to stop. And I lashed out.'

Stevie let the silence fall between them. Somewhere a boiler started, and she could hear water running through the central heating, making a gentle tapping noise.

'What happened then?'

'The ambulance arrived, and they put a mask on him, but he wouldn't stop choking and breathing in gulps. They took him to hospital, where the doctors didn't have a clue either. They thought something was stuck, and kept trying to clear his airways. Nothing was there, and then they took control away from him, had him on a respirator so he didn't have to struggle. And finally he was still, his breathing sounded like some Victorian mechanical device. It was painful to hear. And they still didn't know why it was happening to him.'

'How did they treat him then?'

'They transferred him to the Children's Hospital in Liverpool. Alder Hey. Kept him under constant observation. Ran every test they could. They took so much blood from him. And gave me nothing. They had no answers for me. I wasn't an idiot. I could speak their language, I knew enough. They used to roll their eyes, and make quick exits when they saw me. They weren't used to someone who could get past their medical bullshit.'

'How did he get diagnosed?'

'He started showing other symptoms over the next few weeks. A consultant there said it might be a rare genetic condition he'd come across before. They tested Robert, and he came back positive. It was Findlay's Syndrome Disorder. Robert's body was failing to carry oxygen in his blood the way it should. It lies dormant in people, sometimes for decades, usually never becomes an issue. Robert though, he was one of the unlucky ones. His body started to shut down. And there was nothing they could do.'

'They told you that?'

'Yes. They had no cure, and there were no medicines to manage it. So I sat in the hospital room. Waiting for my child to die.'

Stevie had no response.

'And then AREL happened. My consultant told me he'd heard about a drug that might work for FSD, that it might help repair the mechanism in Robert that was failing. The drug was still in testing stage, but AREL were running trials. And so we made an application. And I thought why wouldn't they? Robert was going to have a future, they were going to save him. I believed he was going to be OK. Before that, I had given him up. I had already planned his funeral, and then all of a sudden, there it was. The possibility that he would live.'

'Only it didn't work out like that?'

'No, it didn't. The drug was expensive. A year's treatment cost half a million pounds. That's what they said. Robert was only the second baby they knew of that had shown symptoms of FSD. Most people didn't get it until they were much older. So to them, testing how their drug worked on a baby just didn't make sense. And where was I going to get half a million pounds from? And so these faceless bastards in some room somewhere made the decision that my baby wasn't worth saving. And they let him die.'

They let him die. There was blame there. All of it understandable. Stevie stared at the broken woman before her. She had lost the thing most precious to her and with him her life too. The question was, was she capable of exacting a cold and total revenge? Was Robert, the innocent baby, actually the first to die?

Chapter Seventy-Four

Michelle watched one of her screens as though her eyes were unable to make sense of what she was seeing. She rubbed her eyelids, and pressed her temples, then stared again. She sighed, sipped at her green tea, started to flick her teeth with her fingernail.

'Everything OK?' said Kate. She was sitting at her own desk, thinking over the links in her head. Esther Lake had lost her infant son. The Kemps in Rochester had lost their thirteen-year-old son after AREL had refused him treatment. Both could be the pieces that brought the investigative loop to a close.

'Yes, I just keep thinking something is obvious and I'm missing it,' said Michelle.

Kate would recommend fresh air to anyone else, but not Michelle. When she was focused her brain needed to stay *in situ* to try to resolve whatever it was she needed to.

'What are you working on?'

'Nathan Lake. Northumbria Police can't make contact with him at his last-known address and his mobile is switched off. In fact it hasn't been used for nearly two months.'

'He's missing?' Kate walked over to Michelle's desk, started to look at her multi-screen set-up.

'It looks that way. I've tried tracing his financial history, but there's nothing, no transactions. Even if he lost his phone or is using a burner, I can't imagine how he would survive without cash or using his credit cards.'

Kate felt her insides tighten, as her mind began to make connections she didn't like. She checked her phone. Nothing from Stevie, although Rob had let her know he had arrived.

'Put out an alert for Nathan Lake. I want the usual channels checked. Hospital emergency admissions, and I want a comprehensive CCTV search done.'

'I've already started. I'm checking all the critical points of interest, running his image through our systems as we speak.'

Kate couldn't hold back the smile on her face. She should know her team by now, and that they were always a step ahead of where she would want them to be.

'Let me know as soon as you find anything.'

Michelle nodded.

'What are you thinking?'

Kate wasn't sure, instead checked her phone again, feeling apprehensive for Stevie. She hoped she hadn't put her detective sergeant into any danger.

Chapter Seventy-Five

Michelle was feeling the tiredness in her every cell. Her eyes were dry, aching, and the images in front of her were blurring. Still she kept on, watching the clips that had been sent to her. Any that had a match to Nathan Lake, no matter how minimal the likeness. So much CCTV was such bad quality that running something like this always ended up with more false hits than actual matches.

Wearily she clicked her mouse, opened up the next video. She sat back, as the screen filled with a man she was sure was Nathan. He looked different to his photo ID, was wearing a baseball cap, but it didn't cover his face. Michelle froze the image, and stared. There was something odd about his features. She dismissed what she was thinking, started to play the video again, and watched as Nathan Lake entered the Seven Dials club. The place where Mark Lynch and his mystery girlfriend met-up after his war-games society meetings.

Michelle watched the retreating form of Nathan Lake, backpack over his shoulder, as he walked up the entrance stairs to the first floor. What exactly was he doing there? Was he going to meet Mark Lynch?

Michelle moved the video forward, until she saw Mark leaving with his girlfriend. Nathan was still inside. She paused the video and pulled up the file containing Esther and Nathan Lake's pictures. She looked from one to the other, trying to make

Esther's face fit. But it didn't. Michelle felt disappointed. Until she changed the angle of the picture, and used a different set of markers. And then she gasped.

'Oh Esther,' she whispered, as her fingers moved over her keyboard and clicked her mouse rapidly.

'What happened after . . .?' said Stevie. She felt her phone buzz. It was three times, a secure alert system Michelle had programmed into it. It screened out all messages and calls but allowed urgent ones DCI Riley authorised to be flagged up.

Esther was staring into space, still caught up in her remembered grief, so Stevie took her phone out and checked the message. She watched carefully as Esther picked up her cold tea, put it down again, and watched as the nails of her right hand started to dig into her left hand.

'Everything ended,' she said, whispering at first, and then her voice hardening again. 'I wanted to sue the world, but I didn't have a case. I became obsessed. I wanted to blame everyone, and I wanted Robert back. And I couldn't. Nathan and I . . . we didn't make it. He had his reasons. And he abandoned me in a way. I moved down south, and tried to rebuild my life. You know they say London is the perfect city to lose yourself in. So many people, so big. But how do you lose yourself, how do you run away, when what you are hiding from is here?' Esther jabbed at her head, then at her chest. 'It's here. Robert is here, always. And he always will be.'

Stevie felt cold, but she had to now turn the conversation to try and find out if Esther could be behind the deaths of four people.

'Did you know the people at AREL that rejected Robert's application?'

The change of topic threw Esther. She looked confused, then seemed to collect herself, before she answered.

'I never met them. Cowards. They didn't have the decency to tell me to my face why my child wasn't good enough. They sat there playing God, and they sent me a letter. A cold, formal letter. With their names signed at the bottom.'

'Do you still have the letter?'

'I tore it to pieces and burnt it after Robert died. I didn't want anything from them in my home, not after they had killed my child.'

'Do you remember any of the names?'

'Oh yes. I remember every single name that signed my child's death warrant. I held Robert while he died you know? As his body shut down. Every day, I held him and felt him suffer. I would have done anything to swap places with him. Anything. But I couldn't.'

'And what would you do to the people who had killed him?'

Esther didn't reply.

'And what about your husband?'

Esther's eyes started scanning the room, the skittishness back again.

'He's not my husband anymore. In a way, he's also dead to me.'

Outside Stevie dialled Kate.

'They killed her baby,' said Stevie. 'I think that sort of pain could do anything to a person.'

'Did you get my message about the husband?'

'Yes. She claims she hasn't seen her husband in months. She said he was dead to her. What exactly is happening?'

'We're not sure yet. How did she seem?'

'Honestly? She's a mess. Or she's doing her best at playing a mess.'

'What do you mean?'

'She went from being a nervous wreck, to being chilling. Her answers made sense, even when they weren't meant to. I've either seen a raw woman at her lowest, or a rehearsed performance. I can't decide. Any news about the other family?'

'Rob is interviewing them now.'

'Esther described what the disease did to her son. I feel for her, what she went through. But I just . . . something in my gut is telling me she's not what she seems.'

'Michelle's tracked her mobile: it doesn't give us the answers we need. But she's working on something, I don't want to say what, not until I'm absolutely sure.'

'In the meantime? Like I said, I don't know about her. Also, she has a degree in biochemistry. That's just too coincidental.'

'Let's watch her movements, and put a trace on her phone. For now, that should be enough.'

Stevie hated feeling like this. If Esther was responsible for these murders, she had to be stopped. That wasn't in question, that was her job, it was what the team did. It was just having to arrest someone that vulnerable, whose life had been so devastated. It felt wrong.

Chapter Seventy-Six

Leanne Birch's eyes fluttered open, the vibrations of the Underground waking her. She didn't know how long she had been there, only that her body was frozen.

She tried to move. There was no pain, only the awareness that she couldn't make anything work. Her eyes blinked, that was all. The rest of her body was locked. She screamed for help, but the words only echoed in her head.

The box was small, barely able to contain her. She could see holes cut into the sides, allowing air to come in, so she wouldn't suffocate. There was no logic to any of this. If she was going to kill her, then why hadn't she done it already?

Or was her game something else? To let her die slowly, and in pain? She tried to move again, with every ounce of strength she had. Still there was nothing.

Why had she come? Why had she agreed to meet her? To talk about her dead child? How could she be so stupid? And yet, she felt she owed her. She felt guilt from those days. She was young, mired by student loans and debts, just launching her career. The money had been good. And she had to make clinical decisions, honest decisions. It wasn't about who was worth more; it was about who would provide the best test cases for the drugs.

People had died. They were dying anyway. And now she was going to die.

Maybe this would give her salvation? After all, who would miss her? Her parents? Her siblings? She hardly saw any of them. If she survived this, she would change that.

Leanne thought about them all. Wondered if they were looking for her, or cared enough to alert anyone. Then again, why would they? They probably thought she was off gallivanting. She promised herself that if she got through this she would spend more time with them.

If she got through this. She knew she wouldn't. That woman wasn't coming back. She was going to let Leanne die. And have her revenge.

Leanne closed her eyes, and tried to move once more. She thought about her parents. And she thought about her life. And she willed herself to move.

Nothing. She swallowed.

She swallowed! She opened her mouth. It was dry, and sore, but it was working. She could feel it, and then she could hear her own voice. And she willed herself to move again.

Michelle was excited as she briefed Kate. This was her domain, this was what she did.

'I couldn't find the link between Mark Lynch and Esther Lake. I tried to focus on his girlfriend, tried to see if I could get her to fit to Esther's features. It's difficult, his girlfriend has her hair in her face as they are leaving.'

Kate looked at the images Michelle was showing her on the screen. They were sitting at Michelle's computer, her three screens full of items being moved and dropped between them. It was true, Mark's girlfriend had her face hidden to some extent, but there didn't seem to be a likeness to Esther.

'And this here? Nathan Lake entering the club?' Kate pointed to the image of Nathan caught on CCTV on the left-hand screen. Michelle tapped away at her keyboard, and the third screen, which was her laptop, filled with another image.

'Yes. And can you see here? It has a date stamp. Nathan was at the club on the same night as the war-games society, and here we can see Mark go in.' Michelle adjusted the images so Kate could see what she was saying.

'What was he doing there? Warning Mark? But about what?'

It didn't make sense. Kate couldn't see the link.

'You see, I was trying to fit Esther's likeness onto the images of Mark's girlfriend. A facial-recognition fit. But with the right make-up and hair, and with the second rate CCTV camera footage, it can easily fail.'

'Is that what happened here?'

'It certainly didn't pick Esther up by facial recognition.'

'So what did you do?'

'This.'

Michelle clicked her mouse, and the three screens started to move, the images flying across them. Kate watched, impressed at what she was seeing in terms of technology, and then horrified as she saw what Michelle's algorithms had managed to pick up.

'Are you sure?'

'Yes. The facial recognition won't work, but I used these other biometric markers instead. Height, weight, proportion of the limbs to the torso, the waist to the legs, even the calf muscles. Anything we can take a measurement of, we can use. And those mappings, they gave me enough of a match for me to be convinced.'

'I need more, Michelle.'

Michelle clicked her mouse again.

'I followed this through, once I thought this might be the case. And so I looked for her in the bereavement group. And, of course, I didn't think she would use her own name; that wouldn't happen, might not even be possible. So I checked the names on the list, and I found this one. She used Natasha Mace. It's a shell name. There was no link to her former life, because she wanted it that way. Her GP had referred her, because of what she had been through, with the fake name and no link to her real identity.'

'Then how do you know it's who we need?'

'Because Natasha Mace made one fatal flaw. This.'

Kate watched as a credit card appeared onscreen.

'This was used to buy the mobile phone Natasha Mace used to register for the bereavement group. It's a phone Natasha has been using for months. I've requested the location history from the provider so I'll be able to tell you pretty quickly what we need to know.'

Kate stared at the name on the credit card.

'Whose watching Esther?' she said.

'Detective Sergeant Harris.'

Kate heard the word 'fuck' run through her mind.

'Well done Michelle. Now go home. I think we have this.'

Chapter Seventy-Seven

Zain had agreed to do the night shift. He was parked outside
Esther Lake's building's front entrance, with another patrol car
at the back entrance, so both exits were covered. She hadn't
made a move to leave.

The flat was in darkness, no lights on. He checked with the
patrol car to see if anything was on at the back. They said there
were no lights there either. Maybe she had had an early night?
But that didn't seem right. He had been in position since seven
o'clock, just over an hour ago. She might have nodded off after
Stevie left, but he assumed she would watch TV or make herself
some food at least.

Kate called him.

'Stay in position, DS Harris. I am on my way shortly. There
have been some developments, but I will inform you in person.
Do not let Esther leave that flat.'

'Do you want me to go and check on her?'

'No. You stay in position and you wait for me.'

Zain didn't trust himself to speak.

'DS Harris?'

'It's risky. I haven't seen any movement for over an hour. I
think I should go in now, see what's happening. If you think
she's a flight risk.'

'What will you say that won't spook her?'

'Just that we have some more follow-up questions.'

'That can't wait until the morning?'

She was right.

'You need to wait for us. We will be there as soon as I have tactical aid set-up. We don't know what we are potentially dealing with.'

He did know. And he didn't like waiting. He felt resentful that she didn't trust him to do this alone. He wasn't an idiot. Of course she wouldn't go in at this time. She was DCI Kate Riley. But DS Zain Harris? Well, he did what the fuck he liked most of the time.

Zain checked the front door but it was bolted solidly. He tried some of the neighbours. One buzzed him in after he showed his ID to the intercom screen. There was no caretaker on site, so he made his way to Esther's apartment and stood outside her door listening. There were no sounds. She couldn't have left the apartment though: the patrol had been in place from the moment Stevie had left.

Zain knocked. He would go with the further questions line, but there was no answer. This is where it got tricky. She was definitely home, so he couldn't break the door down. They either needed a warrant, or he needed to get in some other way.

He was still thinking when Kate called him again.

'Zain where are you?'

'In my car.'

'Zain . . .'

'Outside the flat.' Had Esther called and complained already? Was she watching him?

'I'm on my way, we're bringing a battering ram with us. I have a warrant. *Do not enter*. Do you understand?'

'What's happened?'

'I'll explain when I get there. For now, you need to stand down. That's an order.'

Zain smiled. Orders. Since when? There was a fire extinguisher by the front door he had seen on his way in. He ran down the stairs and grabbed it. Using it as leverage, he rammed Esther's front door until it gave way and he was inside.

The flat was in darkness. He sniffed for gas, when there was none he switched the lights on, and saw the lifeless body on the couch. He called Kate.

'How far are you?'

'About ten minutes. I specifically told you not to go in. An ambulance should be with you shortly.'

'I don't understand?' he said. 'What are we dealing with?'

He listened as Kate explained, shocked as the call ended.

Zain felt the body. It was cold, but definitely alive. There was a cup on the coffee table. He sniffed it, but it was only cold tea.

Zain walked around the flat, trying to find signs of an intruder. He couldn't see anything obvious, until he got into the bedroom. He was closing the wardrobe door when he spotted it. Hanging towards the back, it was the coat he had seen on Mark Lynch's girlfriend. He did a search, and found a blonde wig, the same sort of style that Mark's mysterious woman had had. It was confirmation of what Kate had told him. Zain listened carefully in case he heard anyone else, his senses tuned for the slightest movement. But there was nothing.

He walked into the kitchen where he saw there were a number of dirty cups and plates. Definitely more than one person would need. He opened the fridge, it was well stocked. Again it seemed like too much food for one person.

He heard a noise behind him, and turned around. But it was too late. He felt something stab into his neck, and then he fell, into darkness. The last he thought was that he hoped Kate would get there in time to save Esther Lake.

The front door was smashed in when Kate arrived at Esther Lake's flat. The lights were all on, with Esther on the sofa. Kate let the medics in, who attended to her, trying to wake her.

Kate looked around the flat, her heart hammering the further in she went. She couldn't find Zain anywhere. She tried calling him, and heard his cell phone ring. She found it under the fridge, the door was open, and there were traces of blood on the floor in front of it.

She should have mobilised more quickly, got the back-up team in the squad car to help Zain. Instead she was left with not only Esther unable to help them, but with Zain missing as well.

Kate put an alert out, and called her team back to work. They would need all their resources, it was going to be a long night. She just hoped she could find Zain before anything serious happened to him.

Zain opened his eyes. He could see light, coming in through holes. He tried to move. But he couldn't. Maybe the space he was in was too cramped? He shifted himself, but his body didn't follow the thought process. Only his eyes were moving. His body was locked.

He lay staring out of one of the holes. He tried to open his mouth, tried to make a noise. Nothing came out, not even a guttural plea.

He closed his eyes. And then he heard it. It was a woman's voice.

'Help me,' it said. It was rough, as though said by a full mouth, or someone not used to speaking.

Zain tried to answer, but he couldn't. The voice came again. Followed by a banging. It was gentle, but it was definitely real.

Chapter Seventy-Eight

Kate watched as the paramedics worked on Esther. They had managed to flush her system of the drugs her ex-husband had given her. When Kate explained to her what had happened, Esther didn't believe her.

'He wouldn't do something like that,' she said. 'You don't know Nathan. He's different from other men.'

'We know,' said Kate, looking at her meaningfully. 'You alluded to it, didn't you? When you spoke to DS Brennan earlier? You said he was dead to you in a way. And that's true isn't it? Nathan really is gone.'

'If you know that, how can you suspect him of doing something like this?'

'And Natasha? What about her?' Esther looked at her, as if not understanding. Then she nodded.

Michelle had managed to collate the evidence for her. Nathan entering the Seven Dials club had at first looked normal dressed in jeans and a jacket, carrying a backpack and wearing a baseball cap. Only his face looked odd. His eyebrows were definitely shaped, and his skin had a smooth look, one that could only be achieved using make-up. When Michelle brought up images of the woman with Mark Lynch, doing biometric scans against points of the body, she had seen that the results were similar to Nathan's. He must have changed clothes in the club, and released the wig he was wearing under his cap.

Michelle had then run through the details of the bereavement group, and found the fake ID that Nathan had used. Calling himself Natasha Mace, he had made one fatal error. When ordering the mobile phone he'd used, he had paid with Nathan Lake's credit card. Michelle found the link, and she had her proof. Tracing Natasha's mobile, Nathan was in all the wrong places. On 5 November he was in Earl's Court, St James's Park and Waterloo. Two nights ago he was on Piccadilly, near the Ritz where Dr Lewis was killed.

'She went to so much trouble to remove the batteries of their phones and hide the location of her victims,' Michelle had said. 'And yet she made no effort to conceal her own identity, despite all of that. She doesn't care about getting caught.'

Kate acknowledged that Michelle had been referring to Nathan as Natasha. Kate liked the respect, but still, murderers weren't exempt from justice because they were transitioning. And he hadn't completed the process yet, so she felt OK about using his original name.

'I think you're right,' said Kate. 'He's done what he set out to do. Seek revenge on the people that killed his child.'

And now Kate needed to know where he was, and what exactly his plans were for Zain.

Esther was still groggy. She watched Kate's mouth as she spoke, as though she couldn't hear her voice, couldn't comprehend.

'Do you have any idea where Nathan might have taken DS Harris?'

A shake of the head.

'How long has he been staying with you?'

'For a few months now. He lost his job when he started to become who he is. We lost so much together, I couldn't say no to him. So I let him stay.'

'What did he do while he was here?'

'Nothing. He would go out a lot. I think he spent a lot of time in Soho. I went to a club with him a couple of times. It just didn't work out though. I couldn't bear to look at him like that. Not that I had a problem with who he was. It was more the way he was. He was so . . . happy . . . I hated him for that. How could he be? I was never going to be again.'

'Was he close to anyone in particular? Any friends we might be able to approach and ask about his whereabouts?'

'I don't know them. There must have been. And there was the support group. He went to a bereavement group, to help with . . . you know the details of that already. What happened to us, how we lost . . .'

'I need your help to find him, Esther. Can you please have a think? Exactly where do you think he might be? Are there any places you and he might know, especially secluded places? Anything that can help, *please*.'

Kate could hear the desperation in her own voice. She felt panic and déjà vu. She was going to try and rescue Zain again, and he had played roulette with his life so many times already that this might be the one time he lost. She couldn't let that happen; this couldn't be the one that finally destroyed him.

Esther looked back blankly. Whatever her ex-husband had or hadn't done, it seemed as though she really was totally unaware. Kate was frustrated, knowing there was nothing else she could do to find Zain.

Zain tried to move towards the voice, his whole being attempting to shift towards the woman. She was asking for help, over and over again. She was banging, not loudly, but loud enough.

He wanted to help her, his instinct was to do that. It was his calling. He had a massive saviour complex; it didn't take a therapist to tell him that.

And the fact he couldn't was killing him. The effort inside was terrible, as he pushed with everything he had. The only thing that moved was water in his eyes, leaking out of the sides, the only testament to just how much he was trying.

The woman kept asking for help. And then she started to scream.

Zain heard the footsteps, pacing around them. Stopping nearby, and then a voice, telling the woman to shut up. Zain couldn't place it, the voice was a hoarse whisper.

She screamed louder, and Zain heard a chain being uncoiled, like a steel snake and a lock being positioned to be opened. The hinges to a door creaked, and the screams grew louder. Then a slap, a struggle, he heard grunts and shouts, someone cried out in pain.

Then silence.

Chapter Seventy-Nine

Kate was briefing her assembled team, including her core members, plus SO19 and various DCs and PCs from the PCC office. They were trying to keep warm, stamping feet, rubbing hands and drinking hot drinks from flasks.

'The suspect's name is Nathan Lake but he may also be using the name Natasha Mace,' Kate was saying. 'He is twenty-eight, five foot seven. Pictures are being sent to you all by my colleague, Michelle Cable. It is not spam or a virus, so please open the texts or WhatsApp message or email you receive from her. I also believe that the suspect is armed and extremely volatile. He isn't armed with a gun, but has used a knife, and more than that, is in possession of a deadly neurotoxin. There is no known cure for this neurotoxin, so do not get near the suspect, or you will be putting yourself at severe risk. We have no idea where he may have taken DS Zain Harris, but we're scanning CCTV in this neighbourhood. We are tracking the suspect's van and you have the registration number, or will have when it is sent to you.'

She didn't know what else to tell them, only that Zain and Nathan couldn't have gone far, there was only a fifteen-minute window roughly between Zain entering Esther's flat and Kate and the paramedics arriving. She told them to spread out, and start their search in quadrants, reporting in when they had cleared a section, so that nobody repeated a search and wasted time in the same place.

'Can you see? That's the van that was parked outside Esther's flat.'

Michelle was talking Kate through the CCTV route Nathan had taken. There was no official vehicle registered to his name, but Esther told them about a white van he had recently hired. Michelle had caught it on camera, at first just a glimpse from a block of flats across the road, and then more clearly on Mile End Road. The number plate was a fake, which was confirmation in Kate's mind.

'Where did it go?'

'It went down Mile End Road, until it got to Regents Canal. It then took a right down this side street, Kingston Street. There are no cameras, and from there I don't know.'

Kate was getting updates from Stevie and the other officers under her command, who were out scouring the streets of Stepney Green and Whitechapel, trying to work out where Nathan had gone. They didn't really have a sense of where to go, but they, along with everyone else that was part of the police team, kept moving. Not giving Nathan any more time to put distance between him and them.

Rob was helping, having returned from Rochester. The family there seemed to have coped much better than Esther and Nathan Lake. They had two other children, and had been given thirteen years with the child who had died, at least. That was how they saw it.

Kate called Rob, told him where he should go, and took herself out to the main Stepney Green common. SO19 were waiting for her, Stevie in uniform as one of them. Kate was dressed in her usual outfit. Fitted, one-colour and smart, she felt authoritative in the grey suit. Until she saw the body armour Stevie was wearing.

'You picked the wrong night to abandon me,' Kate told her.

'I thought it best one of us is embedded with them, to keep us live on all fronts.' Stevie didn't have her helmet on, but was wearing the black outfit and her Heckler and Koch was just as loaded and ready as the others.

'Good luck. I think we may have found his approximate location.'

Rob called while she was updating Stevie.

'We followed the back roads through, and I think we've found them. You'd better make your way over here, boss. Could get tricky.'

Kate parked her car, with SO19 in an ARU van behind her. They had turned off a small cobble street, with a warehouse on one side, student accommodation on the other. Next to the student halls was an open yard, full of haulage trucks. Behind it was a row of offices and buildings, with metal grilles guarding the windows. The main gates to the yard were open.

Kate could see the white van Michelle had identified earlier. It was parked between the trucks, at an angle, with no consideration. Definitely someone in a rush.

'You brought the terminator with you, boss?' said Rob.

'I'd watch that mouth of yours DS Pelt, I've got toys and I'm not afraid to use them on you,' said Stevie. She indicated the Heckler and Koch over her shoulder. Rob put his hands up in mock surrender.

'What do we do now?' he asked.

Kate surveyed the location, and the possible places Zain may have been taken.

'We spread out, and we start searching. Stevie, I need you and SO19 to stay here, until we know where they are and whether we need you.'

'Not wanting to question you boss, but the suspect has a lethal weapon on him that has no cure. He's pretty much armed and dangerous, I think you're going to need me.'

Kate thought about it and agreed. The rest of SO19 had to stay put though. There was too much risk involved, and the last time she had used SO19, Zain had nearly ended up being shot. She didn't want to give them the opportunity to revisit that scenario.

Zain breathed in the silence. It was heavy, and he could hear his heart crashing in his ears. He still couldn't move. And then he heard them. Footsteps, slowly approaching him. He couldn't tell who they belonged to.

He heard the chains falling first. He was in a box, and it too was chained and locked he realised. The woman must be in something similar. With a thud the final part of chain lock fell onto the floor. A key was turned in the lock, and then the lid was pulled back.

His eyes saw into the dim light that poured in from the outside. It felt comforting and it felt good that he was now free. He still couldn't move. The woman came into view, smiling at him.

And then she spoke, but her voice seemed odd. It was much deeper than he would have expected.

'This is the end game Detective. I am going to join my son now. And I'm taking you with me.'

Zain didn't understand, but he knew this was wrong. And he heard himself start yelling, only the sound echoed and bounced inside his head.

Chapter Eighty

Kate crept between tightly packed trucks, the air thick with grease and tyres. She could hear Stevie breathing behind her, as the two of them took small steps. While they were between the vehicles, they had cover. Once they broke, they would be exposed. And there was a distance of about eight metres where the ground was clear, to where the outhouses were.

Michelle had texted to say the outhouses were all empty, abandoned. Awaiting demolition, to be replaced by flats. The surrounding land had been leased to a haulage firm that used it to park its lorries overnight.

'Which one?' said Stevie.

She was referring to the doors they could enter by. Other teams of two would be going in with them. Kate decided to take the door dead centre to them. She pointed to it, and she and Stevie began moving forwards.

Stevie raised her Heckler and Koch, looking out of the vision scope, while Kate ran to the door, and tried to open it. It didn't budge, and she motioned Stevie over. The two women stood either side of it. There were metal grilles over the door, and a rusted lock which lay loose.

'It's this one,' said Kate.

The lock had obviously been broken. Kate messaged Rob, and he joined her, with other members of SO19.

'I go in first,' Kate told them. 'None of you makes a move until I say so.'

She creaked open the door. It was so old and broken that there was no way to do it silently. She started to make her way in, followed by her team. There was no time to plan this properly. She was acutely aware of Zain and of the TTX2, how lethal it was, and how quickly it could be given to him.

Inside there was complete darkness, but in the distance she heard voices. She guided her team towards them.

Zain was on his knees, his hands tied behind his back. A needle poised at his neck. He didn't understand who had taken him. It was a man, but he was wearing distinctive make-up. His eyes were kohled and his lips red, with blush on his cheeks. He had tied Zain's hands and feet, and then injected him with something that had made his body wake up. It felt like molten mercury was running through his veins, and he had cried out in pain. He felt weak, but he could at least now speak.

'Who are you?'

'It doesn't matter anymore.'

'It does to me. What is that? In the syringe? Is that what killed Julian Leakey?' Zain swallowed hard.

'Yes.'

'How did you get it?'

'Please, don't. I want to meet my son today. I don't want to explain to you.'

'Your son?'

'Robert. My little boy. My poor wee boy, I want him to know that he was worth more than all of them.'

Robert? The Lake's son? It clicked then.

'Nathan?'

'That's who I once was.'

'I'm sorry for what happened to him. No one should have to suffer that.'

Zain looked into the green eyes that were lined in black. He thought they looked beautiful, which felt a bit weird given the situation he was in. Nathan's eyes filled with the start of tears, but he shook his head, and moved Zain's head to face forward.

'What are you planning on doing? Killing me like the others?'

'Not yet. You are my guarantee. I need to finish this. This syringe contains the right amount of toxin. The same amount I gave to Julian Leakey.' Zain looked sideways and saw the syringe centimetres from his neck.

'You see I made a mistake with her. With Leanne.'

Leanne? The woman he had heard, was that Leanne Birch?

'What sort of mistake?'

'I wanted her to suffer. I wanted them all to suffer. And I was thinking how to do it. And for Leanne, I gave her low levels of TTX. Her body froze, it became zombified. Unable to move, but still her brain functioned. And I wanted her to slowly starve to death. To suffer, like my baby did.'

'What happened?'

'I got the dose wrong. I'm no scientist.'

'No, but Mark Lynch was. Why did you kill him?'

'Poor Mark. He had been through so much. He couldn't cope. I met him at my bereavement group, and when I found out what he did . . .'

'Why did he help you?'

'He understood my pain, really understood it. He was also going through his own issues. And so we became friends. Good friends, fast friends. Those intense relationships where you lose your sense of everything, and you do crazy things you wouldn't even do for family.'

Zain looked around, trying to work out where Leanne was. He couldn't see her, but he could see the two metal boxes, one of which he'd been in. They were empty fridge freezers as far as he could tell, not plugged in.

'Were you lovers?' he asked.

Nathan pulled Zain's head roughly forward.

'Enough questions.'

'What are we waiting for?'

'For that bitch to die,' said Nathan. 'Once I know that for sure, then it's over. But if your colleagues come in before, they won't risk rescuing her if it means you might be hurt. No matter what you say.'

Zain heard it then. The screaming. It was coming from one of the fridges. Leanne was inside, and he knew then she had been given more of the neurotoxin. It was too late for her. But he had to try. There was no other way he knew to be. Even if it meant that he would die too.

Chapter Eighty-One

Zain knew he needed to engage with Nathan. To understand him, to gain time. He had to free himself and at least attempt to save Leanne.

'What will you achieve by her death? Do you think this is what Robert would want?'

Nathan roughly pulled Zain's hair, and spat into his face.

'Do not mention my boy. Understand? Or I will end you right now.'

Nathan shoved Zain's head forward, but in doing so misaligned the needle. It was now resting against the lower part of his skull. If Nathan tried, he might struggle to stab Zain quite as effectively as before. Still, Zain needed a few more minutes to execute his plan.

'Will killing her achieve anything? Let her go. There is still time. Don't you want to live your life? Don't you owe it to Esther? What will she be left with?'

'She will be fine. You don't understand. Esther is a mess, and all she has is a mother's love. I have both. Enough love for a father *and* a mother.'

'This isn't the way. Death is never the way. You know the ones that will suffer will be the people they leave behind. Like you. Leanne will die. What about her family? She's someone's daughter too?'

'They should be ashamed of themselves, raising a cold-hearted murdering bitch like her. And don't tell me anyone will miss Julian

Leakey. The arrogant, selfish bastard. Now keep your mouth shut. Or you will die with them.'

'Not today.'

Nathan looked confused, but he had given Zain a window, and Zain had taken it.

Nathan had made a stupid rookie mistake. Everyone used plastic tags these days to tie people up, but Nathan had used rope and Zain knew how to get out of a dozen different knotted ropes; he had only held firm until he knew where Leanne was and what was going on.

His hands now free, Zain fell to the floor, and kicked out with his legs, toppling Nathan over. He jumped on top of him, and kneeling on Nathan's back, grabbed the wrist of the hand that held the syringe. Nathan tried to manoeuvre and plunge it into Zain, but Zain cracked Nathan's head on the concrete floor, once, twice. Still he tried to stab backwards at him with the needle.

Zain twisted harder, until he heard something break, and Nathan screamed, dropping the syringe.

'Where's the key?' said Zain. 'Where's the *fucking* key?'

Zain could still hear Leanne screaming.

He grabbed Nathan by the throat, and dragged him to his feet, checking his pockets, and then pulled him over to the freezer Leanne was in. He pushed Nathan against it, and asked him again. Nathan just laughed. Zain hit him another time.

He tied Nathan's hands, using triple knots so there was no way he could get free, while he started to break the lock on the freezer.

'Let her die,' Nathan was saying. 'She's a murdering bitch. She killed my boy. And let me die. *Please*. I want to be with Robert.'

'He doesn't want you. You lost all right to him the moment you killed Julian. And the others. Now where's the key?'

Zain tried again, but the padlock on the fridge was solid steel and new, the chains around the freezer thick and heavy. Zain looked around for pliers or anything he could use as leverage. Nothing came to hand.

'It's inside. With her,' Nathan told him.

'You fucked-up bastard.'

'They all deserved it.'

'They made a mistake. They made a bad decision. What about all the lives she *has* saved?'

Zain kicked at the freezer, Leanne's voice louder and more terrible. Her screams had become animalistic. Zain felt helpless. What could he do? How could he open a metal box? There was no phone anywhere; the only thing he could do was go and get help. But it would be too late.

Maybe it was already too late.

Zain heard something smash. A door. He looked up. He realised they were in the basement. Someone had smashed the door to enter it. Finally, help. He started shouting, just as Nathan started wailing. Then there was smoke. They had thrown a gas canister into the room, Zain started choking on it, and fell to his knees. He could see Nathan suffering in the same way.

Then there were boots, and shouting. Zain got up and ran towards one of the figures that had just entered. The figure must have panicked, mistaken Zain for Nathan. The armed and dangerous Nathan carrying a deadly neurotoxin.

Zain heard the gun fire, felt the impact.

Then nothing.

Chapter Eighty-Two

Kate looked at the broken figure of Nathan. He was wearing make-up, wrapped in a cloak, sitting across from her in the interview room at the PCC headquarters. It was hard not to feel sorry for him, despite the things he had done. Yet he *had* done those things, and she would not offer him sympathy. Images of Zain seared her mind.

'Let me die,' Nathan kept saying. 'I want to die. I want to be with Robert.'

Kate was not engaging with those words. She didn't want him to enter an insanity plea, or for his lawyer to claim he had mental-health issues. Nathan Lake needed to face the consequences of his actions.

Kate hadn't even let her own father and brothers get away with the things they had done, so there was no way she would let Nathan do so now.

'Nathan you are charged with some extremely serious crimes,' she told him. 'I need you to explain to me exactly what happened.'

'Maybe you should present your evidence first, before assuming my client has anything to do with these allegations,' his lawyer told her.

Kate provided the evidence they had accumulated. From Nathan's van being spotted near the address in Earl's Court, to a hire car he had set fire to on Bonfire Night.

'You see, DS Harris said he thought something was odd about that night. Just before the explosion. He remembered what it was afterwards. The men facing off with the police, they weren't wearing Anonymous outfits. They were thugs from a right-wing outfit, there to clash with what they perceived to be a threat to security. The only people wearing the cloaks and masks were the figure that set fire to the car, and someone with them. I believe that was you. And Julian Leakey was with you.'

Nathan stared at her, but didn't disagree.

'Why did Julian agree to come with you to St James's Park? Especially after what you did to Freya in front of him?'

Nathan smiled, and touched his lips.

'Is that what you think happened? Julian Leakey killed Freya Rice, the evidence is clear, DCI Riley.'

'Circumstantial, I think,' said Kate.

'No. It's clear. Julian killed her,' said Nathan. 'I watched him do it. Oh that was a pretty sight. I was in control then. They were dancing to my tune.'

'What do you mean?'

'I asked them both to meet me there. Freya, I told her who I was. Julian, the dirty little man, I met online. He thought he was coming to have sex with me. When he turned up, Freya was already tied up. He didn't know what to make of it. And that's when I injected him with the neurotoxin. And then I played him the video, of what it did to that mouse. And he begged me to save him. Do you know what that was like, DCI Riley?'

'Nathan, I suggest you—'

'Fuck off. You're going to get paid whatever I say, so just shut up. I'm talking to DCI Riley here.'

'I can imagine. You had begged them to save Robert.'

'Yes. What Esther doesn't know is that I visited their offices. AREL. And I met with Julian and I begged him to save my child. And I met Freya, and I did the same. They didn't listen to me. And then here he was begging *me* to save *him*.'

'And what did you do? What deal did you make with him?'

'I told him: if he killed Freya, he would live.'

'But there's no cure, you can't be cured.'

'He didn't know that. And the selfish scum, he did it. He barely hesitated, he just picked up that knife and stabbed her.'

Kate watched Nathan as he recalled the details, disgust on his face at what Julian was capable of. And then he smiled.

'And with her dead, I drove him to St James's, told him that's where the cure was. He wanted to live so badly. Just like my Robert did, just like me and Esther wanted our son to. And Julian would do whatever I said to him. I took him to a place in the park I had found before, far enough away from the protests for his screams not to be heard, and hidden away from anyone that might pass by. And then I watched him die. Nobody heard him. Except me. His every last breath leaving him. In agony. And it felt so so good, DCI Riley. Finally, I had done something for my son.'

Chapter Eighty-Three

Stevie was holding Zain's hand. It was cold. The doctors had induced a coma to reduce the swelling to his brain. He'd been this way since the night that he was shot. Since the night *she* had shot him.

She still couldn't recall properly what had happened, what she had thought; only that someone was coming towards her. And she'd reacted too quickly, firing her weapon before she was sure. How could she mistake Zain for Nathan? And now here he was. The bullet had lodged into his head, too close to his brain. He had been saved by his skull, but the bullet couldn't be removed. The surgeons said it could pierce the brain if they tried. Once the swelling had subsided they might try. They said his ventro-medial prefrontal cortex was badly damaged. Stevie had no idea what that meant, but the surgeons said it would mean he would probably not be the same again.

'I'm so sorry Zain,' she said, squeezing his hand tighter. There was no response.

Kate was in the conference room with her team. Minus Zain, it felt incomplete, but also too familiar. Zain in hospital having been injured in the line of duty. His life, her duty of care. She had failed to protect him yet again.

Kate didn't make eye contact with Stevie. She was a mess, clearly hadn't slept or eaten for days. She was at the hospital every chance she got, trying to will Zain awake. She was also under investigation for shooting a fellow officer.

'Nathan Lake has been helpful shall we say,' Kate told them. 'He confessed to killing Julian Leakey using a neurotoxin that Mark Lynch had supplied him with. The two had become intimate friends after meeting at a bereavement-support group.'

'Why did she kill Mark?' asked Michelle. She was still referring to Nathan as Natasha.

'In his mind he was freeing him. To Nathan the only freedom was to be reunited with his son. He wanted to reunite Mark with his parents. It made sense to him.'

'But she did it so grotesquely?'

'Nathan believed you had to suffer before you crossed over. He knew his son was OK, and that was because he had suffered so much. He wanted the same for Mark.'

'That is twisted,' said Rob.

'Nathan Lake suffered the loss of his child in heinous circumstances, and his life fell apart. Through all of that he was also going through a massive change in terms of his biology. The pressure and the stress must have driven him to extremes.'

'Everyone gets stressed; we don't go out and kill people.' Rob looked embarrassed as Stevie held him in a cold stare.

'What about Natalie? Why did he kill her?'

'Natalie had been following Julian, despite the restraining order. She followed him on his last day, to Earl's Court and to St James's Park. She then followed Nathan home, as he made his way back to Stepney Green. After she was questioned by . . . DS Harris, she realised Nathan must have been involved. She went to congratulate him. Only he wasn't done. He still had to kill Dr Sue Lewis, and Leanne Birch. So he played Natalie's own game, and followed her home.'

'Then killed her to keep her quiet.' said Rob.

'Yes.'

'And he knew about Dr Lewis? How?'

'He kept tabs on her. On all of them. We found printouts, files. He was aware of what they all did, the men and women that had killed his son. He was obsessed with them, and had been planning his revenge for years.'

'It's so sad,' said Michelle. 'I can only imagine what losing a baby would do to you.'

Kate didn't know if she agreed. There seemed to be no excuse for doing the things that Nathan had done. Esther had lost just as much, and yet she was managing to cope with life. Whatever form that took.

'Is Leanne going to survive?' Michelle asked.

They had managed to get Leanne out of the freezer, and into an isolation bubble. There was no cure for the neurotoxin, but caught early enough, she might pull through. The medical staff at the Royal Free had transfused blood multiple times through Leanne and put her in intensive care.

'The doctors said if she can survive the first twenty-four hours, there is a good chance she will be OK,' said Kate.

'And Zain? Is he going to be OK?'

'I don't know,' said Kate, looking at Stevie who was leaving the room. 'I hope so.'

Epilogue

Two Months Later

It was another battle she had fought and lost. PCC Justin Hope had demanded that Zain return to her team.

'He is a mess, still in rehab. There is no way on earth he can come back to work for us. The sort of things he will have to deal with, the sensitive nature of the role? No.'

'I want this to happen,' said PCC Hope, from behind his steepled fingers. Kate would be let go if she didn't agree to this.

'Why?'

'He's one of the best. I think he belongs with us.'

'He's managed to get himself stabbed and shot while working for us,' she told him. 'He is not well. The doctors don't think he ever will be. No, sir. I will not have him working with us and putting *all* our lives at risk.'

Hope had to pull out his trump card. The images from the file DCI Raymond Cross has shown him were still swimming in front of his eyes. He could not let that man expose and humiliate him, destroy everything he had worked for.

'My demand is simple enough,' DCI Cross had said. 'Zain is going to come back and work for you.'

And here was DCI Kate Riley, blocking him as usual.

'If you do this, I can make the charges against Stevie go away,' he told her.

There it was. Kate left to choose between two of her team. Her loyal, misguided in their abeyance to her, team. How could she refuse?

She stormed out. PCC Hope watched her go, and called DCI Cross.

Kate was at her desk, her anger in her mouth, unable to speak. How had she got to this stage where someone like PCC Hope was able to control her? She should make the decisions over who was in her team; she had to work with them. Her phone buzzed.

'DCI Riley? This is DCI Raymond Cross.'

What was he doing calling her? Kate didn't respond beyond acknowledging it was her. She wasn't in the mood for pleasantries.

'Zain asked me to look into something for you. Anya Fox-Leakey. He wanted details of her private accounts in Panama. I think he felt he had something to prove to you.'

Kate felt something inside herself soften.

'I pulled in some favours and found you your money trail. You can bring her in for questioning if you wish. The evidence I am about to send you will be enough.'

Kate ended the call and waited for the file to arrive. And considered what to do about Zain.

Zain was in his own room at the rehab centre in Bloomsbury. Kate had visited on multiple occasions, and her presence here was no longer awkward.

'They still can't take it out?' she asked.

'No. They won't risk it. It's stopped moving, but a bang to the head . . . it might pierce the brain. It's sitting there, too far in for them to remove it, not far enough for it to kill me.'

A bullet to the brain. People used that phrase so casually. And here he was, with an actual bullet in his brain.

'Have you still got any symptoms?'

In his mind a litany: my dreams are horrendous, I have hallucinations when it's really bad. Headaches, the need to sleep for twenty-hour periods. I wake up some mornings and half of my body is frozen for hours, so I lie and stare at the ceiling. I feel as though I'm not human, and I know nothing can fix me.

'Nothing serious,' he said instead.

DCI Cross had been the day before. He said his offer for SO15 would have to be rescinded, but Zain would be offered his old job back and he urged him to take it.

'When you're ready though, it's the only offer you will get, Zain. No one else will want you on their force.'

And here was Kate. Offering him his job back again. He accepted, knowing full well he was an even bigger mess than he had been the last time he came back.

He watched her walk. She seemed disturbed, preoccupied. Thoughts that had nothing to do with him, when in fact he was all she should really worry about. The process had begun. Soon Kate Riley's father would be free, and he knew about Kate's whereabouts. Question was, would she run and hide again?

The FBI were under an obligation to protect her. And now that her cover had been blown, she would be a priority for them to move. If anything happened to her, they would have a tough time explaining it away.

But would she run? She had once, and the watcher had no doubt it was for her mother's sake more than anything else that she had done so. Would she do it again? Or stay put, stubborn and determined?

It didn't matter so much for him. He was no longer waiting for her father. He had done his bit; there was money waiting in a fund. And as for Kate Riley, he was about to show her what vengeance and payback were all about.

Kate was tired. She walked through Queen Square, the Institute for Neurology behind her. She found a vacant bench in the square, and sat down.

What had she done? Why had she agreed to go along with PCC Hope? Zain was not ready. He was not going to recover. How could she let a man with a bullet lodged in his brain be part of her team and put him and the rest of her team at risk? And yet, there was Anya Fox-Leakey. Zain had orchestrated that for her. Without him approaching DCI Cross, they might not have uncovered the extent of her fraud for months. He was good. When he was on form.

And then there was the other side. Rescuing a promising officer like Stevie from an uncertain future; almost certainly being asked to leave, if not face charges. What would that do? She would lose two of her officers and their lives would be ruined.

Truth was, Kate needed them both. She had a crisis looming in her own life that meant work would have to be as steady as possible. The doctors thought that Zain would need at least another three months before he was fit enough to have his treatment levels lowered, but they couldn't determine how long it would be before he was fully functioning again. That might give her enough time to save Stevie and work something else out for Zain. Maybe he could have an analytical role instead of being on active duty?

Kate stared into the distance, the sound of laughter reaching her from somewhere. She remembered there had once been a time for both innocence and for laughter. But it was long gone.

She shuddered involuntarily as a chill ran through her. She didn't know what her future was going to be, not for her professional or personal life. She had Eric, and he was fast becoming the only thing she could rely on.

And that in itself was far from ideal. Kate Riley did not depend on anyone. She would be ready though, whatever the future sent her way. She stood up and pulled her shoulders back and her spine straight as she headed into the endless maelstrom of London. And her tomorrow.

Acknowledgements

This novel has been a typical 'second novels are the most difficult to write' nightmare so I owe a lot of thanks to the people that got me through it:

My agent, Luigi Bonomi: He's the best. End of.

Alison Bonomi: Editor, therapist, friend, touchstone and general go to person for everything. There isn't enough black daal in the world to say thank you to you.

Katherine Armstrong: The fates aligned, and I still can't believe you are my awesome editor.

Team Bonnier Zaffre, especially Kate Parkin, the original dream maker, and Jennie Rothwell, you might be new but already have made a huge impact.

All the bloggers and reviewers: I know this is so generic, but there are so many of you I absolutely love for your support. You made *Cut To The Bone* what it was, and I hope I never lose your backing.

Team Twenty 7: We are still together after all this time, and I hope these bonds last a lifetime.

The Whole Kahani: Some of the most talented writers I have ever met.

A.A. Dhand, Vaseem Khan, Imran Mahmood, Ayisha Malik and Abir Mukherjee. Never laughed so much in all my life. Lullah Face. LOL!

Angela 'Real Housewives of Crime' Marsons and Lisa 'Queen of Everything' Hall: the cover queens: I will never forget.

Katherine Sunderland for forcing me to do panels. Nikki East for the same and creating a selfie monster.

My work colleagues for keeping me grounded and regularly making me realise I'm not J K Rowling.

Keshini Naidoo, Joy Kluver, Victoria Goldman, Anita Majumdar, Syed Waji Shah: you know why.

God, my family and friends: The essentials in my life.

Author's Note

I have spoken to a number of experts while researching this novel and tried to make the science as authentic as possible. I think novelists should explore the 'what if's' and the 'maybes', which is what I have done in *First to Die*. Any mistakes in my understanding are my own, and not a reflection of the brilliant minds that have tried to help me understand some very complex issues.

Want to read
NEW BOOKS
before anyone else?

Like getting
FREE BOOKS?

Enjoy sharing your
OPINIONS?

Discover

READERS
FIRST

Read. Love. Share.

Sign up today to win your first free book:
readersfirst.co.uk